ADRIFT JUST EAST OF DENVER

by

MARK BARSOTTI

ADVANCE PRAISE FOR
ADRIFT JUST EAST OF DENVER

"A supremely sleazy and adroitly suspenseful thriller... The 1980's pop-culture ambiance and the regional charms and pitfalls of Denver are meticulously recreated, and Barsotti keeps the accelerator to the floorboards for the whole nasty ride."
   – Paul Di Filippo, award-winning author of *The Big Get Even, The Steampunk Trilogy* and others.

#

It's dark, but don't get fooled - there are tons of great lines and laugh-out loud moments... Characters are drawn so adroitly, you'd swear you knew them. . . a page-turning thriller with sharp, well-crafted prose... Highly recommended."
   – Steve Rodgers, author of the *Spellgiver* series (selected "among the best self-published books we've read" by *Fantasy Book Review*).

For Chelsea

*"The books we need are the kind
that act on us like a misfortune."*
– Franz Kafka

LISTEN

Parts of this novel may disturb you. It contains drug and alcohol use, casual sex, obnoxious rock and roll, smoking, pornography, ecdysiasts and sexual violence, just like real life.

You've been trigger-warned.

ACROSS THE BORDER

"Hot town, summer in the city"
– The Lovin' Spoonful

I crush my cigarette underfoot and glance at the departure times on the screen above the ticket counter. Another hour before my bus rolls out. Sixty more minutes in the lousy Denver bus station where it all began, the Great Summer Road Trip of 1986 that almost got me killed...

1

It was just after midnight when my big brother's voice boomed across the nearly deserted station.

"Welcome to the real world, kid!"

"Dave!" I popped out of my seat and rushed to greet him, not caring that he was an hour late and still calling me *kid* even though I was eighteen. It was great to see him, to be in Denver, even if all I'd seen of it so far was a late night bus station.

"My little brother," Dave said, looking me over from tip to toe, "all grown-up."

"Workin' on it." I grinned like a sweepstakes winner, wanted to hug him, but we high-fived instead. Dave had a dark tan and must have put on twenty pounds of muscle. He exuded rock star cool in black jeans and white tank top, with long, razor cut brown hair. He'd left Garrison three years ago, when the old man kicked him out for being a stoner.

"Baseball?" Dave asked, pointing to the green and gold letterman's jacket draped over my backpack. That was his sport.

I shook my head. "Track."

"I remember you'd really gotten into running," Dave said with a nod. "Any good?"

"Nah," I said. "I just like to go." As we strolled outside the little voice in my head announced, *The Freeman brothers, now embarking on five weeks of Mile High fun!*

Dave's wheels were parked up the block, a dark blue Camaro with chrome rims, just like he always wanted. I whistled my approval. "Nice ride."

"Thanks." Dave put my backpack in the trunk. We climbed aboard and he grabbed two cans of Coors from a cooler on the back seat. "Brew?"

"Sure." We clinked cans to toast my arrival. I took a sip of beer and remembered a conversation I'd overheard in the G&M Cafe, three days ago.

"The fire at the grain elevator sure was a sight."

"Yep."

"'Course with the crop prices we're gettin', might as well burn it all anyhow."

Yep."

—

8

As the farmers grumped, I imagined Greyhound soon rolling me west across a border the cafe regulars would never dare. My life up to then could be summed up by a lyric I wrote for my bud Rick Danson's band, *bookbound in a small town*. But not anymore, and I felt kinda sorry for the cafe crowd, because it seemed like they didn't even know they could leave.

Dave hit the gas and we roared off into the Denver night. "It's really good to see you, Adam."

"Absolutely, bro." I took another drink and gawked up at the skyscrapers like the rube I was, having never been more than seventy miles from Garrison and its fifteen thousand Xerox zombies. They were on their own now, because this was gonna be little Adam's summer to howl.

Yep.

I thought of Wendy, off on her own trip to Cape Cod to visit her ailing grandfather. It had been eight days since I kissed her goodbye and her absence ached like a phantom limb. Yet after only five minutes with Dave, I realized Wen was the only reason I had to go back.

"There's goodies in the glove box," Dave said as we cruised past the state capitol, its golden dome lit up by floodlights.

Goodies turned out to be a fat joint, which I sniffed with approval. "Excellent."

"That's two hundred bucks an ounce shit, so it better be." Dave handed me a Bic. "You do the honors."

"Right here?"

"Sure." He laughed and mussed my hair the way he used to. I still hated it. "We gotta get you up to speed on partying in Metropolis, kid."

I scoped for cops, saw none and so sparked up. "Not bad," I croaked, clamping my mouth shut so I wouldn't bark.

"No shit, Sherlock." Dave laughed and punched a tape into the stereo. AC/DC exploded around us.

She's got the backseat rhythm
The rock and roll rhythm

Passing the joint, I flashed back to me and Wendy at the drive-in, two weeks ago. Her Corvair was parked four rows behind the concession stand, us parked in the back seat, ignoring the Schwarzenegger slaughter as our hands made happy. The thought of *our* backseat rhythm made me smile.

"Hot damn, summer in the city," I whispered, thrilled by all the adventures ahead. A bank clock blinked 12:22.

And the real world felt great.

2

With a nice buzz working, we drove through the wrought-iron gates of the Windhollow West condominiums. The buildings were made of pale gray wood, with roofs that sloped and jutted at odd angles, like popsicle sticks glued together by a drunk. From Dave's occasional letters, I knew Windhollow catered to twenty-something singles.

"Listen," he said as we wheeled into a parking space, "sorry I was late picking you up."

"No big deal." High on weed and brotherly affection, I honestly didn't care. "You out chasing tail?"

Dave smirked. "Actually, I *was* the tail."

"Huh?"

"I'm a male dancer," he said, climbing out of the Camaro. "A stripper."

Trying for a poker face while absorbing this news, I noticed Dave's chipped front tooth had been fixed, to go along with his new gym rat bod. "No shit?"

A quick demo ensued, with Dave twirling around, then kicking a leg above his head. "Meet the Rock 'n' Roll Kid," he said with a laugh. "Had to work a bachelorette party up in Longmont when their dancer cancelled last minute. That's why I was late."

"Well, that's. . ." Remembering him at fifteen, nervously primping for a roller rink date with Nancy Keller, I had to chuckle. "Great."

"The money usually is." We strolled across a parking lot full of Corvettes, Firebirds, RX-7s. The only place back home you'd see such a collection of pricey wheels was at the country club. "And I do get laid a lot."

"Excellent." For Dave I'm sure it was, but the only girl I wanted was Wendy. I stopped dead, grabbed my wallet and flipped it open to her photo. "Check out my girlfriend. Wendy." Her name was like sugar on my lips.

"Nice, very nice." Dave mussed my hair again. "Well done."

"We've been together over six months, since she moved to town last December."

"Six months, huh? Must be some serious heartthrob."

I beamed. "You bet."

"She good in the sack?"

"Yeah," I said, although the question made me kinda uncomfortable. "But it's about a lot more than sex. I'm nuts about her."

"That's great. Congrats, kid."

I wished he wouldn't call me that but didn't say anything as we circled around the pool and approached unit 22-G. Bachelor pad central.

"I'm beat," Dave said as we entered the condo. "Grab some sofa. I hope Derk scored some blow. They got coke out in the sticks yet?" He kicked off his shoes and padded out into the kitchen. "Another beer?"

"Sure." Sinking into a cream colored sofa, I scoped out six crates of albums and a stereo with speakers big enough to rock the popsicle sticks off the roof.

"Here." Dave handed me a Heineken, then grabbed the TV remote off a chrome and glass table. "Check out this tube."

A screen descended from the ceiling and, at Dave's prompting, I turned around and saw wood panels slide open, revealing the multi-colored lens of a beam TV, mounted high on the wall behind the bar on the other side of the living room.

"We usually leave the screen down," Dave said. "But I wanted to unveil it for you."

"Wow." I was duly impressed. "Very Trekian."

"Derk doesn't skimp on toys. He's got three vehicles and there's a full-sized Universal machine in the workout room down the hall."

"Nice," I said, glancing up at a framed poster of an almost naked blonde, draped across the hood of a Porsche. *Take me for a ride* read the caption beneath the girl. "What's Derk do?"

"He's my boss, owns the Bad Boys male review and part of a strip-a-gram service." Dave clicked to MTV, then grabbed a half-pint of Wild Turkey off an end table and did a shot. On the giant TV screen an almost life-sized Joan Jett was loving rock and roll. "Not that Derk *needs* to do anything. His old man could buy and sell ours ten times before breakfast."

I snickered. "Dad still thinks you work for the phone company." Until five minutes ago, so had I.

"Who gives a damn what he thinks?"

"Your secret identity is safe with me, Rock 'n' Roll Kid."

"Fuck it," Dave said, not picking up on the joke. "Go ahead and tell him. Maybe he'll have a heart attack." A car come roaring into the lot outside. "That's probably Derk now."

"What's he drive?"

"It sounds like his 'Vette."

"Gotta go pee," I said.

"Down the hall on the right."

Off to the bathroom, I was pleasantly lit on smoke and suds. "Mirror, mirror, on the wall," I told my red-eyed reflection, "summer vacation an' having a ball."

I thought of Wendy and felt a sudden stab of panic. A month on Cape Cod, with her on the beach in that little pink bikini. . . It would be open season on my baby. All those wolves, with slick come-ons and hot cars, drooling over her dangerous curves and fashion model face.

But she loves you, the little voice reminded me. *So have a little faith.*

"Right," I agreed with a smile. "Wen and I are forever." Back to the living room, I got my first look at Dave's just-arrived roomie, who was wearing designer jeans and a tuxedo t-shirt, a black tennis bag slung over one shoulder.

"Adam, this is Derk." Dave wagged a thumb, both ways. "Derk, my brother Adam."

We shook, Derk smiling as he crunched my hand with a vise-like grip. He was about six three or four, with short, spiky blond hair, chiseled cheekbones and striking blue eyes, handsome like a perfect movie Nazi.

"Since you're Dave's brother, I'll assume it's a pleasure to meet you, Adam," Derk said. "Unless proven otherwise."

"Blow?" Dave asked.

"Of course." Derk dug a silver vial from his jeans and tossed it to Dave. "An aging debutante turned me on to some nice rocks."

Dave sat down and fished a small, wood-framed mirror from under the sofa, opened the vial and tapped out a pearly white chunk of cocaine the size of my thumbnail. He whistled. "I *guess* nice. What'd you turn her on to?"

"Let her suck me awhile in her Volvo," Derk said casually as he stripped off his t-shirt to reveal muscle-mag pecs, and I pegged him as one of those brassy, spotlight guys who make you feel like an extra in your own life.

As Dave chopped up the cocaine with a razor blade, Derk disappeared into what I assumed was his bedroom, soon returning in shorts and tank top.

"I really appreciate the hospitality, Derk," I told him as he sat down in a black leather recliner.

"Happy to be of service." He trained those blue eyes on me with laser-like intensity, and I saw a flash of *something* I couldn't identify. "Just don't bug me, comprende?"

"Don't worry about Adam," Dave said, rolling up a twenty dollar bill. "He's a cool kid."

"Listen, bro. . . You mind not calling me that?"

"What?"

"A kid," I said, pitching my voice slightly deeper. "I'm eighteen now, ya know."

"No prob," Dave agreed, then snorted a fat line of coke through the twenty. He rubbed his nose, put the mirror on the table and pushed it toward me. "Blast off, Adam."

I lit a cig, nibbled my bottom lip as I stared at the white powder.

"Go ahead," Dave urged. "You'll love it."

I glanced up at Porsche girl on the poster, seeking advice. Should I admit that I'd never even *seen* cocaine until now? That maybe I was a little scared? She didn't think so either.

"Don't feel obligated, Adam," Derk said, finishing off the Wild Turkey. "It's not for *kids*."

I plucked up the twenty and snorted, half the line for each nostril. That much I knew from the movies. My nose instantly went numb. "*Oh*-kay," I said as a toasty glow spread through me. I leaned back on the sofa, picked up my beer and grinned. "That *is* nice."

"Stick with the Bad Boys," Derk said with a wink. "You'll get a real education."

Soon polishing off my beer, I went to the kitchen for another, every step feeling like I was crossing the finish line a winner. I thought of the old ad slogan *Coke adds life*.

No shit.

Prince was on the tube when I returned with a fresh brewski. I sat down and my foot started tapping, quickly revved to twice the beat.

Derk did a line then grabbed his black bag off the floor and unzipped it. "Got a new flick," he said, fishing out a video.

"More porn?" Dave asked as he lit a Marlboro.

Derk laughed. "Of course."

"Don't you ever get enough, pussy pig?"

"There's no such thing as *enough*." Derk went to fix a drink, loaded the tape into the VCR when he returned and fiddled with the remote.

I glanced at the screen with anticipation, having never seen a real porno flick before, either.

Welcome to the big city, the little voice said in a congratulatory, adult tone.

Dave lit the rest of the joint we'd started in the car and passed it to me as *New Wave Hookers* began with a falsetto theme song. A pimped-out black dude was soon lecturing three dumb-looking white guys, sitting around in their underwear.

"No boring preliminaries!" Derk barked, fast forwarding to a punk rock chick eating another girl's pussy in loud, slurping close-up. I gawked at the big screen, cheeks burning, but the roomies, thankfully, didn't notice my embarrassment.

My attention was soon riveted on the action, where the girls' butts were now presented side by side for the camera's close-up inspection.

I thought of Wendy and shivered, even as I got a boner.

3

"Pass the suntan oil, bro."

I handed over the Coppertone, although Dave's bronzed body already glistened under the July sun, baking us at poolside. Wanted to jump in to cool off again, but my king-sized hangover made the ten feet to the water seem like a thousand. I'd drunk like a fish last night, so wired on cocaine that I hardly felt the booze.

Then.

"Hey, check out what's coming our way," said Dave, pointing to a gorgeous redhead in a mere suggestion of a swim suit, strolling along the other side of the pool. "How does that top stay on?" he wondered, rattling the ice in his drink.

"Magnets," I suggested with a yawn that, trust me, had *nothing* to do with the girl. Dave had got me up around eleven, prescribing hair of the dog margaritas. We downed half-a-blender full before hitting the pool, and an hour of rays had just about done me in.

"What a bod," Dave said admiringly. "I gotta meet this chick."

I grunted and turned over on the lounge. "Wake me up if her string breaks."

"We need to get you into partying shape, Adam." Dave gave me a playful poke in the ribs. "Go get yourself another 'rita."

"Nah, I'm good."

He stood up and stretched, flexing his new muscles without being too obvious about it. "I'm gonna run greetings and salutations on Red over there."

"Go get her, Rock 'n' Roll Kid." I rolled back over to watch, because, hey, he's my brother. Dave dove into the pool, kicked along the bottom before surfacing close to the redhead and her gravity-defying bikini. Smiles and chit-chat as he established a beachhead.

Some kids strolled by outside the fence with a ghetto blaster cranked. A DJ cried it was twelve-thirty and time to rock the Rockies. Where was I at twelve-thirty yesterday? Still somewhere in flat forever Kansas.

And last week, last month, last year? Nowhere. Zombietown.

Dave swam back over and emerged from the water, all smiles. Shaking his head like a wet dog, he reported, "Terri over there just moved in. I'm off to fix her a drink."

He started toward the gate, then stopped and glanced back at me, flashing his now perfect teeth. "And she's got a sister, Adam. They're coming over to barbecue later, so we both might get lucky."

4

Pain lets you know you're alive.

That slogan hangs on the wall behind Coach Hansen's desk, right above a gold-framed photo of the 1969 Garrison High track team that had won the state championship, anchored by fleet-footed Billy Hansen.

"Pain brings life into sharp focus!" Coach would yell as he drove beside the cross country team in his little green Toyota pick-up on some dirt road, far out of town. "And you'd better *sound* alive, gentlemen, or we'll do a couple extra miles!"

"We're alive!" we'd shout between pants, our wind gone and the wall looming. It seemed like Coach wanted us to embrace pain, when all I ever wanted to do was escape it.

"That sunburn looks like it hurts," said Sherri, younger sis of gorgeous Terri, as she smacked her gum and played with a limp strand of dirty blonde hair.

"Yeah," I agreed. "But pain lets you know you're alive." While Dave was busy touring Margaritaville with Terri, I'd crashed by the pool for another hour, boiling like a lobster under the Mile High sun. "And right now I'm really living."

"You're funny, Adam," Sherri said, then sucked her black Russian through a crazy straw.

"Well, looks aren't everything," I said with a smirk. Sherri was shorter than her sister, pudgy, with a plain, pimply face and pug-nose. Terri got all the good genes. Worse, Sherri's vacant expression and inane comments suggested she read *People* magazine with her lips moving.

"I saw Motley Crue at Red Rocks last week," Sherri said. "They were totally fucking awesome."

I lit a cig as the aroma of grilling steaks drifted in from the patio. "They suck."

"Maybe *you* suck," Sherri said, flouncing out to the patio.

Good riddance, I thought, opening my wallet to Wendy's picture. "Five weeks, beautiful," I whispered, beaming my affection eastward. "But you're in my heart every minute."

Derk sauntered through the front door with a foxy black chick in tow. "Monica," he said to her on their way to the bar, "that's Adam."

"Hi," I said.

Monica waved at me as she sang softly, "My girl wants to party all the time, party all the time." Silver dollar-sized nipples threatened to pierce her tight red t-shirt.

"Derk!" Dave shouted from the patio. "What's up?"

"Just some after work R&R!" Derk grabbed a bottle of Crown Royal and nibbled Monica's bottom lip. "Let's go get nasty."

"Lead on, sugar."

I watched them disappear into Derk's room, then got up and grabbed another beer from the fridge.

"Steaks are ready!" Dave called.

I wasn't very hungry, but maybe food would make me feel better. My head felt like a hallow coconut, my sunburned back like it was being eaten by fire ants. I trudged out to the patio as Dave forked steaks from the hibachi. "Dig in and drink up," he urged, still going strong after umpteen margaritas. Not so Terri, who was clearly crocked and swaying in time to music that wasn't playing.

I wolfed down a couple bites of steak while trying to ignore Sherri, still prattling on about Motley Crue.

"Where's Derk?" Dave asked.

"Bedroom," I said, grabbing a handful of Ruffles.

"I'd kill to get Vince Neil in *my* bedroom," Sherri gushed, smacking her lips.

"Ice cream," Terri said suddenly, a bite of potato salad halfway to her mouth. "Doesn't ice cream sound yummy, Davy?"

"Sure does."

The steak was landing like lead in my stomach, so back to the living room for some MTV. And speaking of those pop-metal hacks, there's the Crue now, big as life on the giant screen and twice as ugly. I cranked the volume to lure Sherri in from the patio.

"Shout," the band shouted, "at the devil!"

On cue, Sherri bounded into the room like an eager puppy. Wait for her to take a seat before her tattooed idols, then. . .

. . .randomly click the remote. A Preparation H ad. Perfect.

"Turn it back!" Sherri squealed.

Click!

Hulk Hogan was thrashing Omar the Filthy Arab, who burned a mini American flag before every match.

"Turn *back!*" wailed Sherri, pounding little fists on the back of the sofa. She looked almost ready to bawl, filling me with the sadistic joy of a six year old frying bugs with a magnifying glass. This might be Denver, but Sherri had Garrison written all over her, small-town in all the worst ways.

Click!

A Mexican soap opera queen swooned.

"Damn you, Adam!" She grabbed a sofa cushion and whacked my deep-fried shoulder. I cursed as she stomped half-way to the patio and called to her sister, "I'm leaving, Terri!"

"Pick up some ice cream!"

"You're a shit, Adam." Sherri pointed at me with a long red fingernail on her way to the front door. "A real shit."

"Get lost, zom." She stormed out, vanishing like a bad dream.

Click!

Gilligan and the Skipper fled from headhunters.

Click!

The Love Boat sailed the Rerun Sea.

Click.

A perky blonde newsbabe reported ". . .the teenage girl was sexually assaulted last night, after being lured into a van at the Westminster Mall. Police wouldn't comment on whether the assault might be linked to other rapes in the Metro area. Coming up next, part three of our In-Focus series on latchkey kids."

"Sure, gorgeous," Dave told Terri as they soon wandered in from the patio. "We'll go get ice cream later."

"Promise?"

He promised as they climbed the stairs to his bedroom. I went to the bathroom for more lotion, although it did little to soothe my extra-crispy skin. Vacation report on my second day in Denver: sunburned and sore, feeling pissy over nothing and everything.

Sitting on the toilet, I flipped to Wen's picture, imagined kissing her as I started playing with myself.

Derk's room was on the other side of the wall. "That's it, baby, suck it," he urged his new friend Monica. "All the way down."

Their sex-noise got louder. I pretended it was me and Wendy. Remembering us at the drive-in made me pop.

God, I miss her.

I cleaned up, flushed, splashed my face with cold water. Back to the sofa, the TV, a fresh cig. I still felt lousy, but jacking off was a lot better than trying to cozy up to dumb-dumb Sherri. And I was being true to Wendy, which was easy, because what we had was the rare *real* thing.

Knowing that made me smile for the first time all day.

5

Up around two the next afternoon — we hadn't crashed until four, Denver party life being *many* time zones from home — I found the roomies prepping for a Bad Boys show in Colorado Springs. Derk had a friend there, where they planned to hang out before their gig. Dave loaded a cooler with sandwiches, soda and beer. Derk phoned last minute details to other dancers and recorded three song sets on the stereo.

This is serious business

Sex and violence and rock 'n' roll

The prep complete, Derk laid out some lines and we fueled up. I noticed the roomies barely mentioned last night's amorous encounters. Instead, they told war stories about the wild chicks down in the Springs. When they were ready to split an hour later, I walked them out to the parking lot. Derk's black van was tricked out with chrome rims, fog lights, and an "Ass, grass, or gas. . . nobody rides for free!" bumper sticker.

"Here, bro." Dave handed me a joint after climbing aboard. "Have fun. Don't burn the place down."

"I'll try to restrain myself," I said with smile. "Any idea when you'll be back?"

"It's an early show, so maybe nine or ten."

"You guys rake in the bucks."

"We always do," Derk said.

Back inside, I fished the phone number of Wendy's grandfather from my wallet. I'd started to call her last night, but hung up after realizing it was too late on the east coast. I punched in the number and stared at her picture.

Four rings, five, then a creaky-voiced *hello* from who I assumed was her grandfather.

"Hello, sir. May I speak to Wendy?"

"She's at the grocery store with her dad. Who's this?"

"Wendy's boyfriend, Adam, calling long distance from Denver."

"Who?"

"Adam. Would you ask Wendy to call me later? She has the number."

"Sure, sure," the old coot said, then abruptly hung up, leaving me to wonder if he'd even remember the call, let alone deliver my message. Still revved up on the coke, I worked out for forty-five minutes, then grabbed a Pepsi from the fridge and clicked on the tube.

Derk's porn flick started playing, the black pimp still jabbering to the dumb white guys. Not in the mood, I turned it off and decided to go exploring. Got forty bucks from the cash stash in my backpack, changed into shorts, and was about to split when I realized they hadn't left me a key.

Shit.

I couldn't just waltz out and leave the place unlocked, but soon decided an unsecured patio door was a minimal security risk. There was a three foot high stack of old newspapers on the patio. Standing atop it, I scrambled over the high wooden fence and marched out of Windhollow, psyched for some Mile High exploration.

Forty-five minutes later, I was hiking along a bike path that snaked through a grassy parkway, heading toward downtown Denver. Warm sun, blue sky, with the Rockies rising before me like craggy dragons teeth. Little Adam was off the leash and feeling fine.

Remembering the joint Dave gave me in my cigarette pack, I wandered off the path into a stand of pine trees, sat down and sparked up. After a couple tokes, I glanced at a high rise apartment building beside the parkway and idly wondered if Mom might be behind one of those windows. Hell, she could just as well be in Denmark as Denver.

It was five years ago last November that Mom ran off with Fred Duncan. *Poof,* she'd vanished like a magician and not a peep from her since, save for a holiday card addressed to Dave and me (pointedly excluding the old man) every Christmas.

God, I miss her, the selfish bitch.

Stretching out on the cool grass beneath the trees, I shut my eyes and smelled sweet and sour pork. That's what Mom made for dinner the night before she split. Five freakin' years, but I still remembered that god damned sweet and sour pork.

All I remember of Fred Duncan was his horsey face inside a teller's cage at the First National Bank and big hairy hands trading crisp dollar bills for a kid's rolled up pennies.

Wherever Mom was, I hoped she was happy. Really, because the old man still tends her stupid roses and busting up a family, even a screw-up one like ours, had better make *someone* happy.

Enough! the little voice declared. *Get up and get moving, Adventure Boy.*

Back on the bike path, I soon broke into a trot. Stayed in first gear until my legs loosened up, then ran faster. The last couple days of partying slowed me down some, but after another five minutes I kicked it up a couple more gears. The world blurred by until it almost felt like I was flying, arms and legs pistoning like a well-oiled machine.

Kenny started me running four summers ago, but *him* I refused to think about.

I just ran faster.

6

Average speed but great endurance, a natural distance runner, that was Coach Hansen's take on me. I finished second in cross country meets six times, my last two years of high school. Nothing to brag about, but had there been an event for running *forever*, I'd own the record books.

Don't take the bus, run home from school. Lazy weekend mornings and dirt road summer nights, run, run. Not to get anywhere but just to *go*, chasing the slip-your-skin moment when the exhaustion and lead-legged agony melts away and you go through the wall and into the blank.

That's what I got out of running, and it was a whole lot better than blue ribbons or gold-framed photos.

Cherry Creek Drive turned into University Boulevard and swung me north into a residential neighborhood. Run. Sixth Avenue slipped by, Seventh. I followed University up the numbered avenues then turned west down lucky Thirteenth.

Run.

My eyes clicked off city snapshots, anonymous apartment blocks and proud old Victorian mansions. Upscale ice cream parlors and punk clothing stores. On the concrete wall of a street-side tennis court a graffito declared *Create Yourself* in intricate, Old English lettering. Two blocks on another message in the same style proclaimed *Freedom is not free*.

I didn't get it.

The Capitol became my finish line, its gold dome beckoning at the bottom of the hill. I began noticing posters on utility poles, promoing a band with the slogan: *Taking rock from this world to The Next!*

There's pretty much only cover bands in Garrison, most flogging Sixties oldies or modern hair metal. My bud Rick's band, Fleeting Youth, did all original stuff, but they broke up last fall when the drummer's family moved to Atlanta. Some of their lyrics were by yours truly, but it's tough to create yourself when nobody wants to listen.

Reaching the Capitol, I discovered it was open to the public. Wandering in, I found a restroom and toweled off most of my sweat. Took an elevator up three floors then mounted a circular staircase leading to the dome itself. Great views from there, the streets and highways of Denver in a swirling grid that seemed to stretch almost to the base of the Rockies. The forever blue sky compared favorably to the humid haze back home, but than gray is the right color for zombies, too small town chicken to ever brave the border.

A last circuit around the observation deck make me smile. There were a lot of places to run.

Back outside, I crossed Broadway to a park, sat on a concrete wall and sneak-smoked the other half of the joint, not two hundred yards from the seat of State Government.

"Ain't that America," I muttered. Yeah, at least until they've got us all pissing into bottles.

At the south end of the park was a small amphitheater. Striding across its cracked, concrete floor, I imagined myself in ancient Rome. The Forum crowd roared my name as I stood over a fallen opponent, arms lifted in victory.

"Need any weed, dude?" asked a Mexican kid who sidled up behind me. He looked about twelve. "Killer bud."

"Nah, I'm good."

Completing a leisurely stroll around the park, I re-crossed Broadway and headed up Colfax Avenue, recognized the name from reading Kerouac. I gave a buck to an old woman, begging in front of a gothic church. She grinned at me like she still had teeth.

A couple blocks further, there was a porn store called Kitty's, which took up most of an entire block. Back home only a couple non-chain gas stations even sold *Hustler* and *Penthouse* anymore, and I stared at the nipples and pubes someone had magic-markered on a life-sized plastic silhouette of a girl.

Feeling like a kid outside a naughty candy store, I was about to wander inside when I noticed a priest walking toward me. That made me feel guilty for some reason, and we're not even Catholic. I adjusted my shades and kept going. No biggie. I had Wendy, all the woman I'd ever need.

Not wanting to hoof it all the way back to Windhollow, I waited at a bus stop plastered with more flyers for The Next. On the bus, I found an abandoned *Rocky Mountain News*, flipped it open to a story about the girl getting raped that was on last night's news.

She had been snatched at the Westminster Mall, after being lured into a black van. The girl was then driven to an unknown location and assaulted, "possibly by the same attacker some in the media have dubbed '"the Shopping Mall Rapist.'" The victim was sixteen and weighed eighty pounds. Her attacker was "built like a football player," had long black hair, and kept at her for over two hours before dropping the girl off on the outskirts of Boulder, almost thirty miles away. The cops had no suspects.

Glancing up from the paper, I noticed we'd reached Colorado Boulevard. I got a transfer, got off, and waited for a connecting bus down Colorado. I couldn't stop thinking about that girl. So horrible. What kind of monster can just grab some chick and use her like that?

Just like that.

7

I got off the bus for some Colonel Cluck's chicken about halfway back to Windhollow, then went to the movies on impulse to cut down on the alone time I'd have, hanging out at the condo.

After catching the second half of a dumb teen movie with a twenty-five year old cast, I watched *The Finish Line,* a thriller about this unpublished writer Max, who went so gaga over rich society girl Alicia that he started murdering his romantic rivals. Alicia began returning Max's affection, even while discovering clues that he might be the killer. At the film's climax, she confronted him with her suspicions in his basement workshop and asked what he was going to do.

He glanced up at her while sharpening the hunting knife he'd used to dispatch her other suitors. There was a close-up of the blade sliding across the whetstone, then their eyes met in a long, conflicted

gaze. Max then kissed the knife, winked at Alicia and whispered, "I think I'll go to California."

Roll credits.

Huh? Did he marry or murder her and what was that about going to California? God, I hate movies that leave you hanging. If you want questions without answers, read a goddamn newspaper.

Hungry again, I grabbed a burger and shake at Dairy Queen then walked the last couple miles to Windhollow. Derk's van was in the parking lot when I arrived, so no need to jump the fence and get in through the patio. Strolling up to 22-G, I suddenly imagined the condo had been ransacked, with the thieves leaving a thank you note for the unlocked patio door. Dave let me in and I saw everything was intact.

Derk was on the sofa, loading a skull-shaped bong, while another guy poured shots of tequila. Fat lines of coke were laid out, not on the mirror, but directly on the glass table in front of the sofa.

"Adam," Dave said, slapping tequila guy on the back, "this is Vance, the first friend I made in Denver."

"Hey, Adam," Vance said warmly, "I've heard a lot about you."

"All lies," I joked, surprised Dave had that much to say about me. "Lies and madness."

Vance laughed. "No, it was all good." We shook then he poured me a shot. On the tube, Cyndi Lauper led a parade of girls who just wanna have fun.

"How was your show?" I asked.

"Great," Dave said. "Excellent tips, and I met a real knock-out named Laura."

"And I doubled my pleasure, doubled my fun, getting head from two chicks at once," Derk crowed, trumping Dave's knock-out with a kinky pair.

"And I did my sayonara strip," Vance said, downing his tequila. "Time to hang up the old g-string and head off into the real world."

Derk snickered. "God, what a horrible thought."

Vance shook his head. "I'm ready for a dose of reality."

"Why are you going back to college again?" Derk asked. "To become a high school custodian?"

"A high school *history teacher*."

"Oh, that's *soooo* much better," said Derk sarcastically.

"Hey," Vance shot back, "somebody's got to wise-up the little shits."

"I think you just want to be around all that teenaged tail," Dave suggested.

We all laughed. Shots, bongs, and lines kept the yucks coming as the roomies ribbed Vance about ditching the dancing life to hit the books and work part-time job in his father's hardware store. He held firm, insisting that twenty-four was too old for full time sex, drugs and rock 'n' roll.

Derk hooted down the idea of being *too old,* swore he'd still be stripping at thirty.

"Well, you're a better man than I, Gunga Dong!" Vance said, hoisting another shot in salute. "And a much bigger perv!"

"Here, here!" Derk agreed.

We drank to some of the memorable babes who'd gotten into Vance's g-string during his Bad Boy tenure. Here's to the pouty blonde who'd decorated his tool belt with fives and tens before attempting an on-stage oral exam up in Fort Collins. To poly-sci major Sally from Yale, who'd left Vance bow-legged but with new respect for the Ivy League, all without taking off her glasses. To Billie from Baltimore, who had a mouth like a Hoover vacuum and a fondness for ice cubes.

The retirement party finally wound down three hours later. Dave suggested Vance crash at the condo, but since I was bivouacked on the sofa, accommodations were at a premium.

"I *am* well-buzzed," Vance admitted as he got up and stretched. "So I'll drive home as fast as I can."

"This'll help get you road-worthy," Derk said, doling out a final line.

"You're a gentleman and a scholar, boss. Oops, newly *ex*-boss." Nose freshly packed, Vance shook hands all around. We followed him out to his Fiero, cheering as he roared away with tires squealing.

"He'll be back within a month," Derk predicted. "History teacher, my ass."

8

Back inside, Dave gave me the rave review on the girl he'd met in the Springs. Laura was twenty-two, drop-dead gorgeous with big brown eyes and jet black hair, but also smart and funny, if a modest tipper. She lived in Boulder and her friend in the Springs practically had to drag Laura to a male review. "She blushed like a school girl at first," Dave said. "It was so damn cute."

"You *sound* like a school girl," Derk joked. "Getting all hot and bothered over some snatch you didn't even bang."

"It's anticipation," Dave shot back. "Delayed gratification trips my trigger."

"Sure, that's why you're *always* turning down pussy."

"Laura's different somehow." Dave shook his head, as if surprised by this himself. "I'm seeing her after our Boulder gig on Saturday."

I frowned, having assumed *my* first Denver Saturday night would belong to the Freeman boys. But then I'd been thinking about Dave, not the Rock 'n' Roll Kid.

Don't whine, the little voice scolded. *He's your brother, not a babysitter.*

I started to ask Dave about bikini girl Terri, but the answer seemed obvious. She was so last night. "*I* think Laura sounds great," I said, toasting Dave's object of desire.

"You always were smart, little brother." Half an hour later, Dave yawned and stood up. "I'm beat, guys. Gonna go sack out."

"Either you're turning into a lightweight," Derk said. "Or you can't wait to yank your crank, thinking about what's-her-name."

Dave laughed and flipped him off. "No, you can't watch."

"Night, bro."

"Night, Adam. If your sunburn's better, we'll get in some pool time tomorrow."

"Sounds good," I said, watching Dave mount the stairs.

"Beer?" Derk asked me on his way to the kitchen.

—

"No thanks. I'm winding down myself."

Returning with a Corona, Derk handed me a slip of paper. "Phone message on the machine from earlier," he said casually, turning the TV back on.

Wendy had called while I was at the movies. Damn. I'd missed my baby to watch killer Max kiss his knife and mutter about going to California. God damn it.

"Anything important?" Derk asked, pawing through a stack of videos.

"Yeah." I scowled and crumpled up the note.

"Who's Wendy?"

"My girlfriend." I starting reaching for my wallet, but decided not to show Derk her picture. I don't know why.

"You're on vacation in the big city. Live it up, son, get some strange!"

I shook my head. "Wen's the only girl I want."

"Good for you," Derk said, loading a tape in the VCR. I wasn't in the mood for porn, but he wasn't asking. The credits for *Bondage Babes* rolled while a handheld camera followed a skinny blonde in a black miniskirt down an alley at ass level and into an apartment building. Derk pulled out his vial and tapped more coke onto the table.

"Line?"

"Ahh, sure."

We fueled up, then I went to the fridge for another brew after all. Tomorrow, Wendy, I thought, glancing at the phone. We'll talk tomorrow for sure.

Derk was fast forwarding the movie as I plopped back on the sofa. It was one-thirty. The zoms back in Garrison were long since asleep, while here in Windhollow the party rolled on.

"Check this out," Derk said, pointing toward the screen. The blonde had stripped down to crotchless black panties and fishnet stockings. She was face down on a bed, ass in the air.

I sparked a cig and stared at the screen.

"You're mine now, bitch," announced an ugly white dude with greasy black hair and a pot belly. He clicked a handcuff around one of the girl's wrists, attached its mate to a bed post, then slapped her ass, hard enough to leave a handprint. His right arm had a shark tattoo, and he was hung like a mule.

"Let me go," the girl whimpered.

"You're not goin' anywhere," Derk said, mouthing dialogue along with the Mule Man, who now scuttled into position behind the girl. He slapped her ass a couple more times, cackling like an undertaker on laughing gas.

I squirmed a bit. This was kind of creepy – no air-brushed playmates here – but it was also compelling, raw and raunchy.

Mule Man drooled on the girl ass. As spit dribbled down between her cheeks, Derk pulled a little glass bottle from his shorts and mouthed more dialogue.

"Yeah, I like a captive cunt."

Opening the bottle, Derk took two big sniffs, then leaned back on the sofa as a goofy grin spread across his face. "Yeah," he whispered, "bone that bitch." The Mule Man obliged.

"What's that stuff?" I asked, pointing at the bottle.

"Poppers."

"What's it do?"

"Here, try some." Derk tossed me the bottle. RUSH read the yellow and red label in capital letters, bracketed by SS style lightning bolts.

I slowly unscrewed the cap, flinched as a nasty smell wafted out, like dirty socks stewing in ammonia.

"You do it for the buzz, not the aroma," Derk said. "To live one must experience, comprende?"

"Yeah," I agreed. On this side of the border, I was up for most *anything*. I took a big whiff, capped the bottle and set it on the table. The stuff hit me fast. My head seemed to expand, swell up like a balloon as warm tingles radiated out along every nerve ending. My tongue felt thick and wet, seemed to take forever to snake out of my mouth and lick my top lip as my gaze returned to the giant screen. . .

. . .where the images now glowed vibrantly as Derk upped the volume. The movie wasn't creepy now, but maybe the sexiest thing I'd ever seen, flesh on fire, and I was suddenly rock hard, at one with the Mule Man as he thrust into the handcuffed girl. Their sweaty skin sparkled, the grunts and groans were primeval love chants.

Pound, pound, pound.

"Do more poppers, Adam," Derk said, maybe a minute later.

My head was starting to deflate as he spoke, the magical sense of *joining* the on-screen action melting away. The camera zoomed in for a close-up, but it was just a movie again. I grabbed the Rush and fed both nostrils.

"Now I'm gonna fuck your ass," the Mule Man declared.

"No, uh-uh," the blonde said, shaking her head. "Vinny knows I don't do anal." She glanced over her shoulder, anger flashing in her glassy eyes. "Where's Vinny?"

Arms entered the frame, stuffed a gag into the girl's mouth as Muley lined up his target. My head was soaring again, up and away, ignoring the little voice, small town scold.

I don't like this. . .

One more sniff and, wow, it was awesome as Mule Man took the squealing girl up the butt. It felt like the scene was being laser-etched onto my eyes.

Derk stood up said he was gonna crash. He didn't ask for the Rush back, and I didn't offer. After he trooped off to his room, I waited five minutes then paused the movie and got some lotion from the bathroom.

Pound, pound, pound.

9

The driftwood clock above the fireplace read 10:30 when the phone rang me back to the land of the living. Through barely open eyes, I saw Derk, sweaty from working out, dash into the kitchen and grab the phone.

The ringing went on in my head. Realizing I had passed out on the living room floor like a freshman at his first kegger, I groaned and crawled up onto the sofa. Sparked a cig that tasted like dirt and spied the now empty bottle of Rush on the end table.

Hard to think with a killer hangover, but it struck me that while poppers were a kick, they also twisted my perception in a way that was kinda disturbing. So maybe no more of that stuff. I pulled on my jeans and t-shirt and trudged to the kitchen for something wet. My mouth was a sandbox.

"Dude, you need to work tonight," Derk was telling one of the Bad Boys. "Sorry about the trouble with your old lady, but I'm not your shrink."

I grunted at Derk and got a glass of ice water. Drank it too fast, sending my headache into *Hulk smash* overdrive.

"As your *boss,* however," continued Derk, "I'll be succinct. You no-show me tonight, no job tomorrow, comprende?" He slammed down the phone. "Fucking amateurs."

"Who?" Dave asked, wandering in from the patio.

"That pinhead Eric," Derk said scornfully. "He's probably gonna blow off the show tonight, leaving us with only four dancers."

"Call Tease," Dave suggested.

"He's in L.A."

"Then we each dance an extra set," Dave said, grabbing a 7-Up from the fridge. "More money for the rest of us." He came over and mussed my hair. "Morning, bro. Tried to nudge you onto the couch earlier, but you just grunted at me. Thought we might need jumper cables to get you moving."

"Yeah," I agreed. "I could use a few hundred volts."

Derk snapped his fingers. "Call Vance! Talk him into working tonight."

Dave laughed. "He just retired *last night.*"

"So it'll be a command performance. Appeal to his camaraderie, his esprit de corps."

Dave looked doubtful. "He'll say no."

"Just call him, Dave."

"Fine, but don't hold your breath."

26

As Dave picked up the phone, I slouched back to the living room and dug into my backpack, in dire need of aspirin and then a long, hot shower. No partying today, I decided, at least not until after dark. I resolved to get out and see more sights.

"Have fun last night?"

I turned to see a grinning Derk, holding up the empty Rush bottle.

"Yeah, I got pretty ripped," I muttered, sure that he knew about the wad of toilet paper, stuffed under a sofa cushion.

"I like you, Adam," Derk said, then walked over and punched me in the shoulder. Hard. "We've got a lot in common."

"Yeah?" I resisted the urge to rub my arm as Dave wandered in from the kitchen, looking weirded out.

"What's the word?" Derk asked, then dropped to the floor and started doing push-ups. "Is Vance gonna bail us out?"

Dave stabbed a Marlboro between his lips and said nothing.

"Well, what'd he say?"

"I talked to his roommate," Dave whispered. "Vance wrapped his Fiero around a light pole on his way home last night. He's dead."

Derk froze for an instant, back stiff, then resumed the push-ups. "You serious?"

Dave went to the bar and did a blast of Jack Daniels, straight from the bottle. "DOA at Denver General."

I replayed last night's endless toasts, remembered the sound of Vance's car, speeding off into the night. I didn't know him, but he seemed like a good guy. God, it was so *weird*. Vance wanted to teach history and now he *was* history. Here one minute, gone the next.

"Well, isn't that a bitch," Derk said as he stood up and sighed. "Now who am I going to get to dance tonight?"

10

"I know Vance pulled a James Dean last night. He's *dead*, I get it." Dave flicked the butt of his smoke into the empty seats below us. "Yet I half-expect him to show up at the gig tonight. Stupid, huh?"

"No, it's not stupid," I said, gazing down at the empty stage and the city rising on the plains beyond. We had spent the afternoon together, cruising in his Camaro, and were now sitting in the top row of Red Rocks amphitheater, in the foothills just west of Denver. Last stop before Dave had to go home and get ready for work. The show must go on. "Shit happens sometimes that's hard to wrap your head around, like when Mom split without so much as a goodbye or go fuck yourselves. What can you say about shit like that?"

"Nothing," Dave muttered, slapping the wooden bench. "Not a god damned thing." He was trying not to show it, but I knew he was pretty torn up. Vance was his best friend in Denver, maybe the world, the guy who got him into stripping as a lark two years ago. If they hadn't met, no Rock 'n' Roll Kid.

I was sorry about Vance, sure, but his death seemed to erase some of the distance between me and Dave and that was a good thing. It almost felt like we were back on our bunk beds at home, trying to decode the world. Until this afternoon, I was starting to wonder if we were ever going to really talk again.

"Can't believe Derk's reaction," I said. "What a cold fuckin' fish."

"Ahh, he's okay," Dave said, without much conviction. "You just have to understand him."

I snickered. "Not sure that I want to."

"What gets me is Vance's big, back-to-college career plan. Doctor, lawyer, I could understand, but a *history teacher*."

"I *like* history."

"Me, too," Dave agreed, "but imagine having to try inspiring a bunch of sixteen-year-old blockheads every day as your *job*. . ."

"Yeah, sounds tough," I said. "But it's cool that he wanted to try."

"I suppose so." Dave glanced at his watch. "Let's cruise."

As we started back to the Camaro in silence, I stared at the huge slabs of sandstone, punched up through the ground like giant red fists, hungry for the sky. It took maybe a million years to carve those slabs out of the earth, I thought, when it only takes a moment to carve out people.

***

As we sped back toward the city, I remembered the band fliers downtown and asked Dave if he'd ever heard of The Next.

"Yeah. Never seen 'em, but they're supposed to be good."

"How 'bout we check them out next weekend?"

"Can't." Dave shook his head. "I'm working both nights."

"Oh."

"You could go. You'd need a fake ID, but Derk has connections for shit like that."

I shrugged. "Even with an ID, I've got no way to get downtown."

"True," Dave said, then a moment later asked offhandedly, "Think you could handle my wheels for a night?"

My eyes widened. "You serious?"

"You're eighteen now, right?" He grinned. "A non-kid."

"Wow, that'd be very, very cool, bro. Thanks."

"You're welcome." Dave sighed, shoulders sagging a little. "I'm really glad you're here, Adam. This is a majorly suckie day, but it's good to have *some* family that gives a shit."

28

I knew he was thinking of the old man and wanted to offer an olive branch, but Dad hadn't even asked me to say hello to his first-born son. I had no ammo for a peace offensive.

"The old man," Dave said, as if reading my mind. "Does he still take care of Mom's roses?"

"Yeah."

"God, that's so weird. And fucking moronic." He punched a tape into the stereo and cranked the volume.

Who the fuck are you? You? You?

Why don't you tell me who are you?

Goodbye, Vance Nathan, former-future teacher, soon to start rotting in a hole in the ground. And who the fuck were you?

11

Back at Windhollow, we smoked a joint and caught the end of *Star Trek,* the episode where they go back to the 1930's and Kirk has to let his new love die to stop Hitler from winning World War II. For the greater good, Spock logically insisted, the captain's heartthrob had to be sacrificed. It made me think of Max kissing his knife in *The Finish Line,* but I didn't quite get the connection.

Is art supposed to explain things, or make us realize there *is* no explanation?

After *Trek,* Dave hit the shower. It was six o'clock and, translating that to Cape Cod time, I debated calling Wendy. Her ancient granddad might be tucked away for the night, but what if her old man answered? He wasn't a fan of mine. I decided to chance it, would hang up if no one answered after four rings.

I punched in the number, then flipped open my wallet to her picture. God, that gorgeous face.

A face I first saw in American Lit class, room 316, a week before Christmas break. I was at my desk early, reading about Captain Queeg rolling marbles when new transfer student Wendy walked in, announced by the final bell. She was a *Creem Dream* pin-up with killer curves, honey-blonde hair, emerald eyes and a warm easy smile. In a word, perfect.

I'd have started rolling marbles if I had any.

One ring. . .

I wasn't the only one enthralled by Wendy. Lots of the hot shot jocks bird-dogged her from day one, but they all struck out. I worked the long game, making small talk before and after class, saying hi in the halls, even joining her in the lunchroom a couple times. Okay, *worked* isn't the right word, since I had no game. I just wanted to be around her as much as possible.

All that miraculously changed around the middle of January, on the Wednesday (*Wens Day!*) we had the final on *The Caine Mutiny*. She got to class early, took the desk beside me and scooted it a couple inches in my direction then leaned over to ask if I thought Queeg was to blame for the Caine almost going down in the typhoon, or the system that produced Queegs.

I said probably both, unless you wanted to go big and blame God. Why, I asked, let the manufacturer off the hook? Wendy laughed and something seemed to pass between us. I couldn't wait to get back to American Lit, the only class we shared, but she was absent the next two days.

Bummed about not seeing her, I looked forward to the distraction of my Saturday morning run: twenty blocks from our house to the water tower, cut through Dillon Park to the high school for a dozen laps around the track, then out across the railroad tracks to the interstate loop, where I'd circle Jim's Auto Scrap and start back.

I was three blocks down Main, outbound, when I saw Wendy across the street, outside the G&M Cafe. I veered toward her and hit the gas, thinking I'd be unbeatable in the 100-yard dash if she was waiting at the finish line.

Two rings. . .

I called her name, but she didn't hear me and walked into the G&M. I followed her inside – completely ignoring my normal reaction, which would have been to assume I *had* been heard and was being ignored – and sat right down in the booth opposite her.

"Hi!" I chirped, but swallowed the *so, been skipping school* wisecrack when I saw the likely reason she'd missed the last two days. Heavy make-up could only partially camouflage Wendy's black eye.

"Nice, huh?" She touched her right cheek below the bruise. I wanted to give her a hug but, being on the wrong side of the booth, asked what happened instead.

"It's so damn dumb, Adam," Wen said, shaking her head. "I tripped on the throw rug in my room and went face first into a bedpost. Graceful, huh?"

"No," I said, figuring if she wanted to joke about it, I'd join in. "Sounds more like just plain clumsy."

"Hey!"

I grinned and held up my hands. "Just kidding."

She pretended to be mad, but a ghost of a smile gave her away and a minute later she asked if I wanted to get hot chocolate to go and give her the Garrison grand tour.

YES!

"Ahh, okay," I said with what I hoped was casual cool. "But the tour won't take long."

"Well," she said with a shrug, "then make stuff up."

Three rings. . .

Cups in hand, we headed out and I explained why I was wearing shorts and a sweatshirt.

"So you love running?" Wendy asked.

"Not really." I sipped what tasted like the best hot chocolate *ever*, licked my lip to make sure it left no mustache. "What I *do* love is that it can take me someplace away from here. Into non-Garrison headspace, if that makes any sense."

"Sure." Wendy batted those big green eyes over the top of her steaming cup. "And I guess you're not with the official town welcome wagon?"

"No, but from *myself*, young lady, the biggest, most welcomey wagon in all the land!" I raised my cup in salute as we strolled toward the park. Couldn't believe I said something that stupid, but she didn't seem to mind. It was an unseasonably warm day but, in her company, it could have been five below and I'd have barely noticed.

"So where is it?" Wendy asked.

"What?"

"This wagon you just promised."

"Oh, it's invisible."

"Cool," she said, deadpan. "I've never seen that kind before."

I laughed. Boy, did I *like* this girl. She didn't mention her black eye again, so neither did I. At the park, we played on the swings like six-year-olds, then I spun Wendy on the merry-go-round. After that we just moseyed around town for an hour, with me pointing out non-attractions like the still empty lot where the movie theater burned down in '79 and the over-grown field near the town limits where the new high school *would* have been if it hadn't been voted down four years ago.

Wendy started to open up, told me her parents had recently divorced, prompting the move to Garrison with her ex-Marine father, who was a manager out at the tire plant. She missed her friends back in Chicago, felt isolated and alone. I offered to be her friend. She said that would be great then leaned toward me like maybe she was going to kiss me, but bent down and picked up a dead leaf instead.

That was one of the best hours of my life, the dawn of us.

When she invited me over to study the next week, her black eye was gone, but I noticed that her bed didn't have any posts to fall against. And her large, loud-mouthed father reminded me of Harry Paul Gattlin, except that he was a *grown-up* bully jerk. Wen insisted everything was fine at home and I tried to believe her.

Four rings, then she said hello. The sound of her voice still reduced me to mentally rolling marbles.

"Hi, babe," I said softly. "It's me."

"It's kind of late to be calling, Adam."

"Sorry." After almost two weeks apart, I had hoped for a more romantic greeting. "Do you need to go?"

"I can talk for a minute, but I'm glad my Dad didn't answer."

"Sorry," I repeated, not wanting to waste precious time talking about her old man. "Having a good time so far?"

"Not really. Gramps seems so much older than he was two years ago."

"The weather nice?" I wanted to kick myself for asking about the god damned weather.

"Muggy." Wendy yawned. "Lots of rain."

"It's great here. Nothing but blue skies." I touched her picture gently. "I miss you so much, I could burst."

"It's only a month, Adam."

"Five weeks."

"I hear my Dad coming," Wendy said. "I better go."

"Call me, okay?"

"I'll try."

She hung up before I could say I loved her, and I wondered how in hell I managed to feel worse now than before we talked.

"Hey, Adam," Dave called from the living room. "You don't have anything going on tonight, do you?"

"Nope."

"Then come check out our show."

"Isn't it for women only?" I asked, wandering out to join him. The thought of watching the Bad Boys peel down didn't exactly trip my trigger.

"You've just been promoted to wardrobe manager," Dave said. "Come on, it's a kick watching all the chicks go ape shit."

"I don't know. . ."

"Hey, I know you're crazy about Wendy and that's great. I'm not saying you should try to get laid or anything," Dave said, fluffing his hair in the mirror behind the bar. "But there's no harm in looking, right? So what do you say?"

"Why not?" All hanging around the condo had to offer was booze and boob tube. And Dave was right.

There was no harm in looking.

12

"Ladies, say good-bye to the work week blues! Because you've been so good, we're gonna get *baaad!*" MC Derk stretched the word out like a rubber band as the Bad Boys pranced across the stage of Trends in time to Prince's "Let's Go Crazy."

Drink in hand, I stood behind the makeshift stage curtain, gawking out at the sea of excited female faces. Trends was packed wall to wall, and the only other males in the place were tending bar. It was girls night out, flesh for fantasy, and they were howling for it.

"Yes, ladies, we are going to make you *hot!*" Derk promised as the troupe high-kicked offstage.

Dave danced his way behind the curtain and started shedding his tux. "Having fun, bro?"

"Yeah, but nowhere near as much as your fans." I was amazed by the boisterous, hooting crowd, had no idea women ever got so whoop-it-up raunchy. "You may not get out of here alive."

"Well, if we don't. . ." Dave grinned. "What a way to go."

"It's almost time to get primitive, ladies!" Derk promised. "Because King Kong Kevin will be right out! To bring out the beast in you!" Derk rounded the curtain, vial in hand. "Who wants a bump?"

"Me," said Kevin, adjusting his tiger skin outfit in the full-length mirror Dave and I had hauled in from the van. Kevin was *huge*, a good three inches taller than Derk, and with a weightlifter's body matted with thick black hair, he looked ready to run down a wounded gazelle on the savannah. Derk spooned him up then pocketed the vial just as a waitress peeked around the curtain to ask if we needed more drinks. Everybody did.

Derk returned to the stage and introed Kevin, who hit the boards to Steve Miller's "Jungle Love." The place went nuts when he shed the tiger skin, dozens of hands holding up money.

"Nothing like this in Garrison, huh?" asked Dave.

"No kidding," I said, watching my bro climb into blue tear-away spandex pants with silver lightning bolts down the sides. In heavy eyeliner, mascara and lip gloss, Dave looked halfway to Ace Frehley. "It's pretty gonzo."

"Give it up, ladies, give it up for the King!" As Derk pumped up the crowd, Kevin leapt off stage and began slowly threading his way through the crush of frenzied, cash-waving females. "Yeah, King Kong Kevin!" Derk trumpeted. "I know you girls would love getting dragged off to *his* cave!"

The crowd roared in agreement, hands squeezing Kevin's butt, kneading his pecs, stuffing bills in his g-string and letting their fingers linger. When Kevin finally climbed back onstage, he appeared to be wearing a skirt made of dollar bills. As "Bungle in the Jungle" ended, Kevin took a final bow then dashed behind the curtain.

"Tick, tock, it's time to rock!" Derk crowed. "And here to rock you all! Night! Long! Ladies, give it up for the Rock 'n' Roll Kid!"

33

Dave hit the stage, Les Paul guitar in hand, spinning and shimmying to Led Zep's "Rock and Roll." Red lights bathed the stage as he put the ax aside and started peeling down. I wondered how many happy homemakers and schoolteachers were screaming for his bod. Soon stripped to boots and blue g-string, Dave grabbed the guitar again and did things with it to make the ghost of Jimi Hendrix blush.

"Let's hear it for the Rock 'n' Roll Kid!" cried Derk as Dave jumped into the crowd. AC/DC's "Bad Boy Boogie" roared from the speakers. "I know you girls want to strum his instrument!" Derk shouted. "And the Kid's very musical, girls. He *loves* yodeling up the canyon."

When Dave returned from the tip circuit the next dancer went out as a doctor, stethoscope twirling. My Seven and Seven was dancing right through me, so I decided to brave the crowd and headed for the Men's, getting pawed some along the way. I didn't like it much, which surprised me at first, but then I realized they were just grabbing meat, not me.

The show was a real education, the lesson being that in the right setting women could be as lewd as a fifteen-year-old boy panting over *Hustler*. I imagined Wendy plunked down in the middle of Trends, wondered if she'd be waving dollar bills.

Emerging from the restroom, I stopped at the bar for a glass of ice water to dilute the booze. Dave was at the mike now, telling the crowd they were about to meet the *baddest* boy of all, Mr. X!

Derk hit the stage, and I almost dropped my glass. He had on black leather pants, with a studded leather harness crisscrossing his bronze, chiseled chest. His face was hidden behind a Lone Ranger mask, but it was the final costume accessory that had startled me.

Derk was wearing a long black wig.

13

Dave and I were sipping early afternoon beers on the patio to prep for Vance's funeral. My sunburn had browned into a nice tan. We were shirtless and in shorts beneath the clear Colorado sky.

"Wish it would fuckin' rain," Dave said glumly. "Vance deserves to be sent off with some thunder and lightning."

"He's probably not worried about it," I said, wondering if *not worrying* was the best life had to offer. I hadn't had a drink since the Bad Boys gig two nights ago, but going to a funeral for the first time in my life seemed occasion enough to work out the old liver.

Dave grabbed his Coors and held it high. "To Vance!"

"Vance."

We drank. Dave wiped his mouth and said he was going up to Boulder tonight to see Laura, the girl he met in Colorado Springs. "I can't believe how much we click, even just talking on the phone. And how much I dig her."

"Sounds like Wendy and me," I said. "It's like we're tuned to the same wavelength."

"It's great feeling connected, huh?" Dave said softly, like we were sharing a marvelous secret.

"Yes, it is," I agreed, deciding to call Wen later. No more waiting to hear from her or tiptoeing around her old man.

Dave pushed up his shades and gave me a long look. "Hold on to her, Adam, 'cause the first cut is the deepest," he said dramatically, as if quoting Shakespeare instead of Rod Stewart. "So try not to fuck things up."

"I won't." Watching Dave finish his second beer and crack open a third, I almost reminded him how drinking and driving had led directly to today's festivities, but instead stuck to the topic, which was more important anyway. "Wen and I are forever," I declared, then burped unexpectedly. We both laughed and, having already expelled some hot air, I added, "Or at least I'm willing to carve that on a tree."

"Have you?"

"No, but I'm *willing*."

"I get it," Dave said. "The impulse to make some romantic gesture, like in the movies. . ."

"Yeah, except it's not make believe."

Dave stretched out on his lounge. "Sometimes I wish we were still kids," he said wistfully, fingers drumming on the beer can. "Playing war in the field behind the post office. Crawling into our beds on Friday night, knowing Mom would make us bacon and egg sandwiches to eat with Saturday morning cartoons."

"I feel that way sometimes, too," I said. "But then we'd just grow up and have go through all the shit all over again."

"True." Dave sipped his beer and sighed. "And I occasionally wish I was more like Derk. Nothing touches the guy, nothing can faze him."

"Who wants to be like that?"

"Me... once in awhile."

"Nah, it doesn't suit you. Some guys are just natural born pricks. . ." I was thinking about Wendy's dad and Harry Paul Gatlin, but Derk seemed like their spiritual relative. "And you aren't in that club, brudder."

Dave shrugged. "Thanks, but Derk doesn't belong to *any* club. He's one of a kind."

I snickered. "Thank God."

Glancing up at the only cloud in the sky, it struck me that around this time eight days ago I was boarding the bus back in Garrison. Only eight days? It seemed like ages.

We soaked up more rays for awhile, then Dave got up and stretched. "I'm gonna shower and get dressed for the fuckin' funeral."

35

"Right behind you." As we headed inside, I remembered what Derk had said to me the other day, that we had a lot in common. I don't see it. Not at all.

14

We'd had all day for funeral prep, but still managed to dick around until fifteen minutes before the service. I asked Dave if we'd make it on time.

"Maybe not, but Vance would have wanted it this way," Dave said as we strolled out to the parking lot. "He was always late and a master of the screwball excuse. We're just following tradition."

We got in the Camaro, and I sparked a cig. "Never expected to be going to a funeral while I was here. Pretty weird."

"Yeah, but you *never* expect it," Dave said as we headed out. He looked both ways then ran the stop sign at the Windhollow entrance. "Never know when the big third strike is gonna come smoking across the plate, and yer outta here!"

I pictured us on another day, driving to another funeral. "Are you gonna come home when it's time to bury the old man?"

Dave bit his lip, considering the question as we motored toward Colorado Boulevard. "Probably," he decided. "If only to tell him he's an asshole one last time."

"Hey, I understand," I said, fumbling for something to say on Dad's behalf. "But when Mom took off, the old man hung tough, right?"

Dave grunted, not prepared to give an inch.

"What happened between you and him later sucked but. . ." I groped for words to rust away the iron in my brother's eyes. "But he never ran out on us in the middle of the night."

"And he never kicked *you* out with no place to go, Adam, so don't defend him to me."

"It's just. . ."

"Just nothing!" Dave pounded on the dashboard. "I don't want to hear it, alright?"

"Okay, forget it." But I'd have to try again, tomorrow, next week, whenever, because we're all scheduled for that Final Strikeout soon enough, so wasting time on old grudges between family and friends was stupid, a pointless waste.

We got on the freeway and headed west toward Fort Logan, a government cemetery. Vance was eligible for burial there, Dave explained, because his father had fought in Korea. It startled me to realize I didn't know if we won that war. They never said on *M.A.S.H.*

———

Arriving at the cemetery, we headed toward a funeral in progress, cruising past long rows of white marble headstones, parade ground straight. We parked and joined the mourners. Vance's coffin had already been lowered into the earth. A woman standing next to the open grave was bawling, sharp rasping sobs, like fingernails on a blackboard. This, I decided, was going to be worse than expected.

"Our brother dwells now with the Lord," a tubby preacher intoned. I glanced around for Derk, wasn't surprised that I didn't see him. The bawling woman managed to dial it down to soft moans. She swayed from side to side, standing so near the hole I feared she might tumble in. A man came up and patted her shoulder, mouthing *there, there's* while looking embarrassed.

Dave was staring down at the manicured turf, eyes damp, and a feeling of melancholy swept over me like a wave. I felt sad not just for Vance and Dave, but sad somehow, all the way back to Garrison.

The preacher droned. The woman sobbed. Finally it was over. As the mourners began drifting back to their cars, we went up to the grave and stared down at the coffin. Dave picked up a clod of dirt and crumbled it into the hole.

"Goodbye, pal."

The gravestone was piled with flowers, but I thought I glimpsed a "B," odd for someone named Vance Nathan. Walking over, I moved some roses and saw that the name freshly chiseled into the white marble was *Barry Sullivan.*

When I waved Dave over, his eyes grew wide. He knelt down to run his fingers over the grooves in the stone, as if needing tactile proof that we'd been at the wrong funeral. Finally he stood up, shook his head and started to giggle.

It was contagious and our giggles soon became guffaws. The remaining mourners glared at us, looking ready to add to the death toll, so we quickly retreated to the Camaro.

"V-Vance would have loved this," Dave said when he caught his breath. "Always leave 'em laughing."

I said finding Vance's actual grave shouldn't be hard.

"We already said goodbye," Dave whispered. "Does standing by another hole in the ground really matter?"

"One dirt nap's enough for me."

"Okay then." Dave fished a coke seal out of his wallet. "Let's do a bump in Vance's honor."

We fueled up and then took off, passing a procession of cars snaking in through the gate, led by a two-tone Cadillac hearse, a gaudy garbage truck. Neither of us said anything for a half mile or so, then I sparked a cig and asked Dave what he was thinking about.

"About why Vance died."

I chuckled mirthlessly. "My guess would be because he got too wasted and plowed his car into a fucking pole." The words were harsher than intended, but I felt grown-up saying them, like I was facing our ultimate destination. We're here today, gone tomorrow, no more substantial than my cigarette smoke being sucked through the sunroof.

"That's how he died, Adam, not *why*."

"You need a reason?"

"There's always a reason," Dave insisted. "And does it mean Vance hung up his g-string too late, or shouldn't have quit at all?"

It seemed to me Vance's career moves had far less to do with dying than his blood alcohol content, but I didn't want to argue the point. Dave turned on the radio and we caught a news bulletin about a terrorist attack on the Paris airport. Sub-machine guns and fragmentation grenades, a bloody valentine from the Mid-East, leaving a dozen or more dead.

"Those bastards," I hissed, picturing broken-doll bodies. "I hope Reagan bombs them again."

"There's a whole lot of bastards out there, Rambo," said Dave, steering around an ancient Buick, which reminded me of the old man. "And bombs deliver random death, not justice."

"Yeah, I know," I said, "but sometimes blowing shit up just makes you *feel* better."

"Aren't we supposed to be the good guys?"

"Sure, but what can we do, bro?"

"Well, I know what I'm gonna do," Dave declared, wheeling the Camaro into the parking lot of Big Dan's Discount Liquor. He was soon back with a little something for what ailed us.

I took a blast from the half-pint of rum and glanced up at the American flag flying above Big Dan's, where every day was the Fourth of July.

15

As we headed east toward downtown, Dave pointed out "Big Mac," a white concrete sports arena that resembled a giant hamburger. The rum went right to my head, and I tilted the seat back and dozed off to dream of Wendy's cool hand in mine as we strolled down Main Street to the Land of Golden Arches.

"Quarter-pounder and fries, babe? Oh, look, there's Dave sharing a McCookie with his first love, Nancy Keller. And in that back booth, it's Mom and Dad, splitting a shake. Gee, ain't it a wonderful life?"

Suddenly Derk danced through the double doors, wearing nothing but a barbed wire g-string and his long black wig, a rifle slung over one shoulder. "Hello, everybody!"

The diners responded as one. "Hi, Derk!"

After pirouetting on tiptoes, Derk slid the gun off his shoulder. "This is a Mannlicher-Carcano rifle," he said, working the bolt to slam a shell into the breech. "It hasn't been fired since 1963. Let's see if it still works." He raised the barrel and fired from the hip.

Wendy's head exploded in a red plume of blood and bone.

I jerked awake, white dots cha-chaing before my eyes as we turned into Windhollow. "Wow," I muttered, shaking my head to dislodge the lingering images, "what a horrible frickin' dream."

"What?" Dave asked.

I started to tell him then just shook my head. "Nothin'. Never mind."

"I don't dream anymore," Dave said as we pulled into his space. "Maybe I just don't remember them."

Thunderheads were beginning to pile up over the mountains. After we entered the condo, I lit a smoke, still creeped out by the dream. "You know your Trends show the other night?"

"What about it?"

"Derk's black wig. . ." I ventured. "How long has he had that?"

Dave laughed. "That's an odd question."

"Yeah," I agreed, following him into the kitchen. "Derk was wearing it in my dream. And shooting people."

"Sounds more like a nightmare."

"Yeah."

"I think he got the wig about six months ago." Dave grabbed a couple Cokes from the fridge and handed me one. "He's always trying out new stage looks."

"Sure, makes sense." Settling on the sofa, I glanced up at Porsche Girl, sprawled on the hood of the car. "And he always gets a lot of chicks, right?"

"No shit, Sam." Dave flipped on the tube. We watched MTV for awhile, then he headed upstairs to take a nap.

I knew the nightmare meant nothing, was just as much a mirage as Porsche Girl's *come-mount-me* smile. Needing to connect with something real, I went to the kitchen and called Wendy.

"Yeah?"

Her old man's rusty tin can voice. Damn. Resisting the urge to hang-up, I gripped the receiver tightly and forged ahead. "Hi, Mr. Daniels," I said, talking loud like him. "It's Adam, calling from Denver."

"Wendy's busy, boy."

"I really need to talk to her, sir."

"You deaf? I said she's busy with her grandfather."

Shutting my eyes, I imagined kicking the big jerk where it counts. "This is long distance, sir."

"Then I'll save you some money." He hung up on me.

"Bastard!" I slammed the phone down, changed into shorts and tank top and went out for a run. When I returned an hour later, Dave was getting ready to split for Boulder to see Laura.

I mentioned how tired I was, but Dave didn't pick up on the hint so when he was about to leave, I asked if I could get a couple lines.

"I guess, *small* ones," he said reluctantly. "I'm almost out. Derk's supposed to be scoring a couple ounces."

"Does he deal, too?"

"He does everything, bro."

Dave doled out some magic power for me and I walked him out to the Camaro. The sky had grown inky and ominous. Lightning crackled above downtown, too late for Vance's going away party.

"Have fun with Laura."

Dave grinned. "Hope so."

Back inside, I considered calling Wen again, but couldn't risk pissing off her old man, not with her as a likely target of his anger. So I did the coke instead and it was just enough to make me want more. My weird tangle of thoughts would unravel with a bit more magic. . .

Tough, the little voice scolded. *Don't whine for what you don't have.*

Retrieving pen and spiral notebook from my backpack, I sat down at the table in the tiny breakfast nook off the kitchen to write Wendy a letter. I needed to communicate with her *now*, even if my words would be days old when delivered. But my pen had gone dry, and a quick search of the living room didn't turn up a replacement.

As rain started to pat against the windows, I noticed that Derk's bedroom door was cracked open slightly. What the hell, looking for a pen was an innocent enough invasion of privacy, right?

His room was dominated by a round waterbed. Exposed colored light bulbs were strung up high in all four corners, like watchful eyes. One wall was covered with gold-veined mirror squares, another papered floor to ceiling with centerfolds. After briefly ogling the eye candy, I went over to his desk and picked up an appointment book that had a pen clipped to the cover.

I detached the pen, hesitated a sec before curiosity won out, then opened the book. Two ruler-straight columns ran parallel down the pages, one listing the Bad Boys nightclub shows, the other "strip-a-grams" for private parties. It was obviously a dance log, tracking B Boys biz.

The entries included date, time and address, contact names and numbers, while the 'grams had more details like "full-sized bottle of Champagne" and "pre-paid except tips." The assigned dancers were identified by two letters: AA, BB, etc., which I figured out from a note below one entry: *EE: car problems. HH subbed instead.*

Some parties were more memorable than others, at least that's how I interpreted the three stars awarded to/by *AA* a couple weeks ago for a gig in Westminster. That was right after I got to Denver, and that girl got kidnapped from the Westminster Mall. . .

Even if that's true, the little voice wondered, *so what?*

"So nothing," I whispered. Turning to leave, I spied a bottle of Rush on a shelf above the waterbed. Wandering over, I saw the shelf also held a hand mirror, piled with coke. I stared at the magic powder and chewed the end of the pen, rationalizing. Derk wouldn't miss a little coke, while I *needed* it to fully focus on Wendy's letter.

It wasn't a hard sell.

I quickly rolled up a dollar, snorted some ill-gotten blow and returned to the breakfast nook. Poised pen above paper, but the words still wouldn't flow. I had so much to tell Wen that it all gridlocked in my brain. Resisting the urge to hijack more coke, I slowly wrung out words to get started.

Hi beautiful,

Tried calling you earlier, but your dad said you were busy, then hung up on me. He hates my guts, and I don't have a clue why. What I do *know is that I wish you were in my arms right now.*

Hardly poetry, but not awful. I lit a smoke and continued.

Went to a funeral today for a friend of my brother who kamikazed his car into a pole a few days ago. We ended up at the wrong funeral (I'll explain THAT later) but it still sucked. And five weeks away from you feels like forever.

Oh, check this out – Dave is a stripper! Wild, huh? He's changed so much in three years, but not really at all, if that makes any sense.

I paused to grab a beer, read what I'd written and realized I was striking random notes. Focus, kid. Get to the point.

I miss you, Wen. My lips long to nibble your neck, your ear lobes, my fingers to stroke your hair, gently tweak a nipple, slowly ease down your zipper. . .

Don't wanna get myself worked up, so back to the tour report. The sky here seems enormous, big and blue, stretching away to forever. Denver's huge, but other than downtown, it's kinda like a lot of small towns stuck together. I'm camped out on a sofa at the Windhollow West condos, where my bro lives with a rich creep of a roommate, who's also the boss stripper.

I was scribbling faster now, hand racing across the page. Thanks, magic powder.

I ache for you, babe. Never realized just how much I love you until now, with all the long, lonely miles between us. God, I wish we were making it right now, on the tiny table where I'm writing this.

XX 'n' kisses!

Adam

I dug a folded envelope from my backpack, sealed, addressed and stamped the letter, then walked out to building G's group mailbox over by the pool and dropped it in the pick-up slot. Soon after I returned to the condo, the TV came on by itself. That freaked me out for a sec, but the VCR must have been programmed to turn on. Probably Derk's doing and, big surprise, it was another porno.

Naughty Nurses began in a doctor's office, where both nurse and patient were soon performing oral surgery on the doctor, who was conveniently nude beneath his lab coat.

"Yeah, ladies, get a rise out of my meat thermometer!"

The beer went down and my blood pressure went up. The nonexistent plot and stilted dialogue were easily ignored, somehow plugging me more directly into the suck and fuck. After maybe ten minutes, I paused the action, then headed back to Derk's room for the Rush.

16

Past noon the next day and Dave still wasn't back from Boulder. I was trying to distract myself by channel surfing but was braced for bad news. Sure, another car wreck was unlikely but there's always plenty of disasters on menu.

The phone *had* been ringing, four calls in the last ninety minutes, but those were all Derk-related. Turning off the tube, I wandered down to the workout room and found him doing shoulder reps on the Universal machine.

"Still no word from Dave," I said, mounting the exercise bike like a weary cowpoke.

". . .twenty-nine, thirty." Finishing his set, Derk got up and stretched, sweat glistening on his bare torso. "Needless anxiety, Adam. Maybe his new chick turned out to be a nympho."

"Sure," I agreed. "He's probably fine."

"Of course he is." Derk snatched up forty-pound dumbbells and began doing curls. "Dave mentioned that you want a fake ID."

"Yeah," I said half-heartedly, having forgotten all about it.

"I'll grab a quick shower after this last set," Derk said. "Then we'll go get you taken care of."

"I should probably wait to hear from Dave."

"He's not in the habit of checking in," Derk scoffed.

"I don't know. . ."

"Jesus, Adam, were you a nervous old woman in a former life or what?" Derk finished his curls and mopped his face with a hand towel. "I'm a busy guy, but happy to do you a favor," he said, sauntering out of the room. "If you want that ID when I'm done showering, we'll go. If not, that's fine. But don't ask me later, comprende?"

42

Enough clockwatching, I decided, following Derk down the hall. "Okay, let's do it."

Forty-five minutes later we were blasting down Speer Boulevard in Derk's red '66 'Vette. He told me about an amateur skin flick he'd been in during a trip to Los Angeles back in May.

"It was a hot tub orgy scene, right? I'm doing this little redhead doggie style, *while* she necks with a blonde getting plowed by this black dude, Cisco, who's hung like a python."

"A star is porn," I wisecracked, mentally contrasting my slow, tender explorations with Wendy to Derk and the Python jack-hammering bimbos for the cameras. "What was her name, the redhead?"

"Tina," Derk said, surprising me that he remembered. "Said she was an art student at UCLA." He chuckled, took a small cigar from a silver case and puffed it to life. "I gave her one hell of a lesson, believe me. Check out *Hot Tub Tarts*, coming soon to a video store near you."

"Hope they changed that tub water." This got a smile from Derk, and in the sober light of day my half-assed suspicions about his black wig seemed foolish. He might be a creep, but one with a full date book.

At a red light on Federal, we pulled up beside a yellow Chevy low-rider. "Check out the bean-mobile," Derk said, then leaned across me to shout out the window. "Hey, Juan! Pick a lot of fruit today?"

"Fuck you, dude!" the driver shot back.

"Got your green card?" Derk asked, then adopted a Cheech and Chong voice. "How much to screw your sister, Juan? Or is she already knocked up?"

The driver's eyes grew wide as the light changed and both cars sped off. The Chevy veered left, like Juan was trying to ram us, but Derk punched the gas and left the Chevy in our dust.

"I don't dislike Mexicans," Derk told me, gnawing on his cigar. "Certainly banged enough hot little Chiquitas. But the dudes tend to be almost cartoonishly macho, so it's fun to whip them into a frenzy."

"Well," I pointed out, like I was trying to score points in history class, "most of the Southwest used to be Mexico."

"*Used to be* is the operative phrase," Derk said. "To the victor go the spoils. Forget all the nonsense you've been fed about *how you play the game* being more important than winning or losing. The *only* thing that matters is winning. Just ask Reagan or Michael Milken."

Gazing out the windshield, I wondered what Derk's game was, then realized big bucks and abundant pussy was how he kept score.

"Hey!" He clamped a hand on my shoulder, scowling. "You listening to me, Adam?"

"Yeah." I tried not to flinch as his fingers dug into my flesh. "Sure I am."

"Good." Derk patted my shoulder before returning his hand to the wheel. "Being ignored really bugs me."

"You were talking about Ronnie and Wall Street crooks."

"Did you ever think about being a dancer?" Derk asked, wildly off-topic.

I blinked at him. "You mean a stripper?"

"An erotic entertainer," he corrected.

"No." I laughed. "Hell, I can barely even pee at a urinal next to another guy."

"You wouldn't be performing for *guys,*" Derk said, then gave me a squinty-eye look. "Unless that's what trips your trigger."

"No," I said, looking down.

"You'd need to bulk up a bit, learn some dance moves," Derk continued, toying with the idea. "But we could have you onstage in a couple months."

"Nah, my girlfriend has exclusive rights."

"You say that now, but it's hard to keep 'em down on the farm after they've seen the bright lights."

We turned off 38th Avenue and were now in a trashy, rundown neighborhood. "Nice area," I said sarcastically.

"Low rent means low profile, just the way Ramos likes it." Derk wheeled into a dirt driveway beside a yellow cracker box house. We climbed out of the 'Vette. The patchy front lawn was dotted with dandelions and toys. Opening a squeaky gate, Derk kicked a Transformer out of the way. I followed him up the walk, glancing around for pimply toughs with zip guns.

Derk knocked. A slender, striking girl around thirteen or so answered the door and waved us in. "Dad's back in his workshop."

"How are you today, gorgeous?" Derk asked her.

The girl shrugged and padded into the kitchen, followed by a small boy in paint-stained corduroy shorts.

"Mmmn, that Teresa's tasty," Derk said softly as we started down the hall. "I'd gobble her up, but then Ramos would get all emotional and might try to kill me." He knocked on the workshop door and winked. "Then I might have to kill him."

"Come in."

We went, stepping into chaos and clutter, with stacks of newspapers and magazines three-quarters of the way up to the low ceiling along the back wall. Two battered metal desks were ajumble with cameras and film cans, stacks of photos, forms, paper stock, and three different typewriters. The room smelled of printer's ink and cat piss. In the middle of this mess stood Ramos, a pudgy, prematurely graying little Mexican guy in a ratty lab coat that had seen considerably more wear than the ones worn by the "doctors" in *Naughty Nurses.*

"Who is this?" Ramos asked, eyeing me suspiciously. His cheeks were dotted with angry boils, his brown eyes narrow and watery. "Derk, you know I don't like strangers."

"It's cool," Derk said. "He's my roommate's brother, fresh off the bus from Green Acres. Adam needs an ID to partake of our cultural pleasures."

Ramos looked me over closely, and I imagined him in a bazaar, haggling over the price of slaves. "I don't like strangers," he repeated.

"And *I* said he's cool."

Ramos picked his nose, then nodded. "One-fifty."

"A hundred," Derk countered.

I suddenly felt like a dope, having neglected to ask what a fake ID would cost. I had maybe thirty bucks on me.

"For you, okay," Ramos agreed. "A hundred."

"Pay him, Adam."

"Ahh. . ." I shuffled my feet, wanting to sink into the floor.

"What?" Derk looked at me blankly, then frowned. "You don't have enough cash?"

"Guess I should have asked the price," I muttered, feeling eight instead of eighteen.

"I fucking guess so."

"You bring over strangers with no money?" Ramos shooed away a fly. "This kind of business I don't need."

Derk asked how much money I had, cursed when I told him, then reached for his wallet. "I'll cover it," he told Ramos. "Just take your pictures."

Told to toe a line of tape in a corner of the room with a white sheet tacked to the wall, I obeyed. Three pix were snapped, dorky looking enough when developed to pass for real driver's license photos. Two shots suggested a recent round of shock therapy, so we settled on the third, in which I only looked slightly retarded.

Ramos ran an ID blank into a typewriter and tapped out my vital stats, one finger at a time. Then he carefully attached my photo and ran the works through a laminating machine. The finished product was still warm to the touch as we compared it to Derk's license. I didn't see any differences.

Derk praised Ramos, paid him with a hundred-dollar bill, then we headed out. Teresa and the boy were racing Hot Wheels on the living room floor.

"Bye, beautiful," Derk said with an exaggerated leer.

"Zoom, zoom," the boy said, playing with a tiny blue Corvette. Teresa said nothing.

"That's one sweet little taco," Derk said, smacking his lips as we crossed the lawn. "If it wasn't for her old man. . ."

"What, is Ramos an overly protective Dad?"

———

45

No," Derk said as we climbed into the car. "He just wants her all to himself."

"Huh?"

"I walked in unannounced a couple months ago and saw Ramos putting the one-eyed weasel to his darling daughter on that ratty sofa in the living room. Fortunately, he was too occupied to hear the screen door open and I backed out, unnoticed."

"That's sick," I said, not sure if Derk was serious or not.

"Sick, sure," he said, "but you have to admit, it's convenient. Any time he wants some tail, all Ramos has to do is ground her." Derk laughed as we sped off in the 'Vette.

I laughed, too, even though I didn't think it was funny.

17

"Time to see if your papers pass muster," Derk said, turning into a strip joint on Federal called the Sly Fox. We tooted up from his vial, then headed inside. Derk exchanged pleasantries with a huge black doorman in a wine-colored suit named James, who ushered us in with barely a glance at my ID.

The small, dim bar was dominated by a long T-shaped runway lit with blinking red lights. There were two tables of biker types and some suits getting their lunch hour kicks.

"I'll get us a drink, Adam."

As Derk headed to the bar, a DJ announced, "Up next, it's sweet Star! And a song about her favorite subject!"

A tiny dishwater blonde took the stage as "Feel Like Making Love" thumped from the speakers. Star strutted along the runway on spiked heels, hips undulating inside denim cutoffs as she fingered her at-attention nipples inside a tight Ratt t-shirt.

Derk returned and handed me a tall skinny glass as we took seats along the top of the runway's T. "Long Island Iced Tea," he said, knocking back a third of his drink. "The perfect libation for a hot summer day."

Taking a sip, I nearly choked on what tasted like rocket fuel. Star was shaking her butt at one of the suits, who'd just laid a five dollar bill on the stage. Soon wiggling out of T-shirt and shorts, Star dropped to the floor, braced her feet against the elevated lip of the stage and began a series of pelvic thrusts in time to the music, each bringing her a bit closer to the suit, who was leaning forward to better enjoy the view, tongue lolling out one side of his mouth. As the song reached its climax, Star lifted her legs, draped one on each of the suit's shoulders and brought her pistoning pelvis to within range of that droopy dog tongue. Then she stopped, froze for a beat or two before bending forward to run her fingers through the guy's close-cropped hair. She then leaned back again to allow him to tuck the tip into her skimpy silver g-string. The suit's pals hooted their approval.

Derk lifted his glass and winked. "To being twenty-one."

"Definitely." We clinked glasses. The second dose of the rocket fuel went down smoother, boosting the coke buzz. I leaned toward Derk and said, "Vacations are all about sightseeing" as the Kinks exploded from the speakers. I had one of their t-shirts back at the condo.

Girl, you really got me going. . .

"Work it, baby!" Derk called and Star now pranced toward us, ignoring other tips along the stage.

"My favorite bad boy," the little blonde said coyly as she rubbed Derk's shoulders.

"Star light, Star bright," he said, reaching for his wallet. "My friend here just turned twenty-one, so turn him on." Derk handed me a twenty. "Tip the young lady, Adam."

Grinning like a goof, I held up the cash as Star spun around in front of me.

"No, honey." Star put a small hand on my shoulder and bent down to flick a tongue tip into my ear. "Tuck it into my g-string when I'm done."

"Sure will."

Grabbing my hand, Star pulled me up out of the chair. She bent backwards like a gymnast, hands braced on the stage and began gyrating her hips and thrusting her pussy towards me. This was a variation of the show the suit got, but being the focus of Star's attention was far more hypnotic, as her feminine mound bucked and swayed beneath a thin fabric triangle.

When Ray Davies' frenzied cries of "Oh, oh, oh!" brought the song to an end, Star sprang to her feet, gave me a peck on the cheek, then pulled her g-string forward, giving me a ringside view of her clean-shaven charms.

Popeyed, I deposited the twenty as instructed.

"That's Star!" the DJ cried. "And she *is* a star, by far! Whoop it up for her, guys!"

I whooped, watching her prance across the stage to one of the bikers and start moaning along with the song "Sex." Star was nearly naked before fifteen horny strangers yet seemed completely in control.

I wasn't. My jeans had grown tight, so I retreated to the men's room to cool off before I dropped trou and started jerking it, stage-side. I smoked half a cig in the only stall and returned to find Derk ready to split.

"You dug that, eh?" he asked as we exited the Sly Fox.

"What's not to like?"

"Women libbers may hate strippers," Derk said, "but where else can a girl with a tenth-grade education make five hundreds bucks on a good night?"

"American enterprise at its finest," I suggested.

"Damn straight," Derk agreed as we climbed in the 'Vette. "And Star's a little wild cat, with a taste for the rough and tumble. Last time I did her, she had to take a couple days off work, until the marks went away."

"You animal," I joked, but Derk didn't smile.

"We're all animals, Adam," he said as the 'Vette growled to life. "The sooner you learn that the better off you'll be."

18

Ted Koppel was covering the Paris bombing on *Nightline* when Dave finally got home. "Hey, bro," he called breezily, tossing his Bad Boys windbreaker on the stairs and heading to the kitchen. "What's shakin'?"

"Not much," I said sullenly, glad Dave was in one piece, natch, but pissed about his long silent absence. "How was Boulder?"

"Great." He joined me on the sofa with a Coke and a big grin. "Laura is one amazing female, in bed and out."

"Good for you." I clicked over to MTV. Vermin Squirm, the latest heavy metal hypes, were prancing around a girl tied to a Styrofoam stone altar, shouting idiot rhymes about big guns and tight buns. "You going gaga over her or is that a violation of the stripper code?"

Dave flipped me off, with a smile. "It's way too early to think about anything serious." He sipped his Coke and proceeded to make Laura's case anyway. "But we did have an *excellent* night. Hit the sheets around ten and barely came up for air until dawn." Dave patted his crotch gingerly. "The girl is a wiz at resurrecting the dead."

He sounded like a kid at Christmas, so I couldn't help but grin back at him. "Spare me the gory details."

"And it's not just the sex," Dave gushed. "I've never really talked to a girl like I talk to her, about *everything*. It's great, but sort of scary at the same time, because, like, where's this been all my life?"

"Yeah." I laughed, suddenly happy for both of us. "That's *exactly* how I feel about Wendy."

"Derk here?"

"In his room with some chick."

"I need to see if he's getting more blow soon."

"Hope so."

We watched a few videos then Dave yawned, grabbed his soda and got up. "I'm gonna go crash, Adam."

"Good night." He started for the stairs and I said, "Hey. . . while I'm here do you think you could maybe let me know if you're gonna be gone this long again? Or should I just expect it?"

Dave glanced back at me then slowly smiled. "What, were you worried?"

"No," I said, glancing at Porsche girl. "Maybe a little."

"Sorry about that, brother." He walked back over to me and tousled my hair. "Do my best to keep you posted."

"Thanks."

After finishing my beer, I went to take a leak and could hear Derk's friend moaning through the wall. Moans punctuated by what sounded like the crack of a whip.

"Harder, you bastard!" the girl cried. "More!"

"Beg for it!"

"Give it to me, asshole! Harder!"

Bladder attended to, I clicked off the light and... stood there listening. The whip cracked. The girl squealed. My hand started moving toward my crotch, but I thought of Wendy and fled down the hall.

"Fuckin' sick," I muttered, but in the dream scheduled shortly it was me wielding the whip, etching red lines on Star the stripper's back. Thirty-nine lashes, then I put down the whip and reached for a chainsaw.

Mental circuits blew. I jerked awake and bolted upright on the couch, scared, sweating, but with a raging hard-on. Staring up at the ceiling, the weird thought struck me that maybe I never should have left Garrison.

19

"Oh, the phone company gave Dave a big promotion," I said, lying on impulse, long distance. Maybe Dave didn't care if the old man knew he was a stripper, but I did, though I don't know why. After two weeks in Denver, I discovered there were lots of things I didn't know. "He's on the rise at AT&T."

"Maybe he's finally growing up," Dad said grudgingly. "Not that I'd bet folding money on it."

"He's got a new girlfriend, Laura, and she's great," I continued, fishing for any positive reaction. "You'd like her." That only prompted a grunt, so I retreated into household trivia. "How's the garden doing?"

"Fine. If Mrs. Johnson doesn't keep her cat out of there, I'm gonna wring the damn thing's neck."

I smiled. The old man had been threatening Figaro for years.

"I'm glad you're having a good time, Adam. Just don't blow all your money on something stupid and then call me, crying for more."

Like a hundred bucks for a fake ID? "I won't."

We hung up, and I started prepping for my rock 'n' roll Friday night. Uniform: black jeans and boots, white and red Who t-shirt beneath my lettermen's jacket. The results in the mirror weren't too bad.

Pocketing the directions to the Big House, I locked up with the key Dave left me and sauntered out to his Camaro like I owned it. Climbing aboard, I gripped the steering wheel and made race-car sounds like a little kid, shut my eyes and got the checkered flag at Indy.

The winner, for the third year in a row, Adam Freeman!

—

49

Victory champagne bubbled down my neck as I snuggled a babe on either arm. *It was nothing, girls, really. . .*

Soon cruising down Colorado Boulevard with the windows down and the stereo cranked, I felt like a million bucks, like nothing in the world could touch me.

Not a god damned thing.

20

The Big House was a converted Victorian mansion, painted prison gray, in the downtown neighborhood I ran through, only a few blocks up the hill from the state capitol. The club's tiny parking lot was full, so I ended up having to park three blocks over and one up. Tried memorizing street names while walking to the club so I could find my way back after a few drinks.

A dozen or so people were lined up outside, waiting to get in. Joining them, I re-examined my new ID, hoping Ramos knew his stuff. The doorman looked like a Hell's Angel, but he only gave the license a quick glance then waved me over to a girl with spiky purple hair, who took my five bucks and stamped my hand.

Made it, I thought, strolling into the packed club. The Pretenders were pumping from the sound system as I found a stool at the end of the bar, next to an Elvira look-alike in a long black dress.

I ordered a Long Island Iced Tea and surveyed the club, which smelled like sweat and stale beer. The dozen or so small tables at the edge of the dance floor were occupied by a mix of long-haired rockers, punks with hair styles ranging from Mohawks to basic training buzz cuts, and an uncategorizable contingent of big city hipsters. Of course compared to me, *everybody* was hip, and I peeled off my lettermen's jacket and sat on it.

Tubes of pulsing blue and red neon ran along the bar and above the stage. Giant album covers hung tilted on the walls. The Beatles crossed Abbey Road at a mountain climber's angle. A pop-eyed Pat Benatar hung upside down in a straight-jacket.

Knocking back a quarter of my Long Island, I asked Elvira the time. She held up a limp wrist: 10:25. I climbed off the stool, hung the jacket on my right shoulder and circulated, getting buzzed on the crowd's expectant energy. Ten minutes later, the lights went down and the band hit the stage.

The bassist was a beefy Mexican guy wearing a white dinner jacket over a black t-shirt, with khakis below. The huge, shaggy drummer was in cut-off jeans and an AC/DC tank top. A tiny blonde girl wearing a pink miniskirt and white go-go boots positioned herself behind a keyboard. The trio went into an instrumental number that grew progressively louder, then stopped dead as the stage went dark.

A single white spotlight illuminated center stage, where a singer-guitarist had stationed himself. Tall and skinny in black jeans and t-shirt, he had pasty skin and a thick black mop of unruly hair.

"I'm Tommy Weathers," he said with a thin-lipped smile as he plugged his Gibson SG guitar into an amp. "We're the Next." The drummer rapped out a martial beat, underscored by a throbbing bass line. Weathers threw back his head and fired off a machine gun burst of metallic riffage. The guitar was *loud*, crashing over the crowd, killing all conversation.

"The past's a flag-wavin' parade, politicians all snake oil charade!" Weathers barked in a raw but melodic baritone as a spook house keyboard run swooped down over the beat. "My bed's not made 'n' I hardly get laid! 'Cause I'm a five round man in a ten round fight! Five round man in a ten round fight! Everything wrong when you ain't got no rights!"

Weathers spun around, lashing his fretboard with desperate fury, like he was fighting off a mad dog.

"Roll the stone up the hill! It rolls down again! Asked a friend where we were, he said man where you been? Five round man in a ten round fight! Seen a lot of what's wrong! Not so much of what's right!"

The lyrics landed hard, because they pretty well described *me,* desperate to roll a stone up that hill, to fight back against the world's endless stream of bullshit. To do something great, when I'm not even really *good* at anything.

But the Next sure as hell were. One song bled into another without any breaks or stage patter. Rock as Serious Business, my fave genre, with Tommy Weathers spitting out hang-'em-high lyrics and detonating his guitar like napalm from a B-52.

"Clown car consumers, living 'n' dying in a hurry! All us half-wits and asses! Give the dollar sign salute! Amid all the sound and fury! Rat race hurry scurry! All us dim-wits and asses! Groove on sex, blood and gloom! Race to our dollar sign doom!"

The rhythm section rumbled like a runway freight train; keyboards added a spiky, haunted house dirge; both barely audible beneath Tommy's pulverizing power chords as he stood at the end of the stage, head bobbing up and down like a paint-shaker. Then he fired off a speedy blues run as he raced back to the mike.

"Buy 'til we die! All us consumer cadre asses! Give the dollar sign salute! Bewitched credit card masses! Bank statement on our tomb! Yeah, dollar sign salute! Dig that dollar sign doom!"

An hour later, Tommy goose-stepped across the stage, unleashing a final orgy of distorted feedback, then jerked the cord out of his guitar and stalked off stage. The band followed and the stage went dark.

The crowd roared, demanding an encore for almost five minutes before a bouncer took the stage to say the Next was done for the night.

I booed with everyone else then grabbed what was left of my third Long Island and shuffled toward the door. The *exact* route back to the car was a bit blurry, but no problem. Playing find-the-Camaro would give me some time to sober up.

Detouring into the Men's, I peed, splashed water on my face at the sink, then emerged to almost collide with Tommy Weathers, who was with a gorgeous chick with fire engine red hair.

"You guys were great," I gushed. "Really fuckin' awesome."

"Unh, thanks," Tommy said, running a hand through his sweaty tangle of hair. "Nice." He pointed to the letterman's jacket draped on my right shoulder. "Real retro."

"Your lyrics are killer, man," I said, ignoring my high school fashion accessory.

"Oh yeah?" He stepped toward me and blinked, like he was seeing me for the first time. "You listen to the words, huh?"

"Always," I said, slurping down the rest of the Long Island. "Without lyrics, music is just. . . *sound*."

"What'd you like about 'em?" Tommy asked.

"Everything!" I enthused. "They're gutsy and real, an angry howl from the heart." God, I sounded like some *Rolling Stone* cliché-slinger. "But it's more than that. . . They sound a lot like *me*, if that makes any sense."

"Actually, it does," he said with a slight nod. "What's your name?"

"Adam."

"Tommy." We shook hands. "This is Raven," he added, nodding towards the sexy redhead.

"Hi, Raven."

"Hi," she said with an utter lack of interest.

"Always good to meet someone on the same wavelength, Adam," Tommy said warmly. "Come see us again sometime."

"Oh, I will."

After watching the pair disappear backstage, I put my glass on the bar and strolled out into the Denver night, where it took me a half-hour to find the Camaro. I climbed aboard and got my bearings: two blocks straight ahead to Colfax, then right all the way to Colorado Boulevard, and from there I knew the breadcrumb trail to Windhollow.

Sounds simple, but less than three blocks up Colfax a cop's cherry top spun to life behind me, siren wailing. Stomach leaping into my throat, I turned into a liquor store parking lot, wondering if I could walk a straight line, but the cop sped on by. I laughed and fumbled out a smoke with shaky hands, feeling like a death row con just reprieved by the governor.

Taking a deep drag, I realized that the porn palace, Kitty's, was directly across the street. I had thirty bucks left and there was no priest in sight. And, I told myself, more time to sober up would be a good thing.

I locked the Camaro and dashed across Colfax, ready to sample the treats in the carnal candy store.

21

Inside Kitty's, I was greeted by a locked turnstile and a gorilla of a man perched behind a high wooden counter to my right. "Fifty cent browsing fee," he said with a foghorn voice. "And let's see some ID."

I fished out two quarters and my fake ID. After studying it for a long moment, the gorilla released the turnstile and I wandered in to take inventory. Magazines and books ran from floor to ceiling on the long wall to the left. The top three racks were filled with slick men's mags. Below *Playboy, Penthouse, Hustler* and their many imitators were maybe twenty rows of thin paperbacks, most with lurid, badly drawn black and white covers.

Hot-Mouthed Daughters. Auntie Loves Horses. Watersport Weekend.

I stood there gawking, somewhat overwhelmed by the kinky cornucopia. One paperback caught my eye, stirring nightmare embers of Derk with a rifle and a shopping mall girl being wrestled into a van. Impulsively, I grabbed *Cheerleader's Rape Night* and flipped open the book.

Rivers of hot cum exploded from Frank's swollen cock. He smashed Jill back against the splintery wooden floor and crowed, 'I'm blowing, little bitch!' as his monster member speared into the girl's quivering quim again and again. The buxom young cheerleader felt soiled and ashamed, yet Jill couldn't deny strange stirrings down below. Feelings of savage animal pleasure tingled now in the red meat folds of her freshly fucked cunt.

My vision blurred as the words rushed into my head like garbage through a sewer pipe. I shoved the book back on the rack, shocked that anyone could actually *write* crap like that, let alone get it published.

Sparking a cig, I moved on to the hardcore photo mags along the back wall, where cardboard signs segregated the selections by kink. Subdividing sex into different kinds of screwing seemed pretty cold, but I guess that's marketing. I thought of a fantasy Wendy had yet to fulfill and felt a tingle in my jockeys as I stared at the cover of *Throat-Fucked Blondes*, on which an achingly pretty girl stretched her mouth wide to accommodate the Mule Man's cousin. I opened the mag to a pic of the guy exploding all over the girl's face like Old Faithful.

A chill raced down the back of my neck. I felt like I was being watched, but a quick glance around revealed an old man eyeing the paperbacks and a black guy thumbing through *Big Milky Boobs*, while the counter gorilla was engrossed in *Sports Illustrated.* No one was spying on me.

What a boozed-up dork.

—

I re-racked the mag and strolled past racks of the video tapes and a big selection of sex toys and leather gear to arrive back at the front counter. On a shelf behind the gorilla were rows of poppers, all aggressively named: Rush, Bolt, Blast, Hardware.

"How much is the Rush?"

The gorilla didn't glance up. "Five bucks, plus the governor's share."

"I need quarters," an agitated bald guy said as he rushed up to the counter. His shirttail was out, zipper down. "Quarters," he repeated, tossing a five on the counter. "Hurry. I don't want to miss the cum shot."

In no hurry at all, the gorilla put the money in the register and leisurely worked the coin dispenser. Quarters in hand, Shirttail scurried back across the store and disappeared through heavy black curtains that I hadn't noticed.

"Freakin' pervs," the gorilla muttered.

"I'll take some Rush," I decided, fishing a twenty out of my wallet. "Ah, what are the quarters for?"

"Movies. There's two arcades in the back with forty-four video channels, plus live girl phone sessions."

Reach out to touch someone. . . "What's a phone session?"

"A private show with a babe behind glass." The gorilla was now salesman smooth as he rung up my purchase. "It's only a buck for five minutes on the phone, plus the girls work for tips."

"Huh." I scratched my chin, pondering.

Might as well see the circus, the little voice agreed.

"Give me the rest of my change in quarters." Pockets jangling, I strolled to the back of the store and went through the curtains, deeper into candy-land.

A few steps down the narrow hall, I came to the open door of a booth about the size of a large bathroom. Inside was a metal folding chair, with a coin box and telephone on the wall. The cramped space provided an up-close view of a girl in the back of the booth, separated by scratched-up Plexiglas. She was a skinny brunette in a black nightie, reading a magazine on a mattress that was raised to eye level for someone sitting in the chair.

"Hi, darling," the girl said with a yellow-toothed smile, "how 'bout a show?"

"Ah. . . no thanks," I sputtered, hurrying on to first open movie booth, where I quickly shut and bolted the door behind me. The message on a small in-the-wall TV welcomed me to Kitty's and said I could deposit up to ninety-nine quarters for uninterrupted viewing pleasure.

The booth was dank and claustrophobic, less than half the size of the ones with phone girls, but see the circus, right? Sitting on a padded bench, I lit a cig and fed a couple quarters into the coin box beside the screen. Channel three glowed to life, showing a guy getting head in the back of a taxi.

54

I watched for a moment then clicked the big red channel button.

Channel four featured a big-butted girl taking it doggie style in extreme close-up. It reminded me of a butcher shop.

Click.

Five was a blank screen.

Click.

Six freaked me out a bit: a guy gobbling a guy.

Click.

Seven was more my speed: two bikini babes necking, poolside. My groin throbbed and I whispered, "Whoa, Petey," then laughed because that was my name for my dick when I was eight years old, and I hadn't thought of it in ages. The blonde started to undo the brunette's top when the screen went blank.

Hey!

They don't give you much time, I thought, depositing more quarters. An ash from the cig dropped into my lap and again it felt like I was being watched, even behind a locked door. I wanted to enjoy the movies, but the spied-on feeling was creeping me out.

I stood up to leave then remembered the Rush and knew it was exactly what I needed. Sitting back down, I broke the seal on the bottle and took a deep whiff up both nostrils. My head swelled as Blondie's tongue flicked in and out of her friend's belly button.

"You're so soft, baby," Blondie cooed, tongue now heading south. Petey throbbed as Kitty's became the *absolutely* coolest place in the world. The girls got to it, and I dialed up the volume. Did two more blasts of Rush then I undid my jeans and took matters in hand. The movie cut off abruptly, but the next channel offered two slutty Girl Scouts giving head to *four* guys at the same time.

More Rush, huge sniffs now 'cause this was awesome, like sex squared, stuff I'd never even *thought* about. My heart was racing. Petey jumped in my hand and. . .

Exploded without warning. Jolts of pleasure arced along every nerve, an electric pulse plugging me into the entire fucking universe and. . .

Suddenly it was over.

My fume-filled head deflated like a punctured beach ball and a headache drummed to life in my temples. Petey quickly shriveled, an empty gun. I dialed down the volume, sucked in air, wiped a sticky hand on the bench.

Shit.

So vibrantly alive a moment ago, I now felt empty, squeezed out like an old tube of toothpaste. Wanted to be away from Kitty's as fast as possible. I stood up, zipped, wiped my hands again on the back of my jeans and slipped out of the booth.

Shirttail was lurking in the hall, a few feet away. He winked at me and flicked his tongue. Forcing myself not to run, I brushed past him and beelined toward the exit at the end of the long hall, banging out the door and into the night.

Down the alley and quickly around the block, I re-crossed Colfax to the liquor store parking lot, where I jumped into the Camaro like a soldier diving into a foxhole. I sat there awhile, head pounding, feeling small and ashamed, like I'd lost a playground fight with the class wimp.

Something's off, I realized, starting the car and white-knuckling the steering wheel.

Something is going wrong.

22

I watched my speed, 'cause in my frazzled state a cop *really* on my tail might spark a chase scene, and there were plenty of light poles out there in the night. And with my head throbbing and hands sticky, the notion of an early check-out had a certain rude appeal. I pictured tear-stained faces around my open grave, boo-hooing for another chance to make things right.

Shaking away the thought, I told myself I had a pocketful of chances left, but still felt like a doomed character in a Next song. Slowing for a red light a few blocks up Colfax, I noticed some graffiti on the side of an six story brick building that had been turned into a storage place. Old English lettering again, like I'd seen on my run downtown.

The Only Rule is Write Your Own the message declared.

How the hell do you do that when you don't even know what the game is? The dirty movies still echoed in my skull - *So soft, baby* - and cranking the music didn't completely drown them out.

Masturbation is so schizophrenic. One sec it's full speed ahead, you'd give *anything* for the pleasure pulsing between your legs, then you blow and feel like a fool, a guilty brat who knew to keep hands off but sinned instead, stabbing Mom, Jesus, and Santa right in the heart.

Jerking off is understandable at thirteen, when you're producing precious bodily fluids by the quart and girls won't even talk to you. But I wasn't thirteen anymore, damn it. And I had Wendy, but right then it felt like I had betrayed her.

I felt the bottle of Rush in my pocket. That stuff turned me into a major porn peeper, drooling to ride a warm chemical wave as I watched strangers fuck for bucks. Steering with one hand, I lifted my ass off the seat, dug the Rush from my pants and chucked it out the window as hard as I could. Hearing the bottle shatter on the street made me feel a bit better.

I turned right onto Colorado and at the next red light pulled up beside a red MG midget. The blonde at the wheel looked like one of the porn girls. Staring straight ahead, I thought of a song lyric I'd written for Rick's band.

What's important in this world, a little boy, a little girl.

I thought about Vance, and how we never know when we're slated for that last ride in a two-toned garbage truck. So you'd better live and love all you can *now*, love your little girl.

That's why porn creeped me out - at the moment anyway - not because of what was on the screen, but because of what isn't. No affection or tenderness, certainly nothing approaching love. I was lucky enough to have those things in my life now. Wen sparked magic enough to make me feel stronger, better, deserving. . .

Arriving back at Windhollow, I was desperate for a dose of that magic.

Yeah, it was real late back east and being awaken by the phone would upset her at first, but this was an emergency. I *had* to hear my baby's voice. . .

I marched determinedly into G-22. Both roomies were still out. I tossed my jacket on the sofa and continued on to the kitchen to call Wendy.

Don't, the little voice said. *Wait until morning.*

"Yeah, good idea," I agreed, even as I grabbed the receiver. My heart ached for Wen *now*. I dug out the number, took a deep breath and dialed. Please, baby, come to the phone. One ring. Two. Three... *"What?"*

Two thousand miles away, I still flinched at her old man's sleepy snarl. Started to hang up but found foolish courage by envisioning Wendy's smile. That and my blood alcohol content.

"I-I know it's late, Mr. Daniels, but I have to talk to Wendy. It's... an emergency."

"Who is this?"

"Adam Freeman."

"What happened, boy? Somebody die?"

"No, but. . ." I fumbled for words, couldn't find any.

"Then there's no god damned emergency."

"Mr. Daniels. . ."

He slammed down the phone. No Wendy, just dial tone defeat. I trudged out to the living room, yanked my boots off and dropped onto the sofa, whispering her name like a prayer. A hot shower would be just the thing, but first I just needed to close my eyes, only for a minute.

But it was nice in the dark and sleep swallowed me, deep and dreamless.

57

23

I awoke with a start, my eyes cracking open on the cruel morning light. I shut them again, tried to will myself back to sleep before finally sitting up enough to fumble for a cig. Smoked it halfway down, then I got up and padded off to the bathroom. Did my business, splashed water on my face, and then remembered the late-night chat with Wendy's old man.

Not the best decision, the little voice said.

"Master of the obvious, ain't ya," I muttered, heading to the kitchen for coffee. I'd have to call Wen and do damage control, but not until I was a fully functioning human being and right then I sure didn't qualify.

Glancing at the clock, I saw it was almost noon in Garrison. The old man had cut the grass by now, just like he did every Saturday morning, mid-April through October. Life back in Garrison felt distant, like a half-remembered dream, and I hated being in Denver just then. Wished Wendy and I were back home, because without her I'm just another five-round man in a ten-round fight.

Coffee soon in hand, I plopped on the couch and reached for the remote, but decided to sit and think awhile, to just be. But just be *what*? Christ, I was eighteen, man enough to buy beer, vote, go to war if Ronnie gets too rambunctious, so how could I have only vague notions of who I was and wanted to be?

It was scary, but maybe knowing I wouldn't settle for being another Garrison zom was enough for now. All the gaps would get filled in along the way.

Sipping my joe, I thought of all the Saturday afternoons spent fishing out at Rook Lake with Dave and Dad. It was at the lake that I met Kenny.

I stopped out at the hospital to see him a few days taking the bus west. It had been three months or so since my last visit, and Kenny didn't know me at all. I stayed maybe fifteen minutes, chattering at him like he understood what I was saying. When he pissed the bed, I yelled for a nurse and then split, deciding it would be my last visit.

Maybe he'll get a miracle some day, whether he deserves it or not.

A second cup of coffee then I hit the shower, where the hot water helped steam away the boozy brain fog. How many days had I been in Denver now? I'd lost count and that was a little scary. Leaning against the tile, I cranked up the hot water and shut my eyes. Images started flashing by like half-forgotten dreams.

Dinner with my unfractured family. Kenny's there, wearing a hospital gown and drooling into Mom's sweet-and-sour pork.

Click!

Dad being chased across the lawn by the mower gone berserk.

Click!

Wendy dashing through the girl's locker' room, with Harry Paul Gattlin hot on her heels.

Click, click, click!

I couldn't shut them off, the dark visions playing in my head like jump-cut videos. I killed the water and toweled off, threw on shorts and sneakers and locked the front door behind me. I sprinted across the grass, already at half-speed, but the home horror movies stuck right with me.

Mom on five-inch heels in slutty underwear, sashaying into the First National bank, home of Big-Hands Fred.

Click!

Dave on-stage at Trends, humping the air fully nude, his dick now a jackhammer.

Click!

Around the fountain, out the front gate and away, I accelerated, determined to run until I ached, until the ache became all. Thirty blocks down Colorado. Fifty. Seventy-five and there's a raging inferno in my lungs, my vision blurred by sweat. The video images stopped changing, stuck now on a grainy loop of me and Wendy at the drive-in in the back seat of her yellow Corvair. I stopped counting blocks and ran harder.

Turn off!

Wen and I aren't meat puppets for porn store pervs, so turn off, God damn it! There was an intersection just ahead, the traffic against me. The loop stopped abruptly so I did, too, tumbling onto a grassy patch next to the sidewalk. I laid there, shut my eyes and sucked air, content now that the creep-peep show had finally run out of quarters.

"Are you okay, son?"

The question sounded like it came through a long cardboard tube. I blinked up at an old man in khaki shorts and a Hawaiian shirt dotted with giant parrots serving umbrella drinks.

"Y-Yeah," I said, leaning up on my elbows. "I am now."

"I thought maybe you had heat stroke or sumthin'," he said, looking worried.

"No, I'm okay," I assured him. Sweat dripped off my chin to splash on my still-heaving chest. "Just finished a long run."

"Oh," the old man said. "Exercise is good."

"Yes." I accepted a leathery hand up, thanked him for his concern then hit the 7-Eleven, half a block back. Self-dispensed a Coke-flavored Slurpee, grabbed a handful of napkins to de-sweatify and arrived at the register as the clerk's radio announced ". . . kidnapped last night from the Villa Italia Mall. The unnamed sixteen-year-old may be the latest victim of a serial rapist, although metro area police haven't publicly linked the crimes."

"When they catch this Shopping Mall guy," the clerk said as he rang me up, "I hope they cut his nuts off."

"No kidding," I agreed, anxious to do damage control back at Windhollow. It was time to call Wendy.

24

Dave was leaning on the bar, eating a bowl of Cheerios and paging through a copy of *Chic,* when I got back to the condo. "Hey, bro," he said, glancing up from the skin mag. "How was that band?"

"Absolutely killer." I plopped down on a bar stool and rubbed my leaden thighs. "Probably gonna go see them again tonight."

"You know *I'm* using the Camaro, right?"

"Sure. I'll take a bus or something."

"So you had fun, excellent." Dave flipped opened the centerfold, then spooned up the last of his cereal. "Meet any babes?"

"Didn't try. I've already got the world's greatest girlfriend, remember?" I nodded toward the phone. "I'm gonna give her a buzz soon."

"Say hi for me." Dave got up and tossed his bowl in the sink. "I gotta go work out. Wanna hit the pool later?"

"Sure." I glanced down at the centerfold girl, spread-eagled on a picnic table. She was holding a butter-dripping ear of corn above her spread-wide pussy lips, but her blue eyes looked as bored as a gourd. I closed the mag and walked over to the phone.

My hand froze on the receiver. This could be the most important phone call of my life, and I had no idea what to say. "Sorry for pissing off your dad, but I was drunk and freaked out after jerking off in a porno palace?"

Didn't think so.

But doesn't love demand honesty?

"I want you, love you, need you, Wen, because you're real in a world full of fakes. You conjure feelings in me that are as close to any heaven as I'm likely to get. I love you because you bring out the best in me, with no need to run away."

Says the world's biggest wimp. . .

Being honest doesn't mean you have to confess every bad thing, the little voice advised. *Be honest about* good *things, and dial down the heart on your sleeve desperation, even if it's true.*

Desperate summed up my feelings exactly, but being scared and screwed up doesn't make for romantic banter, so just try to lie my way through? Maybe, except I've never been a good liar and wouldn't trying wreck the very thing I longed to preserve?

Screw it, I decided. Don't drive yourself crazy. Words are just sound. I trusted Wendy to know what I meant. She always had.

I punched in the number and braced for her old man's growl.

"Hello." It was *her.*

"Hi, beautiful." I relaxed and leaned against the fridge, figuring everything would be all right now.

"Adam!" Wendy's voice cracked like a whip. "Are you *crazy*, calling in the middle of the night? What the hell's wrong with you?"

"I-I thought you'd answer, not your dad," I said lamely, caught off guard by her stormy greeting, even though I deserved it. I'd never heard Wendy raise her voice before.

"Well, you thought wrong."

"I'm sorry, Wen, but I needed to talk to you so bad it hurt. Wasn't thinking so great," I confessed. "I was a little drunk."

"That doesn't make it better, Adam," she said quietly, which somehow cut even deeper. "I mean, you say you love me. . ."

"You know I do."

"Love isn't pulling stupid stunts like that, not with my dad. . ."

"What?" Remembering her black eye gave me a chill. "What did he do?"

"Nothing. I'm fine."

I wasn't convinced. "Babe, you know you can talk to me, right? About *anything*."

"I know, sweetie," she said tenderly. "And that means so much to me, but I really don't have time right now."

"Then I'll call back later, okay? Just tell me when."

There was a long pause then Wendy said, "Around ten. Grandpa will be asleep and Dad usually goes to the tavern for a couple beers."

"Ten o'clock, on the dot," I pledged. "And you *do* know I love you, right?"

"Yeah," Wendy said, then she hung up.

25

"Things were always great with us, Dave, but now they seem to be going straight to hell. I'd be on a bus home tomorrow if Wendy was there, but she won't be back for two weeks, so how do I do damage control?"

"That's a toughie," Dave said, reaching for the Coppertone. We were on lounges, poolside. "And I ain't Doctor Ruth, ya know."

"But you *are* my big brother," I pouted. "If you can't give me advice, who can?"

"Calling in the middle of the night *was* a stupid stunt."

"Jesus, I know that." I took the last swig of my Pepsi and crushed the can. "What I *don't* know is how to make it up to her. And despite what Wendy said, I think her asshole old man may have hit her or something. If so, it's all my fault."

"Let's hope you're wrong about that." Dave frowned as he worked suntan oil into his chest. "But guilt-trippin' won't solve anything."

"I feel like strapping this lounge to my back and walkin' off the damn diving board."

"Belay that thought, matey."

"Summer vacation," I muttered, "turned summer damnation." And watching the taut and tanned Windhollow singles frolicking in the sun while the best thing in my life was slipping away made me want to punch something, mostly myself.

"Listen, Adam," Dave said, "Relationships work themselves out over time. An occasional fight breaks up the monotony."

"But we never fought," I said, slapping the lounge in frustration. "Never."

"Then you're overdue. Look, you fucked up, so Wendy got mad. That's perfectly natural, but it'll blow over."

"Think so?"

"Sure." He shook his empty beer can. "How 'bout running inside for more refreshment?"

"Coming up." Strolling toward the condo, I tried convincing myself that Dave was right but couldn't help but worry. I'd checked the east coast weather in the morning paper. Sunny on Cape Cod and I imagined a mad-at-Adam Wendy on the beach in her bikini. . .

Dave was leisurely backstroking across the pool when I returned. He climbed out of the water, opened his fresh brewski and asked if Wendy liked flowers.

"Sure," I said, watching a fat guy in a too-small Depeche Mode t-shirt do a cannonball off the board.

"Call FTD and send her some roses," Dave said, settling back on his lounge. "With the mushiest card they have."

"Isn't that expensive?"

"Isn't she worth it?"

"Of course." But I scowled at the thought of my shrinking bankroll.

"Roses to solve a thorny problem." Dave smiled at his turn of phrase. "And don't get wasted before calling her next time."

"No duh." I liked Dave's rosy peace plan but couldn't shake the nagging feeling it would somehow wilt on the vine. But enough of my problems. Let's pick at Dave awhile, as a distraction. "How's everything with Laura?"

"Umm, umm, good," he said with a smile. "Can't wait to see her again."

"Does you being a stripper bug her?" Funny how *my brother the stripper* sounded natural after a couple weeks.

"Nah, she knows it's about show biz, not sex." His confident tone chafed. I needed to shake him up a bit, find a chink in his armor.

"That's a crock of grade A bullshit."

"Maybe a little," Dave admitted. "But don't confuse me with Derk, 'cause he's not my role model. Sure, sometimes I take advantage of opportunities at work, but most times I don't. Derk *lives* for it."

"*Opportunities at work,*" I repeated mockingly. "That what you B Boys call the pussy parade down at the office?"

Dave flipped me off. "Point taken, but Laura's got *this* Bad Boy marching to a slightly different drummer these days."

"You fallin' for her?"

"You mean like falling in love?" Dave looked thoughtful, considering the question. "I don't know if there even is such a thing." He lit a Marlboro and sipped his Coors. "But with Laura, I feel like maybe trying to find out."

"What if it turns into more than maybe?" I asked. "And what if things come down to her or stripping?" I wanted him to sweat a little, like me, to remember Mom's vanishing act and Vance's last ride. Never claimed I couldn't be a dick.

Dave shrugged. "I'm not worried."

"Said the ostrich." I got up and dove into the pool, kicking down to the bottom. Air bubbled from my lips. I wondered how gulping water would feel, just like–I realized disgustedly–some thirteen-year-old girl, heartbroken that her fave rock star didn't answer a fan letter. I pushed off from the bottom with a fury.

Why? Van Halen was asking from a boombox as I broke the surface, *can't this be love?*

It *is*, I thought insistently, paddling to the side of the pool. *Adam + Wendy forever.* Sitting down on the hot concrete, I opened my fresh soda and glanced across the pool just as the Barbecue Sisters, Terri and Sherri, strolled in through the gate. I pointed them out to Dave, and we watched as the girls took lounges directly opposite from us across the pool. They didn't look particularly happy.

"Some chicks," Dave grumped, as if describing an alien, unknowable force of nature. "One tango with the ole trouser snake, and they want to skin him for the trophy case."

Perfect Terri and piggy Sherri sat motionless on their lounges, glowering. It was creepy. Dave soon stood up and draped the towel over his shoulders. "I'm gonna go grab a shower."

"I hear ya." We took the long way around to avoid the sisters, were past the diving board and heading for the gate when Terri popped up off her lounge and trotted over to cut off our escape. She was wearing another gravity defying swimsuit.

"Hey, good-looking," Dave said with a paste-on smile. "How you been?"

"Fine, except my phone never rings," said Terri, hips swaying as if under their own power. "You been busy?"

"Always," Dave agreed with a nod. "Just like I told you I was."

—

63

"That's okay." Terri stepped toward me and ran a finger under my chin. "I've decided your brother is cuter anyway." She snapped the front of my trunks and winked. "See you soon, Adam." With that, Terri jiggled back over to her sister, who continued staring at us with serial killer eyes.

I knew Terri was just coming on to me to jerk Dave's chain, but I couldn't resist grinning as I said, "Guess you should have taken her out for ice cream."

26

I still felt lousy and craved magic powder, but didn't want to beg Dave for a line. Instead I got the Yellow Pages. *F* for florists and forgiveness, but I soon learned you can't do biz on the phone without a credit card.

I grabbed the notebook from my pack and sat down to compose a please-forgive-me plea in a hundred words or less. After staring at a blank page awhile, I took out Wen's picture for inspiration then scribbled: *I'm stupid sometimes, but only because I love you.*

Nah. Start again.

I'm a fool in love, with no desire for rehabilitation.

That sucked, too, but before I could scratch it out Derk strolled in the front door, tennis bag slung over one shoulder. "Dave!" he shouted, then sat down and fished for the mirror under the sofa, saying hi to me as an afterthought.

Dave trotted down the hall from the weight room. "You cop?"

"Of course," Derk said, producing a large zip-lock baggie, half-full of pearly white chunks of cocaine the size of baby fists.

Dave whooped his approval, and I closed the notebook, eager to get in on the goodies.

"A moment of thanks before we indulge," Derk said, lifting the baggie toward heaven. "To the campesinos, our brown brothers of the nostril, who tirelessly tend the coca fields so we gringos can ride diamond dust to the stars." His rat-a-tat tone suggested he'd already blasted off.

"Amen," Dave said. "Mission Control reports all systems go."

Derk put a big rock on the mirror and slid it over to Dave, who chopped it up with the speed of a rush-hour fry cook. After laying out six fat lines, he offered Derk the mirror. "Captain?"

"Let the crew proceed," Derk said, grabbing the baggie and standing up. "I'm going to go stash this."

As Derk headed to his room, Dave hoovered his lines through a gold-colored metal tooter shaped like a vacuum cleaner. Leaning back on the sofa, he sniffed and smiled. "Primo."

I fueled up next, the campesinos' handiwork quickly sharpening my senses. All systems *good*. Emerging from his room, Derk went to the kitchen for beers and the three of us were soon babbling about girls, coke, and girls who liked coke. A pro football forecast show on the tube sparked debate among the roomies. Dave had become a Broncos fan, while Derk loved the '49ers. Dumb jocks like Harry Paul Gattlin played football and so had Wendy's old man.

I hate football.

Derk razored up another line for each of us, did his, then went to make some phone calls. Dave did his and went to resume his workout. I did mine and returned to pen and paper, now confident heart-healing words would flow. Poetic couplets soared through my skull yet remained elusive when I tried to coax them from the tip of the pen.

Cupid's wings grow heavy, I scribbled, *could shatter under his weighty load, impale him on one of his own arrows.*

What the hell?

Love burns bright, even in the dead of night. I ache for you and moan. Cries of love long distance on the phone. And I can't really say I'm sorry.

Then it ain't an apology, is it?

Keep it simple, the little voice suggested as I slurped beer. *Just tell Wendy how you feel.*

"Simple," I said aloud. "Sure."

My late night phone call, rejected and disconnected
But the call of love was true, without Wen I'm blue
Forgive my long distance bumbling, late night
In two weeks, I'll make everything right

Wendy knew I wasn't due home for *three* weeks, so that should get her attention. I read the lines several times, decided they'd serve. She was due back in Garrison in thirteen days and, cutting my trip short, I'd be there to greet her, flowers in hand.

And everything would be back to perfect.

27

Happy with my plan to regain Wendy's good graces, I walked the letter out to the mailbox then surfed up an ancient beach movie on the tube. Derk soon left wearing a three-piece suit, briefcase in hand: candy man coke dealer in business drag.

Dave split to run errands and after the Bad Boys' gig tonight he was heading up to Boulder to bunk with Laura.

Alone in the condo, I watched Frankie and Annette rout Baron Von Zipper and his goons, then the couples paired off around a bonfire for the final sing-along. The camera panned over the extras and a blonde in a blue bikini made me bolt upright on the couch, gaping in amazement. It was crazy, but the girl was a dead ringer for Gina Kelly, and never mind that the movie was made before Gina was born.

I clicked over to MTV and sank back into the couch, mumbling, "Gina goddamned Kelly."

She had been a freshman, two years younger than me but light years ahead socially. Pretty and popular, Gina hung with a group of chicks who favored big hair, slutty heavy metal fashion, and dated upperclassmen with the coolest cars and best weed.

We don't need no education. . .

It was mid-December, with the big holiday dance coming up before the Christmas break. I generally hated school events and wasn't planning to go, but then Rick's group won a battle of the bands that decided who'd play the dance the following Friday.

Fleeting Youth's unexpected victory over Thunder 'N Lightning, a pop-metal cover band composed of senior jocks, was announced near the end of the school day, calling for an instant celebration. After the last bell, Rick and I lit a bowl behind the football field bleachers. Strolling by, Gina saw us copping a buzz and sauntered over with a Kool dangling between her lips to ask for a light.

I sparked her and she stuck around – duh – to partake of the herb. High, happy for Rick and acting purely on impulse, I asked Gina to the dance and was surprised when she said yes.

Now I'm not bad looking but was strictly a nobody in the Garrison High hierarchy. I ran track but wasn't a jock, partied but wasn't a stoner, always had my nose in a book, but wasn't a brain. Lacking a group identity left me pretty much invisible, so landing a date with a hottie like Gina was a big deal.

Maybe I existed after all.

Even the old man understood, because he decided to let me use his car. I had access to Mom's old Falcon but never, before the dance, to Dad's beloved Buick Riviera. Dance night started out well, with Gina and I parked out at Rook Lake for some pre-arrival mood adjustment, courtesy of some good red bud and a sixer of Pabst Rick's older brother bought for me.

Well-buzzed after a bowl and a beer, I was psyched to squire my date to the gym at Harry S. Truman High. Gina was wearing a red sequin dress so short you could almost see the promised land. As we drove off, she leaned over, nibbled on my ear lobe and said, "To the dance, Jeeves."

I let out a whoop, both enjoying and trying to ignore my instant hard-on. It was finally starting to deflate when we reached the school ten minutes later, and I was thankful Petey no longer pointed toward true north when we got out of the car. I barely knew Gina but was eager to take the crash course.

As we started across the parking lot, Brad Fredricks pulled in, driving a cherry red Caddy from his dad's dealership. He parked, hopped out of the sled, and Gina dashed over to greet him.

"Get the stuff?" she asked.

"Hell yeah, baby." Fredricks put his arm around Gina and smirked at me. "Thanks for picking up my date, Freeman. I'll take it from here."

They laughed and strolled inside.

I stood there like a wooden Indian, sputtering, unable to say a fucking word. Eventually I drove home, parked the Buick halfway up the street and went quietly in the back door to avoid the old man. Changed into workout clothes and then went for a run. Coincidence must have led me to the alley behind Fredricks Cadillac, where a rock got acquainted with a windshield.

We're just another brick in the wall

The image of Gina's beach blanket doppelganger lingered behind my eyes, and I squeezed the sofa cushions so hard that my hands shook. Thoughts of Ms. Kelly were best repressed because, even after almost two years, I'd happily mortar that treacherous little twat into a wall, one brick at a time.

28

It was almost six-thirty when I woke up from a nap. I didn't feel energetic enough to bus it downtown to the Big House later, but the solution was as close as Derk's briefcase. He sold me a couple big rocks, then left for the night's weenie-wagging after telling me not to sweat it if I didn't see him later, because *he* didn't turn into a pumpkin at midnight.

Jerk.

Dave was already out doing strip-a-grams before the B Boys nightclub gig. I wrote a note to call Wendy at eight, worked out awhile then went for a twenty-minute run. Ate a couple hot dogs when I got back, watched some tube, then shaved and showered. Thus revitalized, I climbed into my cleanest dirty jeans and decided to leave the letter jacket at the condo tonight. It was kid stuff.

I sat down to do a line, determined to jumpstart the night's festivities. Half my nose was attended to when there was a knock at the door. I stashed the mirror under the sofa, nark squad visions dancing in my head.

Through the peephole, I saw hot sister Terri, toting a six pack of Michelob. She knocked again.

I took a deep breath and opened the door. "Hey, Terri. Dave's not here."

"Good."

She sauntered in past me, hips swinging like a hypnotist's watch. The girl definitely deserved to be taken out for ice cream, all 33 flavors.

"It's beer-thirty, Adam," Terri purred.

"Uh, I was about to take off," I said, trying not to stare at her perfect breasts, straining against a purple t-shirt.

"Come on, surely you've got time for *one* beer."

"Ahhh, why not?" I led her to the sofa. "Dave won't be home 'til way late, if at all."

"Perfect," Terri said, sitting down next to me, not two inches away. She handed me a brew, opened one for herself and then slowly licked the oozing foam from the rim. "That gives *us* a chance to get to know each other better."

I was flattered but said, "I really was about to split. One beer, then I gotta go."

"Sure, Adam." Terri smiled and patted my knee. Let her hand linger. "One beer."

Petey sprang to attention. Deciding the situation called for clarity, I fished out the mirror from under the sofa. Terri burbled with approval when she saw the cocaine. Lines went up, beer went down, my jeans grew tighter. I told Terri about the Next and as we finished the brews she offered to give me a ride downtown later.

Don't think, react. "That'd be great."

She scooted closer, brushing up against me. "Can we do another *little* line, Adam?"

"Sure." More coke and suddenly we were necking. Then Terri moved my hands up under her t-shirt, all that firm, ample flesh confirming what my mind couldn't quite believe. The phone started ringing as her nipples swelled at my touch. Terri moaned, "Oh, God, Adam," as I chewed on her neck. The ringing stopped. She stood up, peeled off her shirt and ordered me to suck her tits.

Don't think, *react*, go with the heavy breathing flow, the flesh-on-flesh combustion. After a bit of nip nibbling, Terri pulled my head up and purred, "I want to suck your cock, *bay*-bee."

"Unh. . ." was the only sound I could make.

"Strip," she commanded.

Who was I to refuse a lady? I peeled down quicker than any Bad Boy. Terri ordered me to lay on the sofa and shut my eyes. When I did so, she sat on the edge of the sofa, put one hand on my shoulder and whistled loudly. I heard the front door open, footsteps crossing the room.

"Say cheese," a sing-song voice taunted.

I caught a glimpse of Sherri, right before a flashbulb blinded me. Terri leapt up off the sofa. Two more flashes, then Sherri bolted toward the door, Polaroid camera in hand. I jumped up, cursing, and ran after her, still half-dazzled by the flashbulbs. Racing out the door, I was five strides into the grass before realizing I was stark naked. Luckily, no one was around to gawk.

I darted back inside to find Terri fully dressed. "What the hell's going on?" I asked dumbly, scrambling to climb into my underwear.

"Nothing," Terri said, striding past me with a smile. "Just some souvenir snaps for your asshole brother."

A pithy comeback eluded me, so I chased her out the door, slammed it shut and quickly finished dressing. The phone rang again. I stalked out to the kitchen and yanked the receiver off the hook. *"Yeah?"*

"Sounds like you're in a wonderful mood."

Wendy.

Fuck, I forgot to call her!

"Adam, are you there?"

One deep breath. Another. "Yeah, babe, I'm here."

"I thought you were going to call me at ten on the dot."

"Shit," I said, my eyes cutting to the digital clock in the breakfast nook. I was forty minutes late. "Sorry, the damn time difference keeps throwing me off," I lied, an unthinking *man the lifeboats* reflex. "God, I'm such a dope sometimes."

"Well, you won't get much of an argument from me," said Wendy.

"And I'm *really* sorry about calling so late the other night, Wen. Think you can ever forgive me?"

"Well. . ." She let me dangle above the abyss for a moment. "I know you weren't *trying* to be an idiot."

"No." I'd gladly take some sarcasm if it got me out of the doghouse. "But I *was* an idiot and I'm sorry. I've just been going nuts, missing you." I forced a laugh. "That's not much of a defense, I know."

"You're lucky the judge likes you," Wendy said with a smile in her voice.

"*Very* lucky," I agreed, feeling a bit better, even while knowing I didn't deserve to. "How's your granddad?"

"He had a really good day," she said brightly. "I even took Gramps to the beach for a while."

I felt a pang of anxiety then realized having a doddering grandparent in tow was hardly boy bait. "That's great," I said. "Any beach volleyball?"

"Sure," Wendy said, playing along. "Gramps has a killer spike."

"Oh, a senior volleyball shark." We both laughed. There was something I had to know but hated asking. "How, ah, how's everything with your dad?"

"It's okay, fine," Wendy said, but the warmth vanished from her voice.

I hated killing our banter but couldn't just ignore a hassle with her old man that was my fault. "Good," I said. "Apologize to him for me, if you think that's a good idea."

"Okay."

"Fine."

"Listen, Adam, I can't talk much longer."

"That's okay," I said, then tried kick-starting the jollies. "I know how busy judges are. Plus, you're now managing a volleyball pro..."

Wendy ignored my attempted yucks. Improv-time was over. "I wrote you a letter today," she said.

"Me, too!" I cut in, anxious to offer proof we were still tuned to the same frequency. "I wrote you a letter, too."

"This *is* important, Adam," Wendy said, ignoring my *we're-so-in-synch* interruption. "I'd like you to read it before we talk again, okay?"

"What's the big mystery?"

"No mystery," she insisted. "Can you please just do me this favor?"

"Sure. Of course."

"Thank you."

"Anything for my gorgeous girl," I mooned.

"I should probably get off the phone before Dad gets back from the tavern. You'll get the letter in a couple days, okay?"

"Sure."

"I have to go, but... I love you, too."

Those words warmed me, and as I hung up the bizarre photo session with the Barbecue Sisters seemed as insignificant as a locker room prank. Of course I was curious about Wen's letter, but it had to be good news because "I love you" ain't exactly fighting words.

I wanted to cement my buoyant mood with another bump but couldn't find the coke seal. I searched under the sofa cushions, moved furniture, but it was gone. Terri must have swiped it from my jeans while I was busy chasing her sister.

Bitches!

I stalked around the room, punching air and cursing until my gaze was drawn to Derk's bedroom door. There was a long night of rocking ahead and it wasn't my fault I got ripped off, right?

The little voice didn't contradict me.

I did a couple lines off the mirror on the shelf, then scooped some more into a cigarette cellophane. Turning to leave, I saw the dance log on Derk's desk. Walking over, I flipped it open to the latest entries.

I thought last night's rape had occurred in Lakeview but, no, it was Lakewood, because it said so, right there in the log. The solo stripping Bad Boy was *AA* again, and the entry had been highlighted with five stars.

70

29

Staring at the entry written in Derk's bold, looping hand, I felt a chill but shook it off because even if Derk was "AA," that didn't prove anything. Yet if you factor in the black van, black wig, the description of the rapist as big and muscular. . .

So you're in the teenage FBI now? the little voice wondered.

"Oh shut up," I said, closing the log just as I heard footsteps in the living room. I froze for a split-second, totally confused - *Both Bad Boys are working so who the hell?* - then bolted from the room and pulled the door shut behind me in time to see Derk go behind the bar and grab booze from the bottle rack.

"Hey, Derk," I called casually as I strode down the hall, trying to ignore my thumping heart and fiddling with my zipper, like I was returning from the bathroom. "Thought you guys had a review show tonight."

Ignoring me, Derk poured a big shot of Jack Daniels, downed it, then slammed the glass on the bar and muttered, "Those fucking hagged-out old cunts."

Obviously preoccupied, Derk had no clue that I was just in his room. I sat on the arm of the sofa and stared at him, feeling like a coked-up Perry Mason, zeroing in on a perp. "What haggy old cunts?"

Derk glanced at me and said, "The blue-nosed crones from the CFD." He did another shot then joined me and fished the mirror out from beneath the sofa. "The so-called Citizens for Decency," he continued. "The god-damned anti-sex league is more like it, funded by a prune-faced old dowager who probably hasn't been laid since Nixon was president."

"Was there a protest or something?"

"Threats of one, which were enough to get tonight's show cancelled at the last minute," Derk said. "It was going to be our first gig at the Retreat, an upscale club in Englewood. Took me two months to convince the manager to book us, then the spineless jerk caves under pressure from some geriatric busybodies. The cancellation cost me a grand, plus tips and ten percent of the bar total." Derk produced his silver vial and emptied it on the mirror.

"Well, that's sucks," I said, glancing down the hall to make sure I'd closed his door completely. "But if you need something to do tonight, there's a killer band playing at the Big House."

"What band?" he asked, cutting up the coke.

"The Next."

"Never heard of 'em." He did two big lines and offered me the tooter. I considered refusing, payback of sorts for what I'd just pinched. But that might seem suspicious, so I hoovered and continued touting the Next.

"They really rock, man. Hotter than Chernobyl."

"Okay, Adam," he said with a chuckle. "Since my evening has an unexpected hole, I'll go check out what *you* think rocks.

Derk was semi-sneering at me, if with a fraction of the venom he'd directed at the old hags. I was tempted to tell him to forget it and bus downtown as planned, but my better nature focused on his wheels and cocaine.

We did another line then Derk went to the kitchen to make some phone calls. Rubbing my nose, I reminded myself that the world is rife with coincidences about everything, including wigs and vans. Derk got so much pussy, he qualified as a professional cat catcher. The idea of him snatching teenyboppers was ridiculous.

"I've got a couple deliveries to make before we hit the bar," Derk said, now heading to his room. "I'm going to go change, then we'll motor."

"Cool."

I held my breath as he entered his bedroom, but thirty seconds ticked by, a minute, and he didn't come charging back out with coke-stealing accusations. "Cool," I repeated.

Everything was under control.

30

Our first stop was at a King Soopers on Colorado. Derk said he'd be about fifteen minutes, grabbed his shoulder bag and was gone. The fifteen minutes stretched to thirty, after which I helped myself to a swig of Jamesons from the mini bar in the back of the van. Returning to my seat, I glanced at the store just as Derk emerged through the sliding glass doors.

"Had to weigh out a bunch of quarter grams," he reported when he got in, stowing his bag behind the seat. "The night manager deals to the late shift to boost productivity."

"The genius of capitalism," I said.

"Damn right."

We continued on to a ritzy nearby neighborhood, Cherry Creek. I asked Derk why he sold coke, hoping to glean some insight into what made him tick. He was an egomaniac, sure, but I couldn't forget that *something* I'd seen in Derk's blue eyes. It intrigued and even scared me a little. "Isn't dealing pretty risky?"

"Life is risky," he said with a wink. "And buccaneers rule the world, Adam. Never forget that." We pulled up in the wide driveway of a sprawling two story house. Derk clamped an unlit cigar between his teeth and grabbed his bag. "Come on in and have a drink."

"Sounds good."

We were greeted at the door by Leroy, a flamboyantly gay black guy with a Little Richard pompadour, who looked to be in his mid-thirties and was dressed in a black kimono emblazoned with red dragons and guys having acrobatic sex.

72

"Who's your friend, Derk?" Leroy asked, shaking my hand with a dish rag grip.

"Adam is my roomie's brother," Derk said, "in town from the sticks."

"Welcome, Adam, and aren't you just *delish*," Leroy gushed, causing my cheeks to burn as he led us into a large living room done in cool pastels, with a ten-foot-long fish tank along one wall.

"I think you've got a fan, Adam," Derk joked. My face got redder.

"Oh, dear," Leroy said, noticing my discomfort as he sat in a wicker chair and motioned us to a long white couch. "I'm sorry if I embarrassed you, Adam. That wasn't my intent, I assure you." Leroy fanned a hand in his face and glanced up at the vaulted ceiling. "Heaven knows I try not to entertain wicked ideas, but they *insist* on entertaining me."

I laughed. It was a great line.

"Well, Leroy," Derk said, not ready to give up the rib, "Adam's girlfriend *is* a couple time zones away."

"No, no," Leroy protested, still focused on me, but in a way that somehow wasn't creepy. "Adam's a fine-looking young man, which is all I was pointing out."

"*Lee*-roy," Derk said, still at it. "I saw you flick your tongue like a hungry lizard."

"Did not," Leroy insisted, using his fan hand to brush away Derk's words. "But - and this isn't directed at you, Adam - since you mentioned tongues, I'll put *this* up against girl, boy, or beast." He extended a tongue long enough to make Gene Simmons jealous and rotated it in a slow circle.

We all laughed.

"Okay, enough," Derk said, switching into business mode. "How much cola do you need, you old queen?"

"Is it as marvy as last time?"

"Oh. . ." Derk smiled and patted his bag like a secret agent with stolen plans. "It's even better."

"Really?" Leroy arched a plucked eyebrow. "Then I'll take a half ounce. Raoul's birthday is next week, and booger sugar turns him into a *complete* slut, although honestly..." He tittered. "It's tough to tell the difference."

"You're wicked, Leroy," Derk said.

"Guilty." Leroy got up and glided across the room toward the kitchen. "But against my will, as mentioned." He returned to hand me a Corona with lime, turned on the TV, then he and Derk went off to conduct business.

Summer of '42 was on the tube. Great, a movie about losing your innocence on Cape Cod. I prayed for rain to keep Wendy off the beach. Thought about her mysterious letter, now in transit. Imagined it getting lost or mangled in a mail-sorting machine. Knew I was getting worked up over nothing, and *that* made me feel like an insecure wussie jerk.

73

"My, that blow *is* superb," declared Leroy, rubbing his nose as they returned to the living room a few minutes later. He batted long eyelashes at me. "I assume, Adam, that you have plans for this evening?"

"Yeah," I said, glancing at the door.

"Pity. It was very nice to meet you."

"Yeah. Thanks for the beer." I got to my feet. "Ready, Derk?"

"Yeah, let's hit it."

"You boys have fun," Leroy said, walking us to the door. "Try to do something *I* wouldn't do. And report to me immediately if you discover such a thing."

Back in the van, Derk said we had one more pre-Big House stop, at a video store. I grunted in response.

"What's bugging you?"

"That you invited me in just to be made fun of."

"You're wrong," Derk said, sounding sincere. "I have no clue what makes Leroy's faggy heart go pitter-pat. I asked you in because I thought you'd like a beer while we took take of biz. And you shouldn't be so thin-skinned anyway, Adam. If somebody bugs you, just take control and bug them back, comprende?"

"What, insult your friend in his own house?" I asked, picking at the seam of my jeans.

"Who said anything about insulting Leroy?" We hit Colorado and turned toward downtown. "There are ways to master any situation, and if *you* don't take control, someone else will." Derk gestured with his now-lit cigar. "All the world's a stage. You just need the will to write your own script."

"Maybe," I said. "But is it a tragedy or comedy?"

"Both, of course." Derk smiled. "Just so long as it isn't a god damned sit-com."

***

The smell of popcorn and the murmur of couples debating flick picks greeted us inside Capitol Hill Video. I followed Derk to the five shelf "adult" section in back. "All right, it's here!" he cried, snatching a box off the shelf.

"What?"

"My blue debut," Derk said, thrusting *Hot Tub Tarts* into my hands. The cover showed two bikini-clad chicks emerging, not from the titular hot tub, but a steamed-up shower stall.

"This the skin-flick you're in?" I scanned the cast list on the back. "Don't see your name."

"Jack Hardman," Derk pointed out, "that's me." Video in hand, he marched up to the counter, where a dumpy girl wearing granny glasses and a Patti Smith t-shirt rang up the sale. It cost one-hundred and eighteen dollars. Chump change for Mr. Bad Boy.

———

74

"When do you get off, honey?" Derk asked, clasping Dumpy Girl's hand when she gave him the change. "Want to watch yours truly get nasty?"

"N-No thanks, man." She freed her hand, shut the register, and stared at Derk blankly.

"Come on, sweet thing," he continued with theatrical flair. "The movie's sure to get you wet. If you're lucky, maybe we'll act out some scenes."

The manager appeared beside us, a balding little gnome in a red vest and bow tie. "Now, sir," he said, wagging a finger at Derk. "You can't talk to my employees in a rude and suggestive manner. Kindly take your purchase and leave."

Derk nodded, then grabbed the manager's tie and jerked, forcing him up on tiptoe to avoid being choked. "Say please," a grinning Derk instructed.

"P-Please."

"There, was that so hard?" Derk released the manager and adjusted his tie. "See what a little courtesy can accomplish?"

He picked up the video, wished them a fine evening, and we walked out.

"Desperado leans on frightened shopkeeper," Derk said with a chuckle as we boarded the van. "The classics never get old." Climbing over the console, he grabbed two tall cans of beer from the mini fridge. Handed me one and settled behind the steering wheel. "Let's go rock and roll."

"Hell, yeah." I cracked open the can of Sapporo and tipped it toward Derk. "I'll drink to that."

31

The Next was already playing when we got to the Big House. There were a dozen people waiting to get in. We lined up behind two skinheads. "Dig the junior jarheads," Derk said loudly.

They glared at us, saw Derk's size and said nothing. He winked at me, a reminder to *just take control*, but I wasn't convinced. It's easy to get script approval when you've got four inches and sixty pounds on the competition.

I was anxious to show off the Next, like they were my personal discovery. We paid our cover and found a just-abandoned table bordering the dance floor as the band tore through a thrashy version of "Born to be Wild." Derk hit the bar, returning with whiskey shots for both of us.

Downing mine, I leaned toward Derk to be heard above the music. "Great tunes, huh?"

He shrugged. "They're okay."

"Just keep listening," I urged. "Their original stuff is hot."

"Now *that's* hot." Derk pointed toward a girl with long red hair, standing up by the stage.

"Yeah," I agreed, not bothering to identify her as Tommy Weather's gal pal Raven. Let's see how Derk handled some real competition.

"Save the table, Adam." Derk got up and headed directly toward Raven. When I wanted to approach a girl at school, I'd generally circle my intended target, trying to work up enough nerve to actually speak to them and most times whimping out.

Derk sauntered right up to Raven and whispered in her ear. She nodded and followed him onto the crowded dance floor, where they proceeded to shake it through a long, loud instrumental. He was getting a little handsy and Raven didn't seem to mind.

When the song ended, Tommy growled, "We're takin' a break," then unplugged his guitar and stalked off the stage. His bandmates stood there, looking confused, then followed their leader backstage.

Derk and Raven chatted a moment longer on the dance floor before she made her way backstage. He returned to the table and lit a cigar with a smile. "My new friend will be joining us for a drink."

"Is she with some guy in the band?"

"Who cares?" Derk shrugged. "She'll be here." And not two minutes later, Raven came sauntering towards us, high-heel boots clicking across the dance floor.

"Raven," Derk said, standing up to pull out her chair. I half-expected him to kiss her hand. "This is my friend, Adam."

She sat down, tossed that red hair and said, "Hi," in her throaty bedroom voice. Raven gave no sign of recognizing me and probably didn't.

"What would you like to drink, beautiful?" Derk asked.

"A Cape Cod would be lovely."

Derk produced a twenty and slid it across the table to me. "Adam, vodka and cranberry for the lady. Get yourself something if you want."

I dutifully trudged to the bar, ordered Raven's drink and a double seven and seven for myself. Back at the table, I found the pair sitting shoulder-to-shoulder, chattering like magpies as Derk ran his index finger along her forearm.

"Thank you," Raven said as I delivered her drink and gave Derk his change. A couple minutes later, he asked her if she was ready for a line.

"Absolutely." She lit a Benson & Hedges menthol and shot a glance toward the empty stage. "God knows I could use it."

They got up and headed toward the door before I could ask how long they'd be gone. I frowned and sipped my drink. The club was getting more crowded, so I propped a foot on one of the chairs. Absent-mindedly graded chicks wandering by, but soon gave it up. There was only one ten in the world for me.

"Okay, Big House Saturday night!" a flabby old hippie announced from the stage a few minutes later. "The Next have rocked this joint regularly since we opened eighteen months ago, so it's my great pleasure to announce the band has just inked a deal with Élan Records. They'll soon be headed to L.A. to record their debut album!" Flabby Hippie pumped a fist in the air and shouted, "So once again, give it up for the Next!"

I cheered along with the crowd as the band returned to the stage. Tommy shielded his eyes against the lights and peered into the audience, presumably looking for the wayward Raven. "Here's a new one," he muttered, tuning his Gibson. "About some bad shit, happening right here in Cowtown."

"Shut up and play!" a biker-type two tables away shouted.

Tommy's head snapped up, fire in his eyes. "You don't like it, pal, find the fuckin' door!" The heckler said nothing, prompting a crooked smile from Tommy as he continued fiddling with his guitar. "There's a guy out on the Denver streets right now. . . You've probably heard about him in the news. An evil motherfucker, doin' ugly things to girls my sister's age. This is "Bite of Lust.""

The drummer rapped out a stucco beat, sharp as a rifle shot. The bassist added an earthquake rumble as Tommy spit the opening lines.

"Young girl walking there! So sweet and so fair!

"Her love like a challenge! Her virtue a dare!

"So firm and so fair! A take-a-chance dare!"

Swinging his arm over his head, Tommy slashed the guitar strings and raged into the mic.

"His tweaked-twisted brain! Needs creepy-crawl games!

"Play them he must! Chasin' the ultimate rush!

"So go ahead and take her! Now's the time to break her!

"Take that first bite of lust! Yeah, break the pie crust!"

No one was dancing to this one. The crowd stood mesmerized as the song built like a rising storm. After the second verse, Tommy wrung a howling, homicidal solo from his ax. I shut my eyes and the starred entries in Derk's dance log blazed across my mind like comets, ill omens of disaster.

"Now comes his finest hour! When he has all power!

"That first bite of lust! Yeah, grind 'em to dust!

"Big bite of lust! 'Cause control is a must!"

The song grew louder, more violent, until my brain felt ready to explode through my skull, JFK/Dallas style. The music thrilled but also horrified. I got up and started toward the door, suddenly needing space, fresh air.

Nearing the exit, I saw Raven come back in, red-faced, eyes bright with anger. She glanced in my direction but didn't seem to notice me. I stopped to watch her vanish into the crowd then continued outside.

No sign of Derk, which, it struck me, might mean no ride home. I hurried around the side of the Big House, sighed with relief when I saw the van. I went over and rapped softly on the passenger window.

Derk glanced over expectantly, frowned when he saw it was only me. "It's open."

Climbing in, I saw scratches on Derk's right cheek. They weren't quite bleeding, but almost. "What happened?" I asked off-handedly, though the answer seemed obvious.

"Nothing." He snickered and stared out the windshield. "Just a dumb bitch, playing dumb games."

I looked toward the club to hide my smile. "Yeah?"

"Raven was happy to have some of *my* candy, but didn't want to reciprocate," Derk said stoically. "Well, there's no accounting for taste."

"Nope," I agreed.

"I'm going to cruise, Adam. You coming?"

Not wanting to bus it back to Windhollow, I reluctantly agreed.

As we pulled out of the lot, Derk touched his abused cheek. The muscles in his face twitched, his eyes narrowing to a sniper's squint. More than just a movie Nazi now, I saw him as an embattled Führer, scheming up a scorched-earth policy.

But who was going to get burned?

32

Derk's beeper went off as we hit Colfax. He wheeled into a Shell station and went to use the phone. I had expected to spend my Denver Saturday nights with Dave, but life's what happens when you're making plans, right? And while I wanted to be pissed at my bro for his vanishing-up-to-Boulder act, I couldn't help but hope Dave was enjoying his new romance.

One of us should be having fun.

"Just booked a strip-a-gram," Derk told me as he got back in. Pulling the rearview mirror toward him to examine the scratches, he decided, "Nothing some make-up won't take care of."

"You gonna drop me at the condo first?"

"No time." Stepping over the console, Derk opened the top drawer built into the bar and started pawing through stage clothes. "U.S. Male no-showed this chick's late-night party, so it's Derk to the rescue. It's only a half-hour gig. You can hang in the van or take a walk."

"Whatever." Watching Derk dig through costumes, I realized this was the perfect opportunity to study Mr. X in action. "You get many last minute calls like this?"

"A few a month. Normally I assign them to one of the guys," he said, laying a cop shirt atop the bar. "But I've got the time tonight, plus this party sounds interesting."

"Gonna do a line first?"

"Why, you want one?"

"Sure," I said, trying to turn my question into an invitation.

"The stuff I sold you already gone? Dave wouldn't like me turning his little brother into a coke fiend."

"No, but I managed to lose the fuckin' seal somewhere." I wasn't about to tell Derk about getting ripped off by the Barbecue Sisters.

"Sucks for you." He kicked off his shoes and started undressing.

"Yeah."

"No sweat," Derk said. "Be happy to sell you more."

"I don't have much cash on me," I said, rubbing my nose.

"Sucks for you."

"Yeah, well. . ." I averted my eyes as he stripped, glanced back a moment later to see him snap on a black leather G-string then climb into dark blue pants with a stripe down the side of the legs. "I'm just trying to keep life from being a sit-com."

Derk laughed as he finished dressing and joined me up front. "Point taken," he said, tapping a black billy club against my shoulder, like a king knighting a new royal. "We'll toot up when we get there."

"Excellent."

As we drove off, Derk turned on what looked kinda like a CB radio mounted under the dash. "What's that?"

"Police band scanner. Let's you eavesdrop on some interesting shit." Derk upped the volume on the scratchy transmission.

"Uh, dispatch, this is unit eleven. We're 10-22."

Apparently 10-22's weren't high on the charts, because Derk dialed the volume back down and said, "You separate the men from the boys by the cost of their toys, so the trick move is a hostile takeover of Santa's workshop."

He knows when you're sleeping, I thought, knows when you're awake. I squinted at Derk, and he blurred into a composite of Wendy's old man and Harry Paul Gattlin–all the loud, aggressive jerks who take what they want and leave bones for the vultures. And I wondered again about what I'd seen in Derk's ice blue eyes.

We arrived at his "gram," parking in front of a ranch house in suburban Littleton, just a few blocks off Broadway but miles from downtown Denver. Derk handed me a pocket-sized notebook then climbed in the back of the van. "Check the party girl's name for me, Adam. It's the last entry."

I flipped open the notebook and reported, "Marcy," as Derk took a cosmetics kit from the middle drawer and went about camouflaging the scratches in a lighted mirror behind the bar. "Not to nag," I said, "but are we gonna do that line?"

"The vial's in the left pocket," Derk said, kicking his discarded jeans toward me. "There's a metal mirror in the glove box. Cut us each a fatty."

As I tended to the magic powder, Derk dusted his cheeks with a powder puff then grabbed a boom box, a small bottle of champagne from the mini fridge, and rejoined me up front. We took on fuel then he checked his face a final time in the rearview, collected the party gear and marched up to the house, to be met at the door by a girl in a slinky yellow slip.

A bachelorette-slumber party? No wonder Derk thought it would be *interesting*.

He'd left the keys in the ignition so I could play the radio. I tuned in some Stones and got a can of beer from the fridge. The coke wasn't revving me up much. Nose tingle, ether drip in my throat, but where was the instant energy buzz? Guess I was developing a tolerance.

It was eleven-thirty. I thought of Wendy, in bed a world away. Longed to jump in with her and never have to get out again. I hungered for her...

But what, the little voice asked, *have you done to* deserve *her?*

The question flashed in my mind like Vegas neon. "Nothing," I whispered, started to open the beer, but then got up and put it back in the fridge. A small gesture of restraint, sure, but it felt like maybe a baby step toward becoming more deserving.

Leaning against the bar, I heard that last Next song in my head: *"Go ahead and take her."* I slid open the top drawer and saw Mr. X leather gear, spandex in various colors, what looked like maybe a sci-fi get-up. The middle drawer was a jumble of accessories: cassette tapes, spare batteries, street maps and other tools of the mobile male stripper's trade. The bottom drawer was locked.

I returned to my seat and lit a smoke. Suddenly it felt like the van was growing smaller, pressing in on me. I had to urge to get out and run, just *go* and keep going, through the wall and into the blank, run until I was free at last of. . . *everything*.

But that was just a fantasy, I knew. There's no escaping the world's bullshit, unless I ran off a cliff somewhere. . .

So maybe, the little voice suggested, *deal with reality instead of always trying to escape it.*

I snubbed the cig out in the ashtray and glanced at the keys, dangling in the ignition.

Derk had been gone, what, ten minutes? Fifteen?

Screw it. Don't think, react. I grabbed the keys, scrambled back over the console, and started trying keys in the bottom drawer. The fourth one fit.

A door slammed, scaring the crap out of me. I leapt up, looked out the tinted, diamond-shaped side window, but no sign of Derk so back to snooping before I lost my nerve.

I slowly slid the bottom drawer open and muttered a curse. Inside was a roll of duct tape, a coil of nylon cord, handcuffs, and a tiny pair of red cotton panties.

REWIND AND ROT

> "He who makes a beast of
> himself gets rid of the
> pain of being a man."
> – Samuel Johnson

ADAM
Sketch by Wendy Walker

33

Relocking the drawer with shaky hands, I stood up, snatched the Jamesons from the bottle rack and took a big swig. The whiskey burned down my throat, focusing me on a single searing thought: Derk is *really* doing it. He was the one attacking those girls. Despite my hazy, half-formed suspicions, this was the first time I'd fully expressed the idea, even inside my own head.

I grabbed a Coke from the mini fridge, stabbed the keys back in the ignition and sat down to get my head together.

Okay, suppose Derk *was* the Shopping Mall Rapist. What do I do about it?

Go to the cops, the little voice said. *Obviously.*

And tell them what? The black wig and handcuffs could be dismissed as stage props, while the panties might belong to a petit and *consenting* girl. The police searching the condo for more evidence would require a warrant, meaning hard facts I didn't have. Hell, there must be what, a hundred guys in Denver who fit Derk's description and drove black vans? A thousand?

And there was something else to consider. What if the cops questioned Derk but didn't arrest him, and he then discovered the source of their interest?

Wait a sec, what the hell are the priorities here? If my suspicions were correct then stopping Derk was the most important thing, no matter what. I had to lay it all out for the police and leave it to them to nail him.

Don't react, *think.*

If the cops could. . .

The driver's door suddenly swung open, almost giving me a heart attack. "H-How was the show?" I managed to ask as Derk climbed aboard.

"Can't complain." He stowed the boombox and smiled as he settled into the driver's seat. "Neither will the lovely Donna, who I'll be back to pick up in forty-five minutes."

"Mr. X scores again." I glanced at the house as we drove off, tried sending a psychic warning to Donna then realized Derk was too smart to attack a girl he met while working. Too many witnesses and the victim would surely recognize him.

Thinking of all the chicks I'd seen rotate through Derk bedroom, I almost had to admire the brilliance of his career camouflage. Does a rich man rob banks? Or a stud-stripper kidnap girls from shopping malls?

"What's wrong, Adam?" Derk asked as we hit Broadway. "You look like you swallowed a fart."

"Just feeling kinda burned out." I shook the soda can feebly. "Too much partying for a country boy."

"There's no such thing as too much *anything*," he said, then began describing Donna's ample charms. I relaxed, convinced he had no idea I was on to him.

The Fabulous Thunderbirds came on the radio.

Ain't that tuff enough

Yeah, you're a tough guy, Derk, I mused, but everyone has a weak spot. His was greed. Despite his good looks and workout-sculpted bod, despite the tricked-out vehicles, fancy TV, home gym, and all the booze, dope and chicks, he still lusted after more.

Too God damned much more.

Then it hit me in a flash, what to do. The cops would be called, but after *I* got the goods on Derk myself. I've watched spotlight guys like him win all my life, with me brooding on the sidelines, most times too insecure to even get in the game.

Not anymore though because *this* is what I'd been waiting for, a chance to stand up, fight back, and earn some spotlight time for myself. Bringing Derk to justice would show Wendy, show Dave, Dad and the whole damned world.

Show them that I deserved it.

34

Back at the condo, Derk quickly changed clothes, checked in with a couple of the Bad Boys, then left for his date with Donna. Contrary to what I told him about being burned out, I actually felt revitalized, fueled by righteous purpose. I had a mission now, was tasked to bring down a villain and do my part for truth, justice, and the apple pie American Way that I'd scoffed at since I was twelve.

I made coffee and sat down with my notebook to brainstorm a strategy for the manhunt. The first big hurdle to overcome: I had no car, no budget to play taxi-cab detective, and shadowing Derk without wheels was impossible.

I stared at the blank page for ten minutes before closing the notebook in frustration. Derk's superior smirk mocked me now, but I had no desire to exorcise it by slamming booze or snorting coke. No, to wipe that smirk away *permanently* would require being smart and sober, focused like an avenging angel. Let fury have the hour, Joe Strummer had sung, anger can be power. The Clash knew the score. Harry Paul Gattlin was proof of that.

A big, raw-boned fourth generation farm boy, Harry Paul was a senior football star when I was a sophomore. He took an irrational dislike to me soon after the school year started, apparently for the crime of always reading in the cafeteria during lunch. His nickname for me was *faggy bookworm Freeman.*

85

How I came to his baleful attention remains a mystery, but Harry Paul kept me on edge all year with random attacks, verbal and physical - insults and putdowns, shoves into lockers, tripping, books poked out of my arms from behind - that came in bursts, sometimes two or three a day, then he'd ignore me for weeks. I'd finally become convinced he'd found another whipping boy when the cycle would start all over, leaving me to wonder if the asshole had some meticulously worked out master schedule for my torment, or if it was all purely spur of the moment.

Harry Paul had four inches and at least fifty pounds on me, so avoidance was the better part of valor: ducking down stairwells, listening for his voice before entering a lavatory, walking around the back of the school to stay off his radar.

Our final confrontation came in the middle of May, near the end of the school year. I'd been Harry Paul-free for over a month, but I should have known a natural-born sadist like him would want to get in some final licks. Seniors have to make those final memories, right?

It was a Friday afternoon. After cleaning out my track gear from the boy's locker room, I walked out of the gym to find Harry Paul and two of his pals waiting for me. The snuff-dipping trio quickly herded me behind the building and started tossing me around, laughing and hooting in anticipation of the kill.

With nowhere to run, I'd finally get the *real* ass-kicking Harry Paul had threatened all year. He was about to beat me up for absolutely no reason, other than his apparent hatred of books. And that made me mad. *Furious* that some dumb hick had terrorized me all year for sheer sport, and no one knew or cared.

With nothing to lose, I attacked him first, purely on impulse, launching a rat-a-tat flurry of punches to the face. No doubt as surprised by my vicious assault as I was, Harry Paul remained a stationary target long enough for me to bloody his nose and loosen a tooth, the final punch damn near busting my knuckles in the process. He crumbled to his knees, spitting blood. His buddies took off and so did I, leaving Harry Paul cursing and blubbering behind the gym.

I whipped him because he never saw it coming. To Harry Paul, pounding on "faggy Freeman" was gonna be everyday fun, while I lashed out in righteous indignation, like my life depended on it. Stalking Derk would be just the opposite, requiring planning and stealth, but the lesson was the same. Anger can be power.

And I *was* angry at the thought of Wendy being followed by a black van, angry for all the kids ducking behind lockers, haunted by bullies who groove on torment. Pissed off enough to write a new script, one where the scrappy little guy finally fights back in the final reel.

So have your fun, Derk. Snort your coke and bang your dollar bill-clutching bimbos, because the day of reckoning was coming. The next pair of handcuffs you see may be the one the cops clamp on you.

Comprende?

35

Carrying my coffee out to the patio, I stretched out on a lounge to bask in the morning sun. Dave wasn't home from enjoying Laura's charms up in Boulder and good for him. My bro deserved to find a special girl, like I found Wendy. I wondered if her letter would arrive today, then remembered it was Sunday. Damn.

Yet she'd told me she still loved me, so whatever was in the letter would be pure gravy.

Still, I was curious, because writing wasn't Wen's thing, creatively. She was an artist. Two of her painting hung on my bedroom walls back home. My fav is called *Evening at Xanadu*, a sci-fi vision of a futuristic bar, where humanoids danced to music produced by strange instruments that played themselves while floating in mid-air. In the foreground is a gorgeous girl in a black jumpsuit, her head tilted back, big green eyes staring up through the transparent ceiling. Spidery craft wheel through the starry sky, but those eyes, wide with both promise and pain, gazed beyond them, looking for something she couldn't quite see. Wen gave me the painting for graduation. I always took the girl in the painting to be her, staring across the heavens in search of. . . me.

Well, the search is over, babe, and neither of us would ever be lost again. *That* was the lesson of my great summer road trip.

I went out to run, quickly easing into a rhythm as I wound around the curving street and out Windhollow's front gate. Thinking about chasing down Derk gave me a burst of energy and I picked up the pace. The sidewalk blurred by under my feet and a local late-night commercial I'd seen often the past couple weeks popped into my head.

"Rent-a-Wrecks ain't pretty, but they sure do run!" a cowboy pitchman proclaimed as he sat a saddle, lashed to the roof of a rusty VW bug. "Rent-a-Wrecks are gua-run-*teed* to get you where yer going, partner! For just twelve bucks a day!"

Bingo!

Even my shrinking fundage could handle twelve bucks a day. I'd shadow Derk in some old beater, play gumshoe in a Gremlin. Grinning over this idea, I kicked up my speed. Next, I had to decode the dance log to confirm if Derk was "AA." Dave had shown me their strip-a-gram ad in a weekly paper, so I'd call the service and hire Derk for a party. If the booking then appeared in the log for "AA," I'd be able to monitor his schedule. That could be important, since the rapes might be synched to his solo strips. Maybe there was a psychological link between the two in his sick puppy head.

That part of my case was half-baked, I knew. Intel was needed, not just speculation, but how to come up with hard facts?

Reaching Colorado Boulevard, I ran south for another forty blocks before circling back. My breath came in short, stabbing rasps now, but I soon got my second wind. Was still going strong when the condo entrance came back into view, a quarter mile away.

I imagined Wendy at the finish line with a big kiss for the winner. . .

Breaking into a final sprint, I passed through the wall and into the blank. No pain now as I flew through the front gate. Another block and building G was dead ahead. Here comes Adam Freeman, folks, chewing up the course in record time!

Crossing the finish line, I dropped to the grass on the slope behind the pool, exhausted but happy. Gazing over at the mailboxes, my attention was drawn to the newspaper machines at the end of the concrete slab.

"Intel," I whispered, thinking of the newspapers stacked on the patio. There had to be several months' worth and Derk subscribed to both the *News* and *Post*. Scouring them for details about the Shopping Mall Rapist became my summer reading assignment. The manhunt was gathering steam.

Stretching my legs, I glanced across the pool at Derk's building. A brunette was strolling down the sidewalk, pushing a baby carriage. I stared at her, a grin slowing spreading across my face.

Maybe that's it, I realized, the mystery of Wendy's letter. She couldn't talk on the phone, afraid her asshole old man might overhear the whispered news that she was pregnant with our kid!

Just a guess, sure, but the deep, instinctual flutter in my gut *felt* like the truth.

I got up and went inside, giddy over this terrifying but terrific psychic flash. Boy, so much to worry about, but I decided not to sweat doctor bills and diapers, there'd be plenty of time for that later. The most important thing was that having a kid would bond Wen and me together.

Forever.

36

Derk was counting bench press reps when I glanced in the workout room, sweating to further sculpt himself into some warped vision of a master race super stud. Wendy's stork-related news was so monumental that I was tempted to tell him about it.

No. This was special, sacred even, and telling Derk would be like giving secrets to the enemy. I retreated to the kitchen. No idea when Dave would get back from Boulder, but I had to share the potential papa-Adam news with *someone*. I plucked the phone off its cradle and called Rick, back in Garrison.

Four rings then, *"The number you dialed has been disconnected."*
What the. . .?

Redialing got the same result, three times running. Rick's orthodontist dad could well afford the phone bill, so this didn't make sense. I was still puzzling over it ten minutes later when Dave waltzed in, a sack of laundry over one shoulder.

"Hey, bro," he called, dropping the laundry by the stairs.

"Hey yourself. What's new and exciting?"

"My girlfriend," said Dave, joining me in the living room.

"Girlfriend?" I echoed. "First time I've heard you use that word. Can the Rock 'n' Roll Kid be getting serious?"

Dave shrugged but looked mighty pleased with the world. "Hey, Laura is amazing, so why not?"

"That's excellent." I glanced down the hall to make sure Derk wasn't approaching. "Now here's a bulletin for you. I think Wendy's pregnant."

Dave's smile vanished. *"Think?"*

I explained about her letter and my brainstorm.

"I don't know, man," he said, sinking into the recliner. "Sounds like major conclusion jumping to me."

"Maybe, but I've been running it over in my head." Along with baby names, but I decided not to mention that. "And I don't know what else it could be."

Dave gave me a sad, skeptical look that reminded me of the old man. "I hope you're wrong."

"Why?"

"Jesus, you're only eighteen, that's why," Dave said, then fished half a joint from his cig pack cellophane and fired it up. "Trust me, a bawling bundle of joy is the *last* thing you guys need."

"But we love each other," I protested.

"So?"

"So I guess. . ." The words were thick in my throat, but I managed to get them out. "Maybe I'm a little scared of losing her. If we have a kid and get hitched, I know we'll be together."

"That's total bullshit." Dave took another toke and offered me the weed. "And you know it. Or will when you stop thinking with your dick."

I reached for the pot automatically then remembered my Get Derk mission and waved it off. My mind was focused now, and I liked it. "What bullshit do I know?"

"Getting a chick pregnant doesn't mean a shotgun wedding anymore." Dave leaned back and kicked off his shoes. "I know you loved *Happy Days* as a kid but thank God this ain't the Fifties."

"But I want to. . ."

"Marry Wendy so you can seal the deal," Dave interrupted. "I get the impulse, but marriage doesn't punch your ticket to happy-ever-after-land, Mom and Dad being exhibit A."

"But Wendy and I are different," I protested.

"Yeah, no doubt," Dave said. *"Everybody's* different, but certain facts still apply."

"Like?"

"Having a kid at your age is a disaster. You're just starting to get a clue at eighteen and the *last* thing you need," Dave insisted, gesturing with the joint like some Professor Know-It-All, "is having to care for something that shits and bawls around the clock."

"Maybe," I whispered.

"No maybes, Adam," Dave said quietly. "A kid changes your life forever. You'll get stuck in some assembly line Springsteen nightmare job, just to keep the brat in strained peas. None of which helps you and Wendy keep the hots going." He took another toke. "Sure you don't want a hit?"

"Yeah." I lit a smoke instead, stood up and paced the living room under Porsche girl's watchful gaze. "So you're an expert on marriage now?"

"No expert, but I know three guys who got married in the last three years. Two are already divorced, the other's miserable and so, mostly likely, are the four kids they have among them." Dave snubbed out the roach and cracked his knuckles. "And all those guys are older and wiser than you, Adam. So, yes, I hope you're wrong about Wendy's letter."

"But things *are* different with us," I repeated, struggling to make Dave understand. "I told you I wrote lyrics for my friend's band, right?"

"Yeah, which is very cool."

"What I need, what the soul dreams breed, is the life electric," I recited without preamble. "Some call it fantasy, others insanity, but I gotta plug into the life electric."

Dave stared at me blankly.

"Wendy plugs me in," I explained, walking over to muss his hair. "She makes *everything* electric, and I dig that juice, brud-der. Horror stories about your friends can't affect that."

"Okay, Romeo." Dave grinned, brushing my hand away. "And it's great that you and Wendy have that connection."

"Yes, it is" I agreed, bowing slightly from the waist. "Thank you."

"Then you *don't* need a kid to stay together, right? You two have that spark, the life electric."

"True," I said, smiling over Dave quoting my lyrics back to me "We don't *need* a kid, but if there is one, it's destiny."

He snorted. "So-called."

We fell silent, sat there a moment, then Dave clicked on the tube. I considered telling him about Derk but nixed the idea. Just like with the cops, I lacked enough "evidence" to convince Dave his bud/boss was a sex criminal. Besides, bringing Derk to justice was a solo mission.

Only one seat in the plane.

Speak of the devil: Derk said hi to us on his way from workout to shower. We watched videos awhile then Dave said he needed to go get pumped for an afternoon 'gram at a backyard barbeque.

"When will you be back?" I asked, following him down the hall.

"Probably five, five-thirty." Dave grabbed thirty-pound dumbbells and worked his biceps.

"How 'bout the Freeman boys go out and do something?"

"Like what?"

"Hell, you're the tour guide, remember?" I laughed after saying that but wasn't joking. Dave had been *AWOL* a lot lately and it was starting to bug me. "I don't care what we do, just wanna spend some time with you."

"I haven't been a great host, huh?" Dave finished his curls. "Sorry I've been gone so much, but Laura . . ." Even while apologizing, he couldn't help but smile at his heart-throb good fortune. "I never expected. . . *whatever* this is with her to happen while you're here."

"No sweat, bro," I said, smiling back. "Couldn't be happier for you."

"Thanks."

"So we're going out?"

"Absolutely," Dave said. "I'll come up with something to do."

"Excellent."

After getting his pump on, Dave showered then went upstairs to dress, returning twenty minutes later in tight black dress pants, tux shirt and bow tie. He could have passed for a waiter at an expensive Italian restaurant, except Dave's Velcro-connected tear away trousers contained the main course. After grabbing a mini bottle of champagne from the fridge, he sat down to look over directions to his gig.

"Another bachelorette blow-out?" I asked.

"Just the opposite. Some chick celebrating her divorce."

"Sounds like a case for the Rock 'n' Roll Kid."

———

Dave pocketed the directions and grabbed his keys. "I just hope the new divorcee doesn't expect *extras*. I'm thinking about maybe just being with Laura for a while. See how that goes."

"Wow, you do really like her."

Dave raised a *hold on* hand. "I'm not committing to a one girl policy, understand. But I don't feel like banging rando G-string stuffers right now, either."

I beamed at him, feeling an odd sense of pride. "Imagine my brother," I said, shaking my head. "All grown up."

37

Sandwiched between Talons Nail Salon and the New Age Eateteria in the back pages of *Westword,* the T.J.'s Strip-a-Gram ad boasted pix of a busty blonde packed into a too small t-shirt and a stripped-to-the-waist Derk, oiled-up and preening for the camera.

For the ladies, we feature members of the Bad Boys, Denver's #1 Male Review! the ad copy crowed. *Our men are up to it!*

I quizzed Derk the other night after one of his bedmates split. He loved talking biz and fancied himself a budding entrepreneur. He personally booked the Bad Boys review shows but had found dealing with strip-a-gram phone traffic too big a hassle and so farmed out his troupe's services to T.J.'s exclusively, in exchange for promos in their ads and confirmed bookings, which he doled out among his guys.

After jotting down T.J.'s number, I grabbed the Yellow Pages with an unlit cigarette pasted between my lips, feeling like Bogart in a late show caper. Plenty of junk metal for hire: Cheap Heaps, Rent-a-Wrecks, Jane's Jalopies, all wringing a last buck from aging Detroit steel on its way to the car crusher. I got four numbers and closed the notebook just as Derk strolled into the living room.

"What's are you looking for?" he asked, pointing to the phone book in my lap.

"Cars," I said, seeing no reason to lie. "Might rent a junker for when I want to go out."

"Did Dave really teach you to drive when you were thirteen?" Derk asked, grabbing *Hot Tub Tarts* off a stack of videos.

"He told you that?" Hard to imagine Derk being interested in boyhood tales of the Freeman brothers.

"He did." Derk turned on the TV and fed his porno into the VCR. "I might let you borrow some wheels."

"That's nice but. . ."

"*Damn* nice, I'd say. I'm a generous guy."

"Yeah, but you putting me up is enough." Derk's offer seemed out of character and so made me wary. Why would he suddenly be so accommodating? "Rent-a-wrecks are cheap enough."

———

92

"What, you'd rather cruise the town in some old rattletrap?" Derk asked. "Sure you're Dave's brother?"

"Hey, you want to loan me a ride, I'm fine with that." I couldn't risk tailing Derk in one of his own cars, but didn't want to make a big deal of refusing. "I'll let you know when I need it."

He walked over to the bar. I glanced at *Hot Tub Tarts* opening credits, debating when to make a break for it, since I had no desire to watch Derk screw, or listen to his cocksmanship commentary.

"Here!"

I turned toward Derk just as he tossed a set of keys. I managed to snatch them out of the air.

"Nice catch," he said. "It's a green and white '73 Charger, parked by the wall in the back lot."

"Great. Thanks, Derk."

"No sweat. I'm tired of you always moping around here anyway." He gave me a light punch in the arm on his way to the recliner, then lit one of his little cigars and gestured toward the screen. "Gina Carlucci, now there's one Grade A piece of ass."

A willowy Latin beauty slipped off her pink bikini bottoms - just like Wendy's - and fondled a big black dildo. My eyes tracked up to the ceiling. I wasn't in the mood for second-hand skin but couldn't bolt thirty seconds after he lent me some wheels.

"Want a bump?" Derk asked.

"Umm, sure." I hadn't had a drink since the Big House, but some magic powder would allow me to more intently study my target before I left him to his porn.

Derk cut one fat line and offered me the mirror. I tooted up, but instead of the numbing effect of ether the stuff burned my nose like Ajax. My eyes watered and a harsh, metallic taste filled my mouth.

Gagging, I ran to the kitchen for something wet. Grabbed a Coors, quaffed a third of it, then yelled, "What is that shit?"

"Crystal meth. Pretty intense, huh?"

"Pretty fucking nasty, I'd say." I kneaded my eyes and returned to the living room with an inflamed nose and a beer I didn't particularly want. "And it's not cool to ask if I want coke, then surprise me with some other shit."

"I asked if you wanted a bump," Derk said as he blew a smoke ring. "I didn't say of *what*, did I?"

I glowered and rubbed my poor nose, pissed that he was technically correct while still having tricked me. "No," I admitted.

"Never *assume* anything, Adam," Derk said with one of his cheesy stage smiles. "It will only get you in trouble."

His tone reminded me of my tenth-grade history teacher Mrs. Folger and her condescending *you kids can't appreciate my wisdom* attitude. I never got the chance to wipe the smirk off her face, but Derk would be a different story, right, Bogey?

"What's this crystal stuff?" I asked, glancing at the TV, where Grade A Gina was leisurely stuffing herself with the rubber wang as she sat, as the title promised, on the lip of a hot tub.

"Methamphetamine," Derk said. "*Speed*, baby. The napalm nose burn will stop soon, then you'll be cruising for hours."

"How many hours?"

Derk shrugged. "Six, maybe eight."

I took another slug of beer to combat the foul taste and took stock of the drug's immediate effects. There was pressure behind my eyes, a faint ringing in my ears. "Great," I muttered, "I'll be messed up all day."

"You can function just fine," Derk said dismissively. "Better than fine, actually. It's an energy drug, like a super vitamin."

"Uh-huh." I was skeptical.

After a bit more of Gina's self-servicing, Derk fast forwarded to a scene of two cheerleaders sneaking into the boy's locker room to surprise the team captain in the shower. I was getting a rush from the speed now, coming on fast. I felt warm, had the urge to get up and *move,* get out of Derk's presence and under some sky. Just out.

I popped up off the sofa. "I'm going for a walk."

"You'll miss my on-screen exploits."

"Yeah," I agreed, taking another sip of beer then carrying the rest out to the kitchen trash.

"You could pick up some pointers from the movie, Adam," Derk said jauntily. "Then maybe one day *you'll* get your money for nothing and your chicks for free."

"Later," I said, heading for the door.

Derk laughed and cranked up the volume.

38

The bright sun made me squint, but I wasn't going back for my shades because the crystal made me feel like taking a poke at Derk's smug mug.

The battery acid taste was still dripping down my throat, so I went to the pool and got a Pepsi. After downing half of it, I pulled a chaise lounge into the shade and stretched out. The speed rush was still coming on. My heart beat faster, and I didn't know how revved up it would get. I lit a smoke, sending tingles down my spine. Couldn't decide if I liked the buzz or not, but Derk still shouldn't have tricked me like that.

The bastard did *lots* of things he shouldn't, and maybe that's why I was in Denver, in the Big Picture sense. To slay the Derk dragon and secure fair Wendy's hand. Anything's possible, right?

———

Our daily dot-to-dot existence is usually half-random, half-push button routines, yet occasionally the dots connect in important, unexpected ways. Sometimes the arc of history bends towards justice. Martin Luther King Jr. said that, or maybe Hawkeye Pierce.

But what if the manhunt was bullshit, just another big dream of busting out of my small town cage, doomed to failure? Finishing one cigarette, I immediately lit another and realized my mission to take down Derk was neither doomed nor destined. Not yet. It existed now only in Idea Space, its fate undecided, like that dead *and* alive cat in the box.

Shutting my eyes, I resolved to connect the dots, to *will* the manhunt into existence. If I just got a break or two – which was bound to happen eventually, right? – I could hit the jackpot: Wendy pregnant with our adorably cute kid, while I capture Mall Raper Derk, winning acclaim as an *ah-shucks* hero.

Okay, I had to admit crystal was pretty fucking good.

"Oh, look! There's the pin-up boy!"

That sing-song voice snapped my eyes open. Sherri was giggling with another girl as they came strolling down my side of the pool. I bit my bottom lip, pulse going into overdrive.

"I'm thinking of sending your pix to *Playgirl,* Adam," Sherri chirped as they approached. "Or maybe *Big Jerk Monthly.*" She giggled again, her blubber wobbling obscenely.

I gripped the side of the lounge, tasted blood and so stopped the lip-biting. God, Sherri was ugly, with her beady little pig eyes and bad taste in music.

Ugly.

"I'll show you the photos later, Jan," Sherri told her friend as they flounced past me.

That's when I jumped up, charged after them with a savage war cry and threw a shoulder block into Sherri, sending her tumbling into the pool, arms flailing.

Her friend screamed.

"Not cool, dude!" some muscle-head shouted from across the pool. He got up and headed my way as Sherri bobbed to the surface, spitting water.

"Mind your own business!" I yelled at Muscle Head, then beelined out through the gate. The fat little piggy deserved more than just a dunking, but I smiled at bringing a little justice into the world. *That* should deter Sherri's interest in ambush photography.

Passing building G's group mailbox, I thought of Wendy's letter and wondered why she was playing this dumb game of post office, instead of just *talking* to me. Sure, she had to worry about her old man eavesdropping, but weren't there frickin' payphones on Cape Cod?

Maybe Wendy didn't trust me to do right by our kid.

Maybe she wasn't even pregnant.

Maybe, maybe!

Questions pinballed around my skull, making me mad at Wendy, mad at Dave for being gone so often. I'm his *brother,* god damn it, haven't seen him in years, but some chick he just met gets all his time and attention. . .

Fuck it.

I was just *mad.*

39

The command from my amped-up nervous system was *go.*

Scrambling over the cinderblock fence at the back of the condo complex, I crossed a dirt service road into a plowed-up area the size of several football fields, dotted with surveyor's stakes and large mounds of earth. Bulldozer tracks were imprinted in the ground, but they were old and sprouting weeds, the stakes gray and weathered. Windhollow II had gone bust.

I climbed up the biggest dirt pile in the abandoned construction site, maybe twelve feet high, and gazed down into an open foundation that had a couple feet of stagnant water pooled in the bottom. Two young boys, four or five, were perched on a broken concrete slab at the edge of the foundation, fishing poles in hand. They studied their lines intently, as if expecting a marlin to leap from the fetid water. I watched transfixed from atop mud mountain, picturing a different boy, one that I met four years ago this summer.

It had been a lazy Saturday afternoon, out fishing at Rook Lake with Dave and Dad. Two hours without a nibble. The old man was snoozing under a tree. Dave had wandered off somewhere, probably to get high. I started back to the car to retrieve the new issue of *X-Men*, bought the night before and saved for this exact circumstance, the mid-fishing trip blahs.

A big blond kid was sitting on the bumper of Mom's Falcon (the old man wouldn't dirty up his Riviera at the lake), casually smoking a cigarette. "Ain't hurting the car any," he said with a buck-toothed grin as I approached, wearing a proprietary scowl.

"Never said you were." I'd occasionally bummed a smoke from Dave and so asked the blond kid for one.

He unrolled a pack of Winston from the sleeve of his Black Sabbath t-shirt and shook out a cig. "I'm Kenny Karanski."

I remember being impressed by that exotic last name. *Karanski* sounded like a drunken poet or a Soviet secret policeman. "Adam Freeman."

We shook hands and just hit it off right away. After finishing the butts, Kenny said he knew where to cop some beer.

"Beer, huh?" Two years older than me at sixteen, Kenny's confident, cocky attitude was a glimpse of how I *wanted* to be, while being completely clueless as to how to get there.

"Yeah. You wanna come?"

I decided the X-Men could wait. "Let's go."

By "copping" beer, Kenny meant steal it. "Piece a cake," he said, pointing to a cooler in the back of the Hardy Brothers' pickup, parked by the bait shop.

Bob and Bill Hardy were self-employed handymen, known around the neighborhood for quality work and consuming vast amounts of beer while doing it. They were easy-going but built like bears and ripping them off didn't strike me as the greatest idea. I objected, but Kenny sold me on the *challenge,* plus he'd be the one making the snatch.

So I watched from a stand of trees twenty yards away as he approached the truck. Instead of snatching a six pack – the stated plan – Kenny grabbed the entire cooler, just as Bob Hardy came strolling around the side of the bait shop. I whistled loudly. Kenny looked around, saw Bob, and took off like a rocket.

"Bring that goddamn cooler back!"

"Here!" Reaching the tree line, Kenny thrust the old metal cooler into my hands. It was *heavy.* "Run!"

I staggered forward, with Bob roaring threats as he came chugging after us. Then I stumbled and dropped the cooler. It hit the ground and popped open, scattering cans of Schlitz. I grabbed an intact sixer and hauled ass. Still cursing, Bob settled for reloading the cooler with the remaining brews while we raced away, to soon be toasting our heist. Kenny was living up to that dangerous last name and I loved it.

As we sucked down suds, I learned his family had moved to town a month before. Kenny had big plans to become a race car driver or maybe a stunt man and, caught up in his *the world's-my-playground* attitude, I figured maybe he would.

Dad was still asleep when I got back to our spot an hour later, buzzed on two beers. No fish on our lines, but I'd reeled in a new friend, one halfway into the adult world I only knew through books.

Now, from atop mud mountain, I watched one of the young boys reel in his line, add a second worm to the hook, and drop it back into the dank water with stubborn, childish faith.

The sort of faith Kenny had inspired in me.

"Get out of here!" I yelled, reaching down to grab a dirt clod. "There's no fish!" I flung the clod at the boys, then another. Wasn't trying to hit them, just chase them out of fantasyland. They took off running, poles in hand. I scrambled down to the slab of concrete they'd been sitting on, grunted as I lifted one end and sent it tumbling into the green, smelly water. Flies buzzed around my head as I watched the kids disappear in the distance.

"There's no goddamned fish."

40

"All of our dancers are hot," the breathy-voiced girl at T.J.'s assured me. "I'm sure your girlfriend will be very happy."

"Great, but it has to be this Derk guy," I repeated. "She saw him at a Bad Boys show and that's who she wants."

"Of course," Breathy agreed. "When's the party?"

"Uh. . . when is he working?"

Pages flipped in an appointment book. "Derk's next availability is Wednesday night, between six and ten."

"That should work. Let's go with eight o'clock."

"Perfect," she chirped. "I need the name and address."

"My name's Brad Fredricks."

"Your girlfriend's getting the strip, right?"

"Duh."

"Then what's *her* name?"

"Oh, Wendy," I said instantly, regretted it for a sec but then didn't. Truth is easier to remember, if I had to follow-up with T.J.'s, and the real Wen was no more part of Derk's world than I was Brad Fredricks.

"And what's the address?"

"I don't have the address of this Allison chick who's hosting, but I'll get it and call you back."

"Fine, but I'll need that by the end of the day to hold your booking."

"No sweat, just make sure it's Derk."

"Certainly, but he's very popular so you'll want to firm up the booking today."

"Sure," I said. "I'll get back to you in a couple hours."

"Super," Breathy said. "Derk will take good care of Wendy and all the girls at the party."

"Great." And *I'll* take care of him.

Hanging up the pay phone, I rejoined Dave, waiting outside of Baskin-Robbins. Our brotherly outing wasn't very touristy; we'd spent the last hour wandering around Cherry Creek Mall. Fine by me. It gave us the chance to talk and, still buzzed on speed, I was a motor-mouth, droning on about whatever popped into my head and just glad to be hanging out with my bro.

We'd stopped to get ice cream and Dave ran into a guy, Ben something, he'd worked with at the Hilton when he first got to Denver. While they reminisced over double-scoop cones, I hit the pay phone in the corner to book the bogus strip-a-gram. The manhunt was gathering stream.

Ben had split. Dave and I continued the mall crawl, with him returning to his fave subject, lovely Laura. About her homemade waffles topped with blueberry ice cream and how she once blew bubbles after giving him a blow job.

"You seeing her later tonight?"

"No, she's having dinner with her folks." Dave grinned. "Besides, the girl needs *some* rest."

"You want to go to a movie or something later?"

"Can't," Dave said sheepishly. "I've got a date."

I gaped at him. "What happened to your just-see-Laura plan?"

"Well, it's not really a date," he hedged, sounding like a kid caught at the cookie jar. "More like a test."

I shot him an *oh really* look. "Of what?"

"My feelings," Dave said sincerely, steering us over to a bench. We sat down and sparked cigs. "If I go out with another girl and end up thinking about Laura, that's pretty good evidence she's the real deal."

"So is the fact that you talk about her non-stop."

"Maybe so," Dave conceded.

"Oh, I think the evidence is in." I blew a smoke ring, then intoned with mock gravity, "David Freeman, you've been found guilty of falling hard for Lovely Laura, and this court suggests you accept that verdict."

"Fuck off, your honor." Dave laughed and flicked an ash at me. "But you're probably right."

"Maybe you're just so used to playing the big stud that you don't know how to stop," I suggested.

"Could be, but I still need more time before going completely nuts over her."

"I'd say you're pretty well there, Mr. Peanut."

"Okay, *Dad*," Dave said sarcastically. "I get the point, but I still have to work through things my way."

"Sure." His dad comment made me think of the Humpty Dumpty wreckage of our family. Maybe Dave wasn't interested, but I had to bring it up anyway. "I worry about him sometimes."

"Who?"

"The old man." Dave shrugged but said nothing. I took it as a green light to continue. "He spaces out sometimes. Forgets things he should remember."

Another shrug. "Creeping old age."

"He's only fifty-two. No, it's something else." I studied Dave for a reaction, but his face was a blank mask.

"Why are you telling me this, Adam? It's not like I give a shit about the bastard."

"I don't believe that."

"Believe it, little brother." Dave got up and resumed walking. "And believe me when I say, *fuck* him."

Maybe it was the speed buzz, or my new mission to become more deserving, but I pressed the issue. "Dad can be a dick, sure, but he's only human. And all humans mess up, right?"

Dave snorted. "Him more than most."

"I hated him for kicking you out, Dave."

"Okay."

"But Mom splitting really messed him up," I said. "Everything he thought he had, poof, it was gone overnight, and he's never really gotten over that."

"So what, like we have?"

"Maybe his anti-dope kick was a way for him to reclaim some power," I theorized. "And you *did* kinda rub it in his face, what with auditioning for *High Times* poster boy.*"*

Dave smirked. "You think he went all tyrant on me because of demon weed?"

"What else? Or maybe it was just the trigger. You refused to obey his rules. . ." I lowered my voice, trying to summon the old man's two-pack-a-day rasp. *". . .under my goddamned roof!"*

My impression got the hoped-for chuckle from Dave. "And having lost the battle for his wife," I continued, "he couldn't lose another to his son."

Dave just scowled, like he wasn't buying my theory. "I'm *not* saying we have to agree with everything he did," I continued. "But maybe trying to understand him a little would make things less suckie."

"I appreciate the thought you've given this," Dave said with a sigh. "But you're off-base. The old fart didn't kick me out because I was a pothead."

"No?"

"Hell, I'd been getting high for *years*. It gave him something to occasionally bitch about, but he kicked me out because of the letter."

"What letter?"

"From Mom to him, written shortly before she split."

This was news to me. "No shit?"

Dave nodded. "I found it by accident. Was looking in the old man's room for a pipe that had disappeared, the one carved from an elk antler."

"Yeah, that pipe was cool," I said with a nod. "But what about this letter? What'd it say?"

"It was mostly a laundry list of Dad's faults and failings," Dave said, voice dropping to a near-whisper. "Twenty years' worth, arranged in numbered paragraphs."

"Man, that's pretty hard core."

"That's what I was thinking when the old man walked in, not a minute after I'd finished reading it. He went nuts and chased me out of the house, screaming that I was a no-good sneak, just like Mom."

"Jesus," I muttered.

"I crashed at Billy's that's night," Dave continued, "and when I got home the next day, the old man had calmed down. Never said a word about the letter and *I* sure as hell wasn't gonna bring it up."

I shook my head, trying to absorb this. "Wow."

"Never said a word," Dave repeated as we got up and moseyed toward the parking garage. Frisbee in a local park was next on our agenda. "But his anti-pot bullshit ramped up a couple days later and the next weekend he kicked me out." Dave ground his cig underfoot. "Maybe he was just anti-*me.*"

"How come you never told me about the letter?"

"What difference would it have made?" Dave shrugged and spit on the sidewalk. "Wish *I'd* never seen the god damned thing, so I wasn't gonna dump it on you."

I reached out and touched his shoulder. "What kind of stuff was on Mom's list?"

Dave chewed his bottom lip, apparently debating whether to tell me.

"Spill!" I demanded. "I'm your brother, damn it. If you can't talk to *me* about this, then who?"

Dave remained mum as we walked to the Camaro. After getting in, he fished a roach from the ashtray and lit it. We did a couple tokes then he said, "She complained Dad didn't make enough money. That he wasn't ambitious. Took her for granted but not out to dinner. The part that really got me was at the end, when she started comparing him to Fred Glaston. The old man came up short, in every possible way."

"That's cold," I whispered, feeling a little sick to my stomach. Mom splitting was one thing, but to knife the old man in the back like that on her way out the door. . .

"So *Daddy Dearest* didn't give me the boot over dope," Dave concluded, "but because he couldn't handle me knowing Mom thought Freddy G was a better lay."

"That's fuckin' hardcore. . ." I shook my head. Dave had a right to be bitter, sure, but Dad kicked him out three years ago. I was used to *that*, while the old lady's outrageous letter was poppin' fresh news. "What a low blow, no matter how miserable Mom was."

"That's exactly what I thought," Dave agreed. "Even after he screamed at me, I felt bad for the old man that whole week. . ." Dave's voice cracked slightly. "Up until the minute he gave me the boot."

I could picture the last time Dave walked out of our house, an old army duffle bag on one shoulder, heading for the interstate loop to start hitching west. "I'm sorry, bro."

"It's all ancient history, Adam, but I understand Dad just fine." Dave started the Camaro. "And like I said, *fuck* him."

41

I sucked in an anxious breath, waiting for the approaching vehicle to round the corner. And... it wasn't the postman. Damn. Dave said the mail usually came by eleven and it was now almost noon. The minutes crawled by as I awaited the expected arrival of Wendy's letter.

Don't clock-watch, the little voice suggested. *Think about something else.*

I took off my watch, stuffed it in my jeans, then mentally reviewed the manhunt's progress. I'd firmed up the fake strip-a-gram two days ago, giving them a real address from another condo complex a few blocks from Windhollow.

I'd priced several rent-a-wreck places and gone through some of the old newspapers on the patio with my morning coffee. It was easy to find stories about the two rapes that went down after I got to Denver, but neither provided details beyond the basics and only said they were "possibly related" to other assaults that had taken place the last couple years.

So nothing spectacular, but it was still progress.

The mail finally arrived at twelve-thirty. Unable to wait while three dozen boxes were filled, I marched up to the portly black postman, showed him the box key and asked what he had for 22-G.

"You waiting to hear from a girl?" he asked, grinning at me with a gold front tooth.

I grinned back. "Is it that obvious?"

"Well, I don't think you're hangin' out for the new *TV Guide*." He rooted through his bag, then frowned. "But all I've got for 22-G is a couple bills."

"Crap."

"It'll probably be here tomorrow."

"Sure." Taking the bills back to the condo, I did the math again. Wendy had mailed the letter either four or five days ago, so it should be here by now, damn it. My mind whirled with possibilities—what if it had burned up in a fiery mail truck crash?—and knowing I had to wait at least another day gave me an instant headache.

I took a couple aspirin, lifted weights awhile, then decided to take a spin in Derk's Charger and was soon heading south on I-25. No destination, I just wanted to get some wind in my hair.

The Charger only had an AM radio, so I found a talk station far down the dial.

"...land shark lawyers are a criminal's best friend, working to get violent punks and sleezeball crooks off with a slap on the wrist, while the rest of us put bars on our windows and buy burglar alarms," the nasally voiced host opined. "Enough, I say. When is the public gonna get ticked off enough to collectively scream *Enough!*

"We should consider bringing back hanging for violent repeat offenders. Better yet, the guillotine."

"Don't forget the incompetents in the Post Office," I shouted at the radio. "If Wen's letter's not here tomorrow, off with their heads!"

"Put the executions on cable TV," the host riffed. "Make a buck off it to give a raise to cops and prison guards. Not that I'd want either dating my sister, mind you, but the paid muscle we hire to enforce order deserve a decent living like everyone else. And speaking of making a living, we're gonna sell you something now."

As the commercial came on, my attention wandered to a beach scene billboard. *Bermuda. The First Time.*

I smiled, remembering the first time Wendy and I did the deed. Her old man was pulling a night shift at the tire plant. We were necking in her room, getting really worked up. Just the week before we'd agreed to wait for the perfect moment before surrendering to our fleshy desires (she'd insisted and I agreed), so I broke off a tongue-twisting kiss and told her we'd better cool our jets or I might bust in my pants.

Wen said she was getting overheated, too, turned on the tube for distraction, but we were soon back to the lip-lock. Finally, she pushed me down on the bed, nibbled on my neck and whispered, "Now is perfect, Adam. *Now.*"

It wasn't a hard sell.

Wendy had told me she wasn't a virgin, which made me both more nervous *and* glad one of us had some experience. Oh, I'd practiced hundreds of times, but rosy palm soloing doesn't really count. It's like listening to a tape player with weak batteries, while gen-u-wine *fucking* had to be a front-row concert ticket, right?

And it was, even if the band only played for three minutes. . .

A couple more weeks and we'd be back together, ready to strike up the band. That was my Derk-nailing deadline, because nothing was going to stop me from meeting Wendy's plane. Bermuda's probably great, but paradise for me was anywhere at her side.

". . .like this scum bucket piece of human excrement, the Shopping Mall Rapist."

My attention snapped back to the radio. I turned it up.

"A story in the new *Westword* suggests this guy may have attacked over twenty girls, but don't sweat, Joe and Jane Public, because according to the Denver Police the story's just fear-mongering sensationalism. Chief Mullins said so at a brief press conference this morning, so it must be true. There's no sex manic psycho, folks, the *real* threat is yellow journalism, so tell little Suzie and Cindy to have fun at the mall.

103

"The Chief didn't take any questions, so it was actually just a press *announcement.* I'd like to ask the Chief if his publicly addressing these crimes for the first time the day after the *Westword* story is purely coincidental. Ask him how that story can be dismissed as sensationalism when his own department acknowledged last month that, quote, 'two or three rape cases were likely linked to a single suspect'? Ask about all the evidence suggesting the Shopping Mall Scumbag is working the suburbs.

"Whatever the exact number of victims, just wait: when they catch this bastard some sleazy lawyer will use every trick in the law library to get the animal off, when we should be cutting something *else* off, and not necessarily his head. Maybe give him a choice, in pursuit of more equitable justice: castration or decapitation. Guys, call in and let me know which *you* think would be worse.

"Castration, yeah, you may still be walking around, but is it *really* living, without Mr. Happy? I'd say take the big head and be done with it."

The host was funny and cutting, but I turned him down anyway, needed to mull this latest development. If the cops were holding press conferences, they must have some solid leads or they wouldn't be piping up at all, right? And *that* meant they might nail Derk before I could.

I took the next exit, crossed over the interstate and headed back toward downtown. There was a *Westword* box outside the 7-Eleven near Windhollow, so I'd grab a copy on the way back to the condo and read up on SMR.

Time to press the hunt.

42

No bad boys at the condo, so I went directly to Derk's room to check the dance log and there it was: *AA, Wednesday 8 PM. Wendy, b-day. Three songs, down to G-string. Big champagne & hats. COD.* Confirmation that Derk *was* AA got me stoked. It seemed likely, right then, that bringing him to justice was how the story was destined to end.

Out to the kitchen, I grabbed the phone on impulse to call Wen but fought off the urge. She'd asked me not to call before her letter arrived, and I would honor that. Wasn't some jerk with no impulse control.

Hanging up, I chuckled at the thought of the fake strip-a-gram landing Derk at the door of some middle-aged couple, frantic to convince him that no Wendy lived there as he cranked the boombox and started to peel down. Since I couldn't be there to see it, I called T.J.'s to cancel then grabbed the *Westword* and went out to the patio.

"Charlie Manson With Muscles" Stalks Mall Land was the cover story in the weekly paper, complete with sinister, noir-like art, featuring a black van with jail-like bars on the back windows. "Manson with muscles" was how one of the victims had described her attacker, while the police described *nothing*, having refused to discuss ongoing investigations until today's press conference by Denver's top cop.

The story suggested that much of the local population was beginning to "fear for their daughters, stalked by a serial rapist in the All-American act of shopping, while the police not only refuse to connect the dots, they profess not to see any dots at all."

The rapes had occurred in at least five different municipalities, launching five separate investigations. The Denver cops had admitted "two or three" of their cases *might* be connected, but anything beyond that was media hype. The four suburban departments remained mum about their cases, leading the reporter to conclude, "There is a stubborn bureaucratic resistance to admitting that something far most sinister than consumer conformity in now stalking Mall-Land in the Mile High City."

Behind the official news blackout, rumors suggested that a taskforce of hot shot cops from each department was chasing SMR, but an anonymous detective quoted in the story debunked that, insisting no *official* coordination crossed municipal borders, but that those working the cases were informally sharing info.

While these law enforcement intrigues were interesting, they didn't advance *my* case any, so I paged ahead and hit the motherlode, a half-page box that chronologically listed "twenty-two sexual assaults that may be linked to a single perpetrator, although the evidence is substantial in only the seven cases detailed in the feature."

The list dated back to February 1984, but my eyes skipped down to the most recent rapes.

July 8: a sixteen-year-old, identified only as "Shelly," was abducted from the Westminster Mall between 6-6:30 p.m. She was later picked up on the outskirts of Boulder around 9:30 p.m. by local residents Mr. and Mrs. Hector Sanchez, who saw the girl wandering along Highway 36 'in a daze' and took her to Foothills Hospital.

That's the rape I saw reported on the TV news.

July 18: an unnamed seventeen-year-old from Kansas was abducted from the Villa Italia Mall shortly after 8 p.m. She was found at 11:24 p.m. by state trooper Steve Stutz on the shoulder of southbound I-25, thirty miles south of Denver.

That's the attack I heard about at the 7-Eleven.

After reading the entire main article, I tore out the victim scorecard and went back inside, more determined than ever – the Fearless Derk Hunter.

43

The next morning, I tried calling Rick again but got the same disconnect message as the other day. Losing contact with my best friend really bugged me, but I had no way to find out what was going on. Calling the old man wouldn't help, because *he* wasn't gonna drive over to the Danson's to investigate an unpaid phone bill.

I turned on the radio and spun the dial to some Aerosmith.

I was a high school loser
Never made it with a lady

"Walk This Way" had been blaring from Kenny's beat-up old Nova when he picked up me that hot August afternoon, four years ago. He had a pint of his mom's gin stashed in the barn behind their house. We drank fast up in the hayloft, got sloshed and silly, tossing hay down on the horses in the stalls below. It had been six weeks since we met at the lake, and having a new friend/role model had made for a great summer.

Kenny often talked about running off to L.A. or New York, and I figured he'd make for the bright lights soon enough because he went full bore at everything he did, consequences be damned. He also sort of, I don't know, *glowed* with this weird light. Not literally, like an aura or any of that New Age crap. Words can't really capture it, but Kenny exuded an untamed energy, a freedom vibe that made you believe while he might not be able to actually *do* anything he wanted, he was sure gonna try.

Whatever it was that Kenny had, *I* lacked. It was a rare, precious thing, something I'd only encountered in books, but since he'd managed to tap into this indefinable power source, maybe I could, too.

What a bunch of bullshit.

Changing into shorts and tank top, I went out for a run, logged about five miles before returning to the condo for a long shower. I still ached to call Wendy.

Don't, the little voice advised. *You promised to wait.*

"And heroes keep their promises," I said aloud, knowing I was a very lucky guy, even if life scared me shitless. I wasn't going to college, had no job or prospects waiting back in Garrison, and whatever smarts I possess had never counted for much in the real world. I was scared because most every book that mattered to me made clear that the cruel and ruthless ran the world, and they almost always won. It's the Harry Pauls and Derks who throw the winning touchdowns and get the girls, girls, girls.

There's a devil offering an apple. We're sold a fairytale of females as kind, sensitive and caring, yet most chicks flutter around guys who are complete assholes like giggly moths to a flame. For thousands of years, the strongest hunter got the choice slab of saber-tooth and Raquel Welch in a fur bikini. Evolution seems to have stalled out somehow, 'cause survival of the fittest still favored Fred Flintstone over the math nerd. As we speed toward a new century, who's more important to human survival, some no-neck lunkhead who can bench press three hundred pounds, or a science whiz with a 180 IQ? Yet nine times out of ten, who gets the girl?

So brute force and bullshit run the world, and Derk Flintstone may get most girls, but *I* got Wendy.

Flipping open my wallet, I gazed at her picture, fed off the energy in those electric green eyes. Looking at her pic made me feel better, but I was still scared. Terrified, really, because deep down I knew that I hadn't done anything to *deserve* her.

Winning Wendy's heart had been dumb luck, that's all.

And luck can always run out.

44

"Hey, Rip Van Winkle!"

Shaken awake on the sofa, I blinked up at Derk and mumbled, "What time is it?"

"Six-thirty. I'm taking off soon and didn't think you'd want to snooze the night away."

"You're right." I sat up and yawned. Wendy's letter hadn't show up again today. In a funk, I downed four or five beers before nodding off in the middle of the afternoon. "Is Dave home?"

"Here and gone," Derk said. "And he's heading up to Boulder after work."

"Figures. You working tonight, too?"

"Of course."

I stood up and stretched. "Where at?"

"At soon-to-be-delighted bachelorette parties around town," Derk said airily, heading toward his bedroom. "Some final prep, then I'm off."

And I *could* have gotten a rent-a-wreck this afternoon and been all set to tail him, but instead I'd zonked out. Pissed at myself for blowing a manhunt opportunity, I lit a smoke, turned on the tube and channel surfed.

Vanna smiled and turned a letter.

Andy counseled Opie on standing up to bullies.

Frickin' Motley Crue on MTV.

A five car pile-up on the local news.

Derk emerged from his room, dressed like the electric horseman, from white Stetson and pearl button shirt to red and black cowboy boots. "Line?" he asked, grabbing some sofa.

"Is it coke?" I asked, nudging down the TV volume with the remote.

"Yes," he said, fishing for the mirror under the couch.

"No thanks."

Derk shot me a surprised, sideways glance but only said, "Suit yourself."

An eye-opening bump was tempting, but I needed a clear head after the day drinking. Derk tooted up and went to the kitchen. I turned up the news and was suddenly all ears.

". . .just released a composite drawing of the so-called Shopping Mall Rapist," a serious but sexy news babe declared as Derk returned with a protein drink. He froze in his tracks, blue eyes riveted to the police sketch on the giant screen.

"The suspect is approximately six foot three, two hundred pounds, has long black hair and is believed to be in his mid-twenties."

Derk's gaze shifted to me. "Later, Adam."

"Have fun."

"Always do," he declared with customary bravado as he grabbed his black bag and started toward the door, now conspicuously ignoring the sketch on the TV.

The face was angular like Derk's, but the dimpled chin wasn't. The nose was too big, the eyes a bit too close together. Still, it *could* be him, inaccurate details chalked up to multiple descriptions from traumatized victims. And I wasn't fooled by his nonchalant exterior. The news bulletin had knocked Derk off balance, if only for a moment. His mask slipped and just then I saw something in his eyes I *could* name.

Fear.

That flash of vulnerability made me smile, but as the door closed I knew I should be running to my rent-a-wreck to tail him and... Oh, shit! What if the police sketch spooked him? Derk might decide to lay low until SMR disappeared off the media radar and I was long back in Garrison.

Totally bummed, I tramped out to the kitchen for a Coke and glanced at the phone. Another "I love you" from Wen would sure be nice. I grabbed the phone, but restraint kicked in and I called the old man instead. We talked a couple minutes before he dropped a bombshell.

"Your friend Rick stopped by last week to drop off a note with his new address."

"What new address?" I asked, confused. "Where'd he go?"

"Guess him and his folks up and moved to California."

"What? Why?"

"Something about his grandparents getting in an auto accident," the old man said as nonchalantly as if he was talking about changing the blade on his lawn mower.

Stunned, I made chit-chat on autopilot for a couple minutes and then said good-night. I returned to the living room and sank into the recliner.

Son of a bitch.

My shock over Rick's mysterious move quickly morphed into anger. He *could* have gotten Dave's number from the old man and called me with the news but apparently, I only rated a note. I remembered Rick sitting cross-legged on the Persian rug in his bedroom, acoustic guitar in hand, putting my words to music.

Night falls sadly/In a dream-killing town
Night falls badly/Threatening meltdown

Our friendship had meant more to me than him, but that was only natural, considering Rick had a lot more friends to go around. Still, we shared something special, the act of co-creation. Now he'd up and gone to California like killer Max, was halfway across the country and out of my life, all without a fucking word. So much for the silly *someday* notion of me and Rick as rock troubadours, a songwriting team like Elton and Bernie.

What a joke.

Fuck it. It didn't matter. *He* didn't matter, and I idly wondered if he had really ever been my friend at all.

Hadn't Kenny taught me that there was no such thing?

45

Eager to blot Rick from my mind, I went out to the patio, grabbed a fistful of newspapers from near the bottom of the stack then hunkered down in the breakfast nook and got to work.

I found two more stories about suspected SMR attacks, both with bare bones reportage: time, location, age of unnamed victims.

Disappointed, I re-seeded the papers in the pile, mindful not to leave the slightest hint for Derk that I was on to him. Then I read the *Westword* cover story again and was rewarded with intel that hadn't registered the first time: fragmented descriptions of SMR sprinkled throughout the piece, culled from the reporter (and others) having tracked down and spoken to many of the victims or their families.

I numbered and copied down everything the victims were quoted as saying, from the headline worthy "Charlie Manson with Muscles," to a terse "grody." Twenty-nine separate quotes and after reading the complete list twice, I concluded what the story had only suggested, that if taken at face value, the girls *couldn't* have been talking about the same guy.

The earliest description, dating back to April of '84, reported a rapist with "curly red hair" and "a weird mole on his chin." Obviously not Derk, unless he was going full Lon Chaney with a make-up kit. From August '84, "he was really skinny." March '85, "Flabby, with a pot belly and bow legs." February, this year, "Just average, normal looking, kinda short."

All non-Derks.

An October '85 victim nailed Derk's body type, but her attacker's van was *gray* and empty in the back, except for a "ratty mattress on the floor."

Three assaults last summer took place during or after concerts at Red Rocks, far from any mall.

Although the reporter noted several times that most of the rapes were "only tenuously linked" to a single assailant, it was clear to me that many weren't linked at all and had only been included to run up SMR's score, hyping the story to draw more eyeballs.

Dave had told me Derk got the black wig six months ago, so I zeroed in on more recent attacks. It stuck me that maybe *none* of the pre-wig crimes were connected at all, maybe Derk's fake hippie hair signaled SMR's actual debut, with the earlier crimes cobbled together in the media's never-ending hunt for a Big Story. But rereading the chronology disproved that instant theory, as six pre-wig victims mentioned long black or dark brown hair, which suggested Derk's innocence. . .

No.

I wasn't prepared to consider *that*, not after pushing so many emotional chips into the manhunt pot. But wait. . . Derk could have had the wig for years, only adding it to his Bad Boy's routine six months ago.

A possibility, the little voice agreed.

Two of the four most recent victims mentioned "blue eyes," one of Derk's most striking features, as did four of the '85 girls, putting him squarely back in the bullseye. I started to like the "old wig" theory.

The girls who mentioned blues eyes also called SMR "attractive but creepy;" "like a male model;" "real handsome, which is why I was dumb enough to trust him;" and "built like a gym rat."

Nothing non-Derk there.

Ditto: "muscles everywhere;" "tall and striking;" "could have been an underwear model." Not only did those descriptions fit Derk, right down to earning a buck by undressing in public, but according to the story those were the rapes most strongly linked to a single attacker.

I realized that if Derk had five-starred any recent solo strips in his dance log, it could be evidence of an attack that hadn't been made public. Knowing I might be on the verge of a case-cracking lead, I dashed to his bedroom, but the log wasn't on his desk, or in it. I quickly searched his room, without success. He probably had it with him. Any *eureka* moment would have to wait.

After retracing my path around the room to make sure the search hadn't left anything out of place, I returned to the living room and stashed the *Westword* and notebook deep in my backpack. Then I changed into shorts and tank top and went out for a run, confident that I was hot on SMR's tail, if not yet literally.

I liked my chances. Bringing Derk down felt like destiny.

Even more, it felt like I *deserved* it.

46

I was singing in the shower after logging thirty early morning laps around the condo complex. My sunny mood stemmed from the certainty that Wendy's letter would arrive today. I just knew it.

Emerging from the bathroom, I found Derk watching porn at 9:15 in the morning, one of his own "Jack Hardman" scenes. He was absently playing with himself beneath his bathrobe, and I thought of Nero, fiddling as his decadent empire awaited a spark. Jesus, what a piece of work.

Well, fiddle about, Derk. It will keep you from noticing me, striking matches at your feet.

His beeper went off, breaking his reverie. Derk paused the movie and said hi to me on his way to the kitchen to retrieve the message. On the big screen, his frozen face was twisted with lust, but videotape failed to capture the *something* behind those blue eyes.

Soon back to the living room, Derk turned off the video and asked if I wanted the TV left on.

"No."

"I'm going to shower and then head out on cola delivery," he said, clicking off the tube.

"Sure."

"Any plans for the day, Adam?"

"Nothing special."

"Every day should be special, comprende?"

"You're right," I said, watching Derk pad off to the bathroom. When he left on coke biz, I'd look through more old newspapers, knowing what dates to focus on now. I no longer expected to find anything useful in the dailies, but looking would keep me from going buggy while waiting for the mail, still at least a couple hours away.

After Wen's letter arrived – assuming my pregnancy theory was confirmed – I was planning to call her and propose. Of course she'd say yes. The wedding would have to be fast-tracked to avoid an at-the-altar baby bulge. Maybe on my birthday, September Tenth.

How fast things change, I thought. A couple weeks ago, I'd have agreed with Dave's low opinion of marriage, been terrified at the thought of having a kid. But my trip west had wised me up to what really mattered. I was ready to step up and be a man, to do anything necessary for the woman I loved, even if that's corny and old-fashioned.

The tire plant had the best jobs in Garrison, and Wendy's old man was a manager there. No matter what the bastard thought of me, he wouldn't want an unemployed son-in-law, right? It wouldn't be forever, maybe a couple years of timecard tyranny while plotting our great escape. I could buckle down and do it, with a smile.

Thinking again of Derk as Nero, I realized that the coming fire could serve as *my* spotlight. Just delivering Derk to the cops and heading home would be passing up a media bonanza. Bernie Goetz became a folk hero by shooting some punks in the New York subway, so why not a Big Fuss over the young Sherlock who caught the dreaded Shopping Mall Rapist? Hell, they might even give me the key to the city. And playing this right could mean an early ticket out of Garrison for me and Wendy, because once the world knows you're a hero a lot of doors crack open.

Two hours later, thoughts of my coming heroics had been replaced by nervous jitters as I marched up to the mailbox, having just seen the postman drive off. Taking a deep breath, I inserted the key and opened the box, feeling all pins and needles.

Yes!

There was the letter, addressed in Wendy's spidery handwriting. A warm glow spread through me as I extracted it from of the box and headed for the condo, resisting the urge to tear open the envelope on the spot. This was a Major Moment – life was about to change forever – and I wanted to savor it.

Derk was back from coke-slinging, so I cloistered myself in the bathroom and slowly opened the envelope, ready for a love song from Cape Cod's rocky shore.

47

Dear Adam,

What we had was very special. . .

Had? Squirming a bit on the closed toilet lid, I figured the tense was just inexact grammar.

. . .but everything has to change, even us.

Of course, Wen. The baby will change everything.

We've had tons of fun and maybe that's part of the problem. We're not high school kids anymore and "fun" isn't exactly an adult priority, at least it can't be top of the list. You know I want to go to school for my art and Garrison doesn't provide any opportunity for that.

Duh. Garrison doesn't provide much opportunity for anything.

Yet I have no idea what YOU want to do, and I don't think you do either. So I've been thinking a lot since I got here.

Me, too, babe. Thinking about our future.

I remember Gramps carrying me on his shoulders when I was little, spinning me around over his head, but now he can barely carry himself up the stairs most days. It's scary. . . This is real life, and it goes by real fast. There are so many things I want to do, places I want to see.

But what about the most important thing, Wen? What about us?

And I've decided I need more space for myself.

My heart started to hammer and my throat went dry. I read on.

You'll always be special to me, but we promised never to lie to each other, right? We've shared some awesome moments and maybe there's more to come, I don't know. What I do know is things have to change. This is all about me, Adam, it's nothing you did wrong.

Like pissing off your old man with a drunken late night phone call?

And I know your heart is big enough to understand.

But I don't understand. And my heart is shriveling. . .

I've been accepted by an art school in Chicago. I'm moving back at the end of August to live with my mom and until then I have to be free. I still want to see you, but I guess not as my "boyfriend." And honesty, right? I met a guy I like. Sam's an artist, too, does air brush.

My skin suddenly felt too small, like my ribs were about to snap through my chest.

I'm not trying to hurt you, but I have to focus on my future now. I do love you, but I guess I'm not "in love" like I thought I was. Let all this sink in a while, okay? We'll talk when we're both back in Garrison.

Wendy.

My fingers went numb, and the letter fluttered into the wastebasket beside the toilet. I sat there a moment, stunned, then got up and beelined straight for the bar. Poured a big shot of Chivas Regal and gulped it to the sound of Derk banging weights around, down in the workout room. My head felt stuffed with cotton, which was okay because it kept a primal scream lodged in my throat. I did another shot then carried the bottle with me over to the sofa.

Oh god, *Wendy.*

How could this be happening?

Oh fuck.

I clicked on the tube for distraction, anything to drown out my thoughts, racing like rats in a cage. *Hot Tub Tarts* came on and I stared dumbly at the screen. If only the world could really be reduced to the old in-out, the simple piston action of the fuck machine in motion.

I took another drink because I wasn't feeling the booze at all. Muted the TV sound as a fiery pain needled through my chest. I put the bottle on the table and dropped my head into my hands.

"A little early in the day for bottle-drinking, isn't it?" Derk asked from behind the couch.

I just grunted.

"What's wrong, Adam?"

"Nothin'." Except my dreams being aborted with a rusty coat hanger. This *can't* be happening, I prayed, tugging at my hair. It's a bad dream, so wake up, wish it away, blot it out. I looked back at Derk and asked if he had any coke.

"Of course."

113

"Can I buy, like, a half gram."

"Certainly. For you, I'll only charge twenty-five."

I dug cash from my pocket and paid him. As Derk headed to his room, I glanced up at the on-screen tangle of bodies, silent now but still in motion. In, out, in, out, and all's right in Machine Land. No soul crushing rejection there.

Returning with the coke, Derk asked again if anything was wrong.

"Nope," I insisted, wasn't about to parade my wounds in front of him.

"If you say so. Oh, Dave called earlier. Wanted me to tell you he'll be gone all day and is going to Boulder after work tonight."

"Sure," I muttered. Who's got time for Adam?

"I'm taking off soon, too" Derk continued, "and won't be back until late tonight, if I all."

"So?" I shrugged. "You won't turn into a pumpkin."

Derk chuckled then walked over and picked up the whiskey bottle. "There's nothing wrong with an occasional morning eye-opener, but it's going to be a beautiful day, kiddo. You've got wheels now, so take my advice and go have some fucking fun, okay?"

"Sounds good," I said with a wane, wax museum smile.

"Attaboy."

After Derk left, I did a couple lines, continued sucking down whiskey and watched the fleshy automatons on the giant screen. In out, in out. It was reliable, predictable, with a gooey *mission accomplished* payoff every time. A machine doesn't need to *deserve* anything, it just runs the program.

By the time the movie ended the Chivas was almost gone, but I didn't feel drunk at all. Just vacant, vacuumed out. I got up and careened down the hall to take a piss. Suddenly dizzy, I slumped against the wall and thought I heard laughter.

Who's that?

Kenny?

His legacy was to harden me, toughen my skin so that something like Rick moving across country without a word barely drew blood. Ditto Wen tossing me overboard like yesterday's garbage. . .

That lying *bitch!*

She'd betrayed me, betrayed us, but fuck it, a knife in the heart doesn't have to be fatal, right? So survive it, I thought with bitter determination. It will make me tougher, stronger, maybe finally smart enough to never trust anyone again.

My kidneys felt about to burst, but my fingers didn't quite work right as I fumbled with my zipper. My knees turned into noodles. "Wen-*dee*," I muttered, sinking to the floor like a deflating balloon. I felt something wet running down my leg as my eyes fluttered shut.

It seems, the little voice whispered, *all that alcohol is finally catching up to. . .*

48

I was content in the dark, floating through a warm chemical sea. It felt safe, with no broken families, false friends, unfaithful lovers. I wanted to stay there forever, drifting in the welcoming wet. . .

Jerking awake like a dog from a dream of chasing rabbits, I found myself face down in carpet. The *wet* was piss in my pants, not womb juice. I vaguely remembered trying to hold up the bathroom wall but had no idea how I got out into the hall. Still half-drunk, but not so much that pissy underwear didn't feel gross, I slowly craned myself off the floor. The pulse-beat in my ears was like a brass band as I stepped forward gingerly. Left, right, left. Yes, that seems to be working.

It was dark outside. The clock over the fireplace read nine-fifteen. I vaguely remembered Derk saying he and Dave would be home late, maybe not at all. Thank God. After changing clothes, I staggered back to the bathroom and left my jeans and rinsed-in-the-sink underwear hanging on the shower rod. The coke seal that had been in my left pocket was pee-soaked, so I flushed it down the toilet with disgust.

Next, out to the kitchen for ice water. I chugged it too fast, sending the brass band into a clamorous frenzy as the memory came back to me through the thick whiskey fog. The letter. Wendy's stinking goddamn letter.

She had run out on me, just like Mom.

I plopped down on the sofa with a groan. The smoke I lit almost made me gag. Leaving it burning in the ashtray, I kneaded my tired eyes.

This is real life, Wendy had written.

Yeah, too fucking *much* real life.

I needed magic power and so got up and went to Derk's room. Get fuel, that was the program. Damn. The mirror on the shelf was bare. Back to the living room and a hair-of-the-dog shot of Jack Daniels. Nasty, but it settled my stomach and after a while I could think semi-clearly.

I'd lost Wen.

She *knew* I wasn't deserving, could see through my skin to the weakness and writhing insecurities beneath. I didn't deserve shit, and the whole idea of proving myself by bringing Derk to justice suddenly struck me as hysterical, a sick joke.

I pictured the manhunt unfolding Keystone Kops-style, with me tooling along behind Derk's van in some ramshackle, exhaust-belching rent-a-wreck, disguised by glasses with a big rubber nose. How many nights would I have tailed him, waiting for SMR to strike?

And what was the game plan if he did, super sleuth? Rush up to the van with piggy Sherri's camera, snap a few crime-in-progress pix, then make a citizen's arrest?

I hadn't figured out that part.

No, the little voice agreed. *I guess you hadn't.*

I remembered something Derk said one night about fathers screwing daughters, brothers doing sisters. Extend that thinking and the wicked family of man is one big cluster fuck.

"And fuck Wendy," I whispered, wondering what girls had ever done for me. Nothing but serve up embarrassment, hurt and heartache. I realized that I didn't give a shit what Derk did. Let the cops save the bubble-headed mall chicks, 'cause it sure as hell wasn't my job.

The world gets what it deserves.

I loaded the coffeemaker and thought about calling Wen. Maybe beg another chance, maybe just scream that she was a lying two-faced bitch, then I realized I didn't want to talk to her at all.

Since magic powder was unavailable, revival measures stronger than coffee were called for. I changed into my swimsuit, grabbed a towel and headed for the pool. Some splish-splash would give me a jumpstart, but the damn gate was locked.

"Wanna go swimmin'," I insisted out loud, then started climbing the wrought-iron fence. Swinging one leg over, I held myself directly above a spike and toyed with the idea of letting go, a final, bloody gesture to my treacherous Juliet.

Nah. She wasn't worth it.

Dropping down inside the fence, I tossed the towel on a lounge, ran to the pool and dove in wildly. My right cheek smacked the surface and I must've swallowed a pint of water on the way to the bottom. Kicking back to the surface with arms flailing, I coughed up pool water and paddled to the side. After a moment to catch my breath, I climbed out and headed for the diving board.

"Hey, the pool's closed!"

Ignoring the shout, I raced up and off the board. Big cannonball splash.

"Get outta there!" the fatso manager ordered as he waddled across the grass toward the gate. "The pool closes at nine."

While he fumbled with his keys, I was back up the diving board for a final splashdown. Fatso was waiting for me when I got to the side of the pool.

"You dumb ass, kid! Want me to call the cops?" he asked, half-hauling me out of the water.

I twisted out of his grip. "Get your damn hands off me. I'm leaving, so back off!"

"Damn right you're leaving!" he barked as I ran over and grabbed the towel. "What unit are you in?"

"Z-50!" I raced around him and through the gate, slamming it shut behind me. "And I know where *you* live!"

That was a lie, but it wouldn't be hard to find out. So watch out for flying rocks, Butterball, 'cause this was little Adam's summer to raise hell.

Comprende?

<h2 style="text-align:center">49</h2>

"Here you go, boys," our waitress said with a smudged lipstick smile. "Denver omelet with hash browns and two eggs sunny side with a short stack, both with extra crispy bacon." The busty, thirty-something brunette put down the plates and looked us over. She had kind eyes and a crooked nose. "You two brothers?"

"Yeah," Dave said, attacking his omelet with gusto.

"Our parents could only afford the one model," I added.

"Huh," she said, then was off to greet a couple truckers who had just sat down, three booths away.

Dave rhapsodized about Laura while scarfing down his breakfast. "She does this thing, nibbling on the tip of my tongue, that drives me *crazy*."

"Yeah?" Hearing about his erotic exploits wasn't helping my appetite. I picked at my food, but the first couple bites of pancake settled in my stomach like wallpaper paste. I pushed the plate away and fumbled out a cig.

"I haven't been crazy about a chick for a long time, bro," Dave said between forkfuls as I stared out at the traffic buzzing by on Colorado Boulevard. "It almost feels like I'm sixteen again."

"Enjoy the zits," I grumped, nibbling a piece of bacon. It tasted like ashes. I had planned to tell Dave about Wendy's betrayal, but with all his gooey hearts and flowers crap, I was too bummed to admit how big a fool I'd been. He couldn't help me anyway. No one could. I had to stew in my own miserable juices, like always.

"Oh, I actually remember a dream I had last night," Dave said, lifting his coffee mug to signal for a refill. "You and me were having a double wedding in this huge gothic cathedral. Wild, huh?"

I scowled. "Dreams don't mean shit."

Dave smiled. "Except that Laura's seeping into my subconscious."

"Better call roto-rooter."

"Here's some fresh," our waitress chirped as she returned with the coffee pot. Much more of that lipstick grin and she'd wind up wearing my pancakes.

"Something wrong with your food, honey?" she asked, gesturing toward my barely touched plate.

"No," I said, resisting the urge to blow smoke in her face. "Just not very hungry."

"Well, let me know if you want something else."

"Okay," I muttered.

"You used to eat like a horse," Dave said. "Not becoming anorexic, are you?"

"I'm just not fuckin' hungry, okay?" My voice was loud enough to turn heads our way. I felt like giving the audience the finger, but just went back to staring out the window.

"Wow, you're touchy today." Dave pushed his empty plate away and lit a Marlboro. "What's wrong?"

"Nothing." I said, spooning sugar into my coffee. It tasted like forty weight, but I needed the caffeine. "I just got too hammered last night."

"Laura gets really *wild* after three drinks," Dave said, launching into another god damned story.

Breakfast had seemed like a chance to spill my guts, ask if Dave had ever felt like he was being eaten alive from the inside out by tiny, razor-sharp teeth. But he was on another god damn planet, jabbering away about stupid Laura, the World's Greatest Girlfriend.

Maybe she was. Wendy was out of the running.

Not up to parading my pain in Dave's starry-eyed face, I stayed mum as we left the diner and headed to a dry cleaner to pick up some of his dancing clothes. Passing the theatre still showing *The Finish Line,* I thought of killer Max sharpening his knife while staring at the object of his desire.

I think I'll go to California.

Ain't that the script? When dreams die, just whistle up a fresh batch from the Hollywood dream factory. Better yet, peddle them *your* sticky-fingered fantasies and screeching nightmares.

Runaway Mom.

By a Bitch Girlfriend Betrayed.

This is boffo box office, C.B., pulpy red meat for the masses. . .

The dry cleaner was in a little shopette. Dave parked next to a pick-up loaded with hay bales. I stared at them, flashing back to Kenny and that hot August afternoon. We'd downed almost the whole pint of gin in a half-hour, and the hayloft was like a steam bath. We took off our shirts, then smoked a joint and thumbed through some skin mags. *Boy's Life* high jinks by way of Larry Flynt, right down to an impromptu wrestling match to see who got the last belt of gin. Kenny got on top of me, put a knee in my kidney then twisted my right arm behind my back. It hurt, and I had the first flash that maybe he wasn't just horsing around.

"Service sucks anymore!" Dave cursed as he jerked his door open.

"What happened?" I asked, rubbing hay from my eyes.

"They totally missed a red wine stain on a white shirt," Dave said, tilting the driver's seat forward so he could hang dress shirts on the hook behind it. "Then they wanted two more days to redo it, until I gave them a ration."

"Bastards," I said. "The guillotine for the lot of them."

Back at 22-G, I stuffed my dirty clothes into a garbage bag and headed to the laundry room. Got a wash started and returned to find the roomies arguing.

"When's the last time I had a weekend off?" Dave asked.

"I don't remember, but you can't have *this* one," Derk said, sorting mail on the bar. I hate fucking mail. "Not when you wait until the week of to ask me."

"I *told* you this chance to go to Vegas with Laura just came up," Dave protested. "And I need the r 'n' r."

"Go next week," Derk said. "You know we're booked solid this weekend. Vegas sucks in the summer anyway."

I sank into the recliner and tried to be invisible.

"The plane tickets are non-refundable, like I've explained *twice*." Dave spoke softly, but I recognized the quiver of about-to-erupt anger in his voice, from all the times he went at it with the old man. "I know the weekend's busy, but the other guys won't mind making more money."

"Sorry about the tickets, but I didn't tell you to make an impulse buy," Derk said, turning around to look directly at Dave. "And the answer's still no."

"Fuck it." Dave stomped over to the stairs and started up toward his room. "Maybe I'll just no-show."

"Do what you want," Derk called after him. "Eric did."

What?" Dave stopped halfway up the stairs and spun around. "Are you threatening to *fire* me?"

"We're pals, David, but I have a business to run."

"I realize that."

"Then don't leave me hanging," Derk said, lighting one of his small, smelly cigars. "Comprende?"

They stared at each other a moment, then Dave tried again. "How 'bout I work Friday and take off Saturday."

Derk blew a smoke ring, then sighed like an indulgent parent. "Fine, whatever."

They'd split the baby, but I knew that if Derk hadn't thrown Dave a bone, that would have been the end of it. Derk knew how to get his way.

I was very jealous of that.

50

Rerun Friday night: the roomies out stripping, me alone with the tube, sucking down suds. Wanted some coke but tried to ignore the craving.

I re-read Wendy's letter for the first time in three days then broke down and finally started to call her, but hung up before it connected. She was probably out with the asshole *artiste*. I imagined them screwing on a moonlit beach and hoped for a freak tidal wave.

Back to channel surfing. A local music video show reported that the Next were playing a gig tomorrow at the Big House before heading to L.A. to cut their album. Great, that would fill my Saturday night dance card.

I'd been telling myself all week that I didn't need Wendy, didn't need anybody, but I was out of smokes and definitely needed nicotine. Off to 7-Eleven in Derk's Charger, I decided to go cruising after getting cigs, get my sorry ass off the couch and out of the condo for awhile.

At the store, I squeezed the Charger into a tight space between an old station wagon and a sweet silver Jaguar. There were four people in line at the register. We waited as Abdullah fussed with the drop safe, failed to get it open it, then went to get the manager. Dave was right about lousy service everywhere.

Finally out of there with my Salems, I fired up the Charger and threw it in reverse. There was a metal-on-metal crunch as–shit!–I sideswiped the Jag's rear fender. Pulling forward a bit, I cranked the wheel around and tried again. Easing out of the space, I eyeballed a foot long gash in the Jag's hi-gloss silver pant.

"God damn it! Who taught you to drive, asswad?"

The screamer was a aging hipster with a gray goatee, who'd emerged from the store with a six pack of Pepsi and a bag of ice right after I nailed his Jag. Cursing, he trotted toward me, face turning beet red. "You god damned idiot!"

Well, I sure didn't need *this* shit and so slammed the Charger into drive and took off.

"Stop!" Goatee screamed. "Come back, you fuck!"

I flipped him off and roared out of the lot. Screw that rich asshole, but maybe going cruising wasn't the *best* idea, not with several beers in me. Retreating to Windhollow, I drove to the rear of the complex and backed into a space to hide any damage to the Charger from casual inspection.

That's not *too* bad, I thought, running my finger along the scrape in the right rear fender. The Jag got the worst of it. Goatee was probably out prowling for young pussy in his fancy sports car and was no doubt insured up the ass. So fuck him.

Fuck everything.

Back inside, I got a fresh beer and then pawed through Derk's stack of porn tapes. Loading *Bondage Babes* into the VCR, I watched the skanky chick in the mini skirt walk down the dark alley. No piston-pounding action yet, so I snatched Wendy's letter off the coffee table and glanced at that fatal line.

I do love you, Adam, but I suppose I'm not "in love" like I thought I was.

Way to twist the blade, honey. She didn't even say in love like she *had* been, no, turns out our love was only a wayward *thought*. Just a silly notion these last seven months, one that turns out never to have been true at all.

"Arrrgh!"

Jumping to my feet, I tore up the letter, threw the pieces in the air like confetti, then went to the bar, grabbed the nearest bottle and downed a couple gulps of gin. I wiped my mouth and whispered, "I don't love you either, you dumb bitch. I *don't*."

To prove it, I pulled her picture out of my wallet and read the inscription on the back.

You do incredible things to me, Adam. Don't stop!!!

Three exclamation points of incredible, and I never would have stopped, Wen, you had me, heart and soul. Now her words mocked me and I began to tremble. I paused the movie and sank back onto the sofa. Felt like crying but no tears would come.

After a few minutes, I realized what I had to do. I took a last, long look at Wendy's picture, gazing into those spellbinding green eyes.

"You who I thought my soul mate," I announced dramatically to no one as I walked over to the fireplace, "have been instead revealed as Miss Judas." I tore the picture in half, quarters, then dropped the pieces onto the ashes. "I don't need you, Wen," I declared, giving a finger to the heavens. "Don't need anybody, so bring on the Mule Man."

Back to *Bondage Babes,* I fast forwarded to where the girl was handcuffed to the bed. "Told Vinny I don't do anal," she was whining.

I moved closer to the screen, wanted to lose myself in the action, but I couldn't stop thinking about Wendy's picture. The initial rush of triumph had evaporated, leaving an empty ache in the pit of my belly. It felt like I had sinned somehow, and I don't even believe in that hocus pocus.

"You're mine, bitch," Mule Man crowed. "All mine."

No.

Leaping up off the sofa, I knelt before the fireplace and dug out bits of the photo, desperate to put Wendy back together again.

Too late, the little voice declared. *Humpty-Dumpty and all that.*

I knew he was right. It was too late, for everything.

On-screen, the girl strained against the handcuffs as the gag was stuffed in her mouth. The Mule Man laughed. I turned off the movie, gathered up the scraps of Wendy's letter, deposited them in the kitchen trash and was out the door.

Running.

I raced to the back of the complex, scrambled over the cinderblock fence and raced through the abandoned development, chased by phantoms.

"Faster, Freeman!" I heard Coach Hansen growl. "Faster."

121

I was at a full sprint now. Didn't see the hole that tripped me. Landing hard on my right shoulder, I cartwheeled into some weeds and laid there, sprawled out and panting beneath a smirking sliver of moon.

It felt like I had been running forever, getting nowhere. I was eighteen and had nothing and nobody. And maybe this was as good as things get for Adam Freeman, on either side of the border. Maybe I've been a twistoid zom all along and had just never realized it until now.

And zombies don't deserve love.

They don't deserve anything.

51

I woke up to see a Pink Floyd poster directly above me on the ceiling. Groaning, I dimly recalled climbing the stairs last night to crash in Dave's room and a real bed, since he was staying in Boulder with Laura. Again.

I sat up and stretched. A stab of pain reminded me of my shoulder-first landing in the field behind Windhollow. Didn't see a clock but it felt like early afternoon. I stumbled downstairs in search of coffee.

Derk was cooking a steak in the kitchen. "Adam! Where'd you come from?"

"Dave's room," I said, fumbling with the coffee maker.

"Didn't see you when I got home last night, so I assumed you were shacked up somewhere," Derk said, chopping up some onion. "Good for you, I thought, particularly after that *Dear John* letter from your chick."

I was suddenly wide awake. "How do you know about that?"

"You left it in the bathroom the other day," Derk said, forking the bloody-rare steak onto a plate. "Not the best way to organize personal correspondence, so I tucked it in the top of your backpack."

I wanted to rage at him for invading my privacy, but said nothing as Derk carried his plate to the living room. I figured *I'd* put the letter in the pack in a drunken stupor, but since I had no actual memory of doing so, there was no reason to doubt Derk. I saw that it was one-fifteen, half the day slept away.

"A word of advice," Derk called. "If you give chicks a chance to break your heart, be prepared to bleed."

"Yeah," I agreed, wondering if a zombie's choices were limited to breaking things, or being broken. I sugared up my coffee and joined him in the living room.

"You need to get that chick out of your head," Derk advised. "Get crazy and go have some fun."

"Yeah, that's the mission from now on."

"Go get 'em, tiger."

The Next were playing tonight, and magic power would maximize the fun quotient. I considered counting my thinning bankroll but didn't really want to know. Derk was right. I needed to get out and howl. And you really can't blame someone for reading a letter left lying around their own house. After Derk finished eating, I told him I needed some coke.

"Later," he said, washing his plate. "I need to get rolling."

"Just trying to take your advice about fun," I said with a shrug.

He smirked and took care of me before he left. I wanted a bump but summoned the willpower to stash it in my wallet for tonight. I got more coffee instead then walked over to the fireplace and looked down at the scraps of Wendy's picture. They have no power. That "sin" stuff was boozed-up rubbish. I'll be just fine without you, Wen, I swore as I changed into my swim trunks and headed to the pool. You'll see.

Shit.

Butterball the manager was hosing off the concrete by the shallow end. He glanced in my direction, so I turned my head and continued down the sidewalk instead of veering across the grass toward the pool. If I remembered him, drunk as I'd been the other night, he'd surely remembered *me*. And another confrontation would do nothing to goose the fun-o-meter.

After circling the building, it was back to 22-G. I remembered seeing *Debbie Does Dallas* among Derk's tapes. There's not many skin flicks famous enough to know by title, so what the hell, a sleazy bit of fun still qualifies, right?

But I couldn't work up much enthusiasm for the business at hand. I wasn't high, didn't have poppers, and the first couple sex scenes in *Debbie* were too mellow for my mood. I switched tapes, back to *Bondage Babes* to watch the Mule Man piston-pound the handcuffed skank while Tommy Weather's voice howled in my head.

Go ahead and take her/Now's the time to break her

Stroking away like a good little zombie, I completed the program with a shudder. Then I turned off the tape, sat there and smoked a cigarette with a sticky hand.

Ain't we got fun.

52

Examining the Charger's fender again before leaving for the Big House, the idea hit me to tell Derk the car got dinged in the club's lot *tonight*, while I was inside rocking. I'd still be responsible, having borrowed his wheels, but surely not *guilty*.

Pleased with this defense, I decided to confess the next time I saw Derk. Such forthright honesty could only bolster my credibility. Not bad for a zom.

After stashing a half-pint of Jack under the seat, I motored toward downtown, psyched to see the Next again. Tommy Weathers was a dangerous voice for dumb, dangerous times. His best stuff told the truth - a commodity always in short supply - screamed it out raw and rabid. But the band would just be the soundtrack. The *most* dangerous thing I was after tonight walked with a wiggle.

By hook or crook, I resolved to get laid.

Heavy traffic on Colfax. Passing a van full of Cub Scouts, I felt sympathy for the boys, being stuffed like Thanksgiving turkeys with smiley-face lies. But they'd have to fend for themselves, because I was done boo-hooing over the world. From now on, it was all about looking out for number one.

I calculated that simple math would get me some pussy. Hit on every hot chick until finding a jackpot girl who just wanted to have fun.

My luck started out good, as I arrived early enough to snag a spot in the Big House parking lot. There was no one around, so I rolled up a dollar and did a big bump out of the seal. Wouldn't be able to buy much more coke, but all that mattered was tonight.

Once inside, I began scouting the talent. The opening band had just taken the stage, but the club was already pretty packed. A little blonde standing in back by the jukebox caught my eye. Channeling Derk, I marched right toward her, was about to invade Blondie's air space when a guy rejoined her with drinks and got a kiss for the bar run.

One babe down, however many as necessary to go. . .

Over to the crowded bar, I maneuvered behind a redhead with a killer ass in jeans so tight they looked painted on. As the thirsty patrons inched forward, I bumped up against Red's behind. Target acquired, Captain. She didn't seem to mind and I popped wood. Damn, I might get lucky before even buying a drink. Wine cooler in hand, Red turned around and smiled. Woof. She was a complete bow-wow.

"I'm upstairs," Red said, fingers brushing my thigh as she squeezed by me. Resisting the urge to make a cross with *my* fingers, I got a seven and seven and resumed the poon patrol. There was a brunette who looked like Valerie Bertinelli, standing by herself on the dance floor.

Don't over-think, the little voice urged. *Just go for it.*

Pasting a cig between my lips, I ambled right up to her and asked for a light.

"I don't smoke."

"What *do* you do?" I asked with my best Derk-like leer.

"Nothing with you," she said witheringly, then stalked off in a huff.

"Stuck up twat," I muttered, heading for the balcony to do recon from above. But the railing was already lined with people. I couldn't see much and didn't want to run into Bow-Wow Red, so back downstairs, ignoring the itch for more coke.

Focus on Jackpot Girl.

Two hours later, nursing my fifth Seven & Seven, I was convinced J-Girl had a thing for hide and seek. I'd asked five chicks to dance while the opening band played covers, racking up four rejections. Lisa said sure. She had a plain, math club face, but it was framed by thick brown hair that smelled like wildflowers. She had a sexy smile and decent tits. No Wendy, natch, but after dancing to a couple songs, I decided she'd do and offered to buy her a drink

"Sure," Lisa said. "But don't even *think* about hitting on me. I'm into the new celibacy."

"Really?"

"Yes, really," she said with chastity-belt conviction.

"Then buy your own goddamn drink."

I'd mostly been holding up the back wall since, watching the Next.

"We're just about done," a sweat-drenched Tommy Weathers announced. "Gonna end with a new one. Rewind and Rot."

A heart attack bass line and paint-shaker drums laid down an insanely fast beat. Tommy hit the opening chords and spat out lyrics which seemed aimed directly at me.

"Crank it up loud! Every moan and groan, yeah!

"Forty channel fun that never gets done!

"Crank it up proud! All that bone and moan, man!

"'Cause the groin is the link! We got camera crews! For every kink!

"Yeah, forty channels, son! All that suckie fuckie fun!

"Love you long time, bay-bee!"

The keyboardist let out an orgasmic yowl. The guitar solo screamed like a demon out for blood and pussy and the end of the world. I stood mesmerized. Squeals of tormented feedback washed over me like a riptide then Tommy wrestled the demon back in its cave and hammered out the main riff.

"For just a quarter in the slot! The babes get hot so hot!

"My Dad's a drunken old sot! Taught me to rewind and rot!

"Grubby quarter in the slot! Rewind and rot!

"Forty channel fun! Slip a quarter in her slot!

"Give it all you got! And rah-rah-rewind and. . . *ROT!*"

Draining the last of my drink, I maneuvered around the back of the crowd toward the exit as the band bought the song to an abrupt, crunching end and walked offstage.

Back in the Charger, I snorted half the coke left in the seal, took a big swig of whiskey and realized that while the last song sounded like a warning, to me it meant *welcome*. Who needed snotty, stuck-up bar bitches anyway?

"Forty channel fun," I said, firing up the Charger.

Time to hit the candy store.

53

Gorilla guy at Kitty's counter collected my fifty-cent browsing fee without a hint of recognition. Pervs must be pretty interchangeable to him. I bought Rush, got twenty bucks in quarters and retreated to the arcade. Locking the booth door, I sat down and fed the coin box a couple bucks. The screen served up a girl humping a mop handle on a men's room floor. I watched awhile, then dropped trou and clicked through the channels.

Landing on two blondes blowing a Mexican guy, I opened the Rush and fed my nose. Warm fog filled my head. The TV's phosphor dots sparkled like jewels. The guy soon got off and, on the brink myself, I released Petey and lit a smoke, planning to stretch out fun time.

I clicked around the channels before finding a fresh-faced couple humping like mad on a pool table, shredding the girl's white wedding dress in the process. Leaning back against the booth wall, I smiled and realized I felt at home here, tucked away from the world amid a banquet of secondhand flesh, free to indulge every fantasy impulse.

I wasn't a misfit in my little booth. No pain or rejection here, so load up on coin and bolt the door. There's camera crews for every kink and all the chicks want is to be fucked harder. In Candyland, a brazen celebration of raw, nasty sex *was* the program, the jizz-bang eruptions all that mattered, not the anonymous suck-fuckers, mere interchangeable body parts fueling the Machine.

The bride was starting to moan when the screen went dark. I fumbled more quarters into the box and rooted the couple on to climax.

Clicking around for the next kick, I realized I'd hardly thought of Wendy all night. Good. I needed to blot her out completely, delete the memory banks, 'cause they were turning rotten.

A three girl dildo squad on channel four was juicy fun. Huffing Rush kept me plugged into the action. With the coin box well-fed, I stroked away to the fuck parade at a measured pace, all that sweet on-screen meat in service of throbbing King Petey. Time blurred by.

Pound, pound, pound.

I cycled through every channel a couple times before finding a really cute Latin girl gobbling four guys on channel sixteen. They stood circled around her, cracking knuckles and jokes, their big dicks fleshy special effects for her busy hands and hungry mouth. This chick's really into it, I thought, 'cause if *that's* acting then she deserved an Oscar.

I decided to blow when the circle jerks did, but the screen again went blank and – shit! – no more quarters.

Yanking my pants up, I scrambled back to the front counter and slapped down ten bucks. "Quarters please!"

Making my change, the gorilla mentioned they were closing in twenty minutes.

"Okay." A quick dash back to my booth, but the boys had finished without me. I cursed and clicked around for fresh inspiration, but the movies had looped back to stuff I'd already seen.

Hungry for fresh meat, I hurried to the other arcade. As I started down the hall, a booth door opened down by the exit and I stopped dead, shocked to my socks to see Tommy Weathers emerge, tucking his t-shirt into his jeans.

Then I got it. He and Raven had popped over for some dirty bookstore fun after the gig. But it wasn't Raven who followed Tommy out of the booth.

And it wasn't a girl.

My American Lit teacher last year was Mr. Wilson, pudgy and balding, and the guy trailing Tommy out of the booth could have been his twin, right down to the bad comb-over. Totally freaked, I turned and bolted back up the hall.

"Hey, handsome," one the phone booth girls called. "Want a show?"

I ducked into her booth and shut the door. Stood there slack-jawed, heart racing, trying to process what I'd just seen.

"Put some quarters in the phone. At least a dollar, hon."

"Yeah." I fumbled coins into the box and sat on a metal folding chair. Coughed and lit a cigarette, barely aware of the scantily clad girl behind Plexiglas, three feet away.

"The phone works better if you pick it up," she said, but *my* voice from four years ago buzzed in my head.

"Quit messing around, Kenny. Let me go."

I snatched up the phone and mashed it against my ear as footsteps went past the door. Weathers and Mr. Wilson.

"I'm Tish," the little peroxide blonde said, stroking a nipple through her frayed red nightie. She had a cute button nose and a dusting of freckles on her cheeks. I latched onto the fact that Tish wasn't a movie. She was real and *right here*.

"Hi, Tish. I'm Adam."

"I work on tips, Adam." This with a big *Hi sailor* smile.

I fished a five out of my wallet, rolled it up and fed it through a circular hole – too small to accommodate any dick wider than my little finger – cut in the Plexiglas.

"It's almost closing time," Tish said cheerily. "Get those jeans down so we can have some fun." Cradling the phone against her shoulder, she slipped the left side of her nightie down, exposing a small but lovely breast. Her fat nipple looked exactly like an eraser on a pencil.

I considered her offer, but after all the Rush I had no interest in flogging now-shriveled Petey in front of a stranger. "Nah," I said. "You must get bored with sex talk anyway."

She dropped a hand between her legs. "That's why I'm here, hon."

"The name's Adam."

"Show me your dick, Adam."

"Nah," I repeated, scooting the folding chair back slightly on the grimy linoleum floor. "Can't we just talk like regular people?"

"Sure," Tish said with a shrug, "why not? So what's a cute kid like you doing here this time of night?"

"Don't call me kid," I growled.

"Sorry." She fumbled a Kool from the pack next to her on the thin mattress and lit up. "You're just a lot younger than most customers, is all I mean. And *way* cuter." She spread her legs a little, drawing my eyes down there like a magnet. "Having trouble with your girl?"

"Just trouble," I said, refusing to credit Wendy with anything. There was a knock on the door. The gorilla announced that we had ten minutes.

"Okay, Ricky!" she called, puffing on her Kool.

Tish *was* attractive, in a hard, Dust Bowl sort of way, girlish behind the heavy make-up, with pale, distant eyes. On impulse, I dug out another five and tipped her again.

"Thanks, hon." Tish spread her legs wider and pulled her panties to one side, revealing pubic hair shaved into the shape of a heart. Petey perked up, just a bit. "Sure you don't want to get off?"

"Yeah, but what are you doing when you get out of here?"

"Sorry, I can't date customers." She put her cig down in a full ashtray and started playing with herself a little.

"Who said anything about a date?" I kept my eyes locked on hers now, hoping to impress her by not gawking at her pussy. "It's just. . . I'm buzzed, bored, a thousand miles from home. And you seem nice, Tish." I crushed my smoke out on the dirty floor. "I could use a little nice right now, that's all."

She smiled and this time it didn't seem like a come-on. "Me, too."

"Then let's grab some coffee or something." I returned her smile, although I felt more mannequin than man. "Trust me, I'm harmless."

"You got wheels?"

"Sure."

"If you can give me a ride home, then okay, why not?"

"Great."

"There's a Circle K a couple blocks up Colfax," said Tish. "Meet me there in twenty minutes."

"You got it." I figured it was maybe fifty-fifty that she'd actually show up, but I had no particular place to go. "I'm driving a green and white Charger, Tish."

"Okay, hon."

54

Exiting Kitty's, I knew the notion of impressing a talk-dirty girl by not talking dirty was pretty ludicrous, but it seemed important to try connecting with Tish. Not sexually, just one screwed-up human to another.

Back in the car, I did a slug of whiskey, shoved the bottle under the seat and drove up to the Circle K. I roamed the aisles slowly, killing five minutes or so, then bought a Snickers and went back outside.

By the time I'd eaten the candy bar and sucked down two smokes, I saw Tish crossing Colfax, a block down. I leaned in through the Charger's open window and gave the horn a quick toot.

She waved. Tish was wearing baggy jeans and an oversized pink sweatshirt. As she walked beneath a streetlight, I saw dark circles under her eyes, the hard set of her narrow jaw. She looked nineteen going on forty.

Strolling up to the car, she tossed her tote bag into the back seat. "Hi, hon."

"Adam," I reminded her.

"Let's go, Adam," she said, climbing aboard.

I pulled out slowly, keeping an eye out for cops. Tish said she lived over by Big Mac, the hamburger sports arena. We headed west on Colfax, down the hill past the capitol and its gold dome, still lit by flood lights at two in the morning.

"Where are you from, Tish?"

"I'm a native. You?"

"A little hick town called Garrison."

"Never heard of it."

"Who has?" I asked with a laugh.

She lit a Kool. "Got any dope?"

"No," I lied. Didn't feel like doing more coke, or sharing it. "But I've got some whiskey."

"That'll work."

I fished Mr. Daniels out from under the seat. "Maybe this is a weird question," I said, handing her the bottle. "But do you like your job?"

"Yeah, most times," Tish said matter-of-factly then took a drink. "Old guys kinda gross me out, and I get a complete freak now an' then, but mostly it's pretty fun. And it beats hell outta flippin' burgers."

"Sure."

We drove a couple minutes in silence, crossing a viaduct over the railroad yards, then she motioned with her Kool. "Take a right up on Federal, Adam."

"You got it."

After another shot of whiskey, Tish leaned back against the door and looked me over like she was deciding whether to bid at an auction "You're not a cop, right?"

I snickered. "Fuck, no."

"Didn't think so, but I had to ask."

"No problem."

"What'd you have in mind then?"

I blinked at her. "What do you mean?"

"Head costs forty," Tish said, ticking off the menu on purple paste-on nails. "Screwing is seventy-five, but I don't do anything *real* kinky."

"Hey, I just want to talk, remember?"

"Yeah, yeah," she said sarcastically, waving the words aside. "Guys always wanna *talk*."

I scowled.

She smiled, missing the signal, and put a small hand on my shoulder. "Look, Adam, we don't have to do it in the car, 'kay? We can use my place."

I shrugged off her hand, annoyed. "People like to do things other than screw, ya know." There was a nasty edge in my voice I hadn't intended.

"Like what?"

"Like just trying to fucking communicate with another individual. Machines *can't* do that," I stressed, taking the exit onto Federal. "Only people."

"Okay, I get it," Tish said, but her blank expression suggested otherwise. "Take a left at the fourth light." She flicked her cigarette butt out the window. "So you really just wanna rap, huh?"

"*Yes*," I said desperately. "You already gave me the price list, right? I'd tell you if I wanted to mess around."

"Okay, Adam," she said agreeably. "I'll only charge you twenty-five for a half-hour."

Unbelievable.

I wheeled the Charger hard right, into the parking lot of a Denny's, and slammed on the breaks. "Get out," I said, voice a dry croak.

What?"

"Get the hell out of the car," I ordered. "Now!"

"Fine!" Tish leaned over the seat and grabbed her bag. "You think I've got time for every drunk jerk-off who wanders into my booth with a sad story?" She climbed out of the car then spit through the window before storming off.

I was tempted to chase her once around the parking lot, but two guys were watching from the sidewalk in front of Denny's, so I took a couple deep breaths and just slowly drove away.

"Fuck yoooou, Adam!" Tish shrieked.

The perfect end to the evening, I thought sourly. Yet I didn't feel pissed off, even with the spitting and shrieking. I was too hollowed out to feel much of anything.

55

The parade is done/Time to put a price tag on fun

Those Next lyrics rang in my head as I motored east up Colfax. What was the price of Tommy Weathers porn-booth fun? There's no tolerance for gays in hard rock, so was he just using the gorgeous Raven as a macho man disguise, while dreaming of rutting with Mr. Wilson, or did he swing both ways? Either option meant Tommy was a phony, so his music had to be fake, too, despite its chaotic fury. Another false idol crumbles.

It's enough to make you puke.

Stopping to buy cigs, I discovered three bucks was all I had left from the sixty I'd started the night with. Time to start squeezing nickels, before I ended up begging on a Denver street corner. I dig Kerouac, but didn't want to live out his empty pocket scrounging. Back on the road, I thought how weird it would be if that really *was* Mr. Wilson in Kitty's.

Today class, we're discussing latent homosexuality. Skip it, teach. I've already got that credit.

On the radio, Eddie Money sang about two tickets to paradise, but they only let you on the plane if you're *really* in love, right, Wen?

"I'll love you, hon," I heard Tish whisper. "For a hundred bucks an hour."

My stomach suddenly churned in revolt. Afraid I might *really* have to puke, I turned into the next alley, brought the Charger to an abrupt halt and shifted into neutral. The headlights framed a guy maybe a hundred feet away, spray-painting the back of an apartment building. I gawked at the Old English lettering with a shock of recognition. It had to be the same street sage.

He looked in my direction with haunted eyes that hinted at news too awful for TV talking heads, fit only for alleys that never saw the sun. I killed the headlights, but he turned and fled up the alley, spray can in hand.

"Wait!" I shouted, popping the door and getting out of the idling car. "I wanna talk to you!"

He ignored me and kept running. Hopping back in the Charger, I threw it into gear and gunned it, had almost caught up with him when he cut left, darting between two buildings. I sped up, then had to stand on the breaks for a stop sign at the end of the alley. 14th was one-way, against me, but there was no on-coming traffic in sight so...

"Fuck it!" I shouted, mashing the gas to zoom up 14th the wrong way as fast as possible before navigating a hard left at the next corner. No sign of the shy philosopher. I parked mid-block, jumped out and trotted a hundred feet in each direction, looking between buildings, eyeballing shadows. Nothing. The sage was gone, had no reason to chat up a zom.

Then I remembered I'd interrupted him at work and so circled back to the alley and his waiting words.

The answer is

I stopped him from finishing the lesson! Parking by a dumpster, I walked over to the building and touched the still-tacky paint.

"What?" I whispered. "What's the god damned answer?"

There isn't one, the little voice said. *No Sage Santa, toting a big bag of truth.*

Maybe not, but I stood there awhile, staring at his unfinished words on the wall. They seemed to mock me like a lost last chance.

56

"Seems like something's stuck in your craw, so it's best to just go ahead and spit it out."

"It's hard, Dad," I said. But then I'd never really been able to talk to the old man, not about anything important, so why should now be any different? "And it hurts like hell."

"It, ah, it's okay, Adam," the old man said, gravel voice softening. "You can tell me."

"W-Wendy dumped me." There it was. The awful truth made more awful by saying it out loud.

"I'm sorry to hear that," he said quietly. "She's a lovely girl."

"Yeah."

"Heartbreak hurts, that's for sure," the old man continued. "It's probably about the shittiest feeling in the world."

That was maybe the tenth time in my life I'd heard the old man use language stronger than *hell* or *damn.* "Yeah," I agreed with a sniffle.

"I don't expect you to believe this right now, but it *does* get better. And you'll meet lots of girls."

"But I don't want lots of girls," I protested, gripping the phone so tightly that my hand trembled. "I want *Wendy.* We love each other."

"It sounds like maybe she doesn't, kiddo, not anymore." I said nothing. The silence stretched between Windhollow and Garrison. I heard the old man strike a match, inhale deeply on one of his Camels before resuming the rah-rah for team Adam. "A good-looking guy like you, you'll have the girls lining up."

Sure, I thought grimly, all wanting to charge me by the hour. I know the old man was trying to cheer me up, but happy talk bullshit only made me feel worse. "There's only one Wendy, Dad." My voice cracked. I hated how pathetic I sounded. "You just don't get it."

"Like hell I don't," he said sharply.

From the depths of my pity party, I remembered that he certainly *did* get it, which made me feel even shittier.

132

"A broken heart will mess you up bad," the old man went on, "and all you can do is just hang in there and be a man. Not in the tough guy sense, but a man smart enough to know that the world craps on all of us, now and again. Smart enough to realize you have to fight your way through it, simply because there's no other way."

"Uh-huh," I agreed, then started to sob.

"Oh, Adam. . ."

The old man's voice trailed off and maybe he was remembering the cold November night, shortly after Mom split, when I found him sitting in his Rivera in the dark garage, bawling like a hungry newborn. I stood there for what felt like a long time before he glanced up at me through the windshield. Our eyes only locked for a second before I clicked off the light and retreated back into the house, terrified by the look of abject loss and desperation etched on my father's face.

Neither of us ever mentioned it, so he doesn't know that I grabbed my coat, went out the front door and stood in the driveway for a half-hour, shivering in the wind to make sure he wasn't going to start the engine. Finally, I heard him climb out of the car and go back inside.

So, yeah, he gets it.

"Just hang in there, son, and things *will* get better."

"O-Okay," I said, wanting to believe him but unable to stop blubbering. "Thanks for that, Dad. W-We'll talk later."

"Call me whenever you want."

"I will."

After hanging up, I slumped against the kitchen counter, wondering just what the hell it meant to be a man. Was the old man the model, still tending to his run-away wife's roses five years after her great escape?

He had spoken to me with a sympathy and understanding I'd never heard him express before. It struck me that maybe Dad was more than a bundle of clichés: middle-class, middle-aged divorced guy, surprised to find himself knee-deep in the wreckage of his own life. That maybe he was more than the sum of his flaws, and just because you're old doesn't mean that you're always wrong, or unworthy of some sympathy yourself.

But warm fuzzies aside, the old man couldn't help me. Dave couldn't help me, nobody could. It was time I started helping myself, and the only rule would be to write my own. I briefly thought of calling Wendy, but screw that. What was there left to say?

Better to stop thinking about her at all.

I got a beer and walked into Derk's room. Coke on the mirror, so I fueled up then went to take a shower. Petey sprang to attention while soaping up and I realized I never got off last night. Started to whack it, but all I could think about was Wen and I refused to go there.

Toweling off, I decided on other erotic inspiration. Kitty's was fifteen minutes away and, despite last night's Tish fiasco, I still had the itch. Needed to blot out the white noise in my head with the grunts and groans of the Fuck Machine.

I got quarters and hit the arcade. Same vids as last night and they just weren't doing it for me. When the four bucks in quarters I'd dropped ran out, I returned to the bookstore and strolled over to the paperbacks. The wide-eyed girl was still there, cowering before three leering guys on the cover of *Cheerleader's Rape Night*.

It's only a book and…

Go ahead, the little voice sighed with resignation. *Admit it.*

I *wanted* to dive into the gutter, fantasize about grabbing some chick and using her any god damn way I pleased. Just like that. I snatched the book and headed to the counter before changing my mind.

Purchase safely tucked away in a paper bag, I sped back to Windhollow, where I didn't think about backing the Charger against the wall to hide the scraped fender. I strode quickly toward the condo, eager for some bad book learning, but then stopped dead in my tracks.

A cop was standing outside the door of 22-G.

57

My first impulse was to rush up to the cop and tell him about Derk's black wig, about the handcuffs and tiny panties hidden in his black van. This was as close to playing hero as I was likely to ever get.

Then I remembered my dirty book in the bag and felt like a co-conspirator.

Circling around the swimming pool, I considered stashing the book somewhere and then talking to the cop, but why should I? Derk had never hurt me and the same certainly couldn't be said of girls. Maybe *all* people, regardless of sex, color or creed, are greedy, grasping shits, locked in an unending cannibal dance of domination. Trying to sort out the lot was no business for a zombie like me.

I sat down in the grass behind the mailboxes and had a cig before again scoping out the condo. The cop was gone, but him being there in the first place must mean they were closing in on Derk. That wasn't my business, either.

Once inside, I made a whiskey and seven and smoked half a joint I found in the ashtray on the bar. Copping a buzz, now *that's* a skill I'd mastered in Mile High. First rule: score by any means necessary.

Buy, beg, scrounge, or steal.

Back to Derk's room, I stared at the wall of centerfolds, yards of exposed young flesh. Thinking of Wendy screwing her new guy, I muttered, "Bitches." Two lines to fuel up then I locked myself in the bathroom with *Cheerleader's Rape Night*. Sipped my drink and smiled at the irony. Derk was living out his rape-o fantasies and they would be coming to take him away for it. But little Adam could enter that dark world by merely opening a book and do so in complete safety.

I flipped to page one and started reading.

Jill was cold. The blonde, big-titted teenager had been waiting in the chill October twilight for twenty minutes, dressed in her skimpy cheerleader's outfit. A gust of wind bit Jill's shapely ass, while the thin, tight sweater molded to her ripe melon breasts offered little warmth as dusk fell on the school parking lot.

Jill was pissed off at her boyfriend. This was the second time this week Paul had been way late picking her up after school. Screw it, she decided, tossing long, honey-colored hair over one shoulder. Grabbing her book bag, Jill started toward the bus stop, three long, dark blocks away.

The Machine hummed on.

58

The next afternoon on the sofa watching MTV, my insides gray and numb. Tried to run earlier, but managed only a couple miles and had been anchored in front of the tube ever since. Bored with music vids, I found a spring break movie on cable.

Every time I heard a car pull into the lot outside, I half-expected a SWAT team to come busting in after Derk. But it was Dave who soon strolled in the front door with his travel bag, right after the move's first gratuitous tit shot.

Surprised to see him, I called "Hi!" and muted the TV. "Why aren't you in Vegas with Laura?"

"She couldn't get the extra time off after all," Dave reported, hanging his bag on the stair railing. "So we came back after one night, but still had a great time. We were up until four, talking. I figured some things out."

"Yeah?" I finished my rum and coke and studied Dave's serious expression as he went behind the bar. "Like what?"

"Well, first. . ." Dave let the question linger as he retrieved the skull bong and sank into the recliner before announcing, "I'm in love, little brother."

I snorted. "That's just your dick talking."

"Maybe," he said, "but I don't think so. I also figured out something about Vance. He quit dancing too late."

"What's that mean?" I shook me head, confused. "Are you saying Vance died because he was a stripper?"

"No, that'd be ridiculous. What you do isn't who you are." Dave did a bong hit then continued. "But our lives have an ebb and flow, right? It's like we're paddling along on some great river, navigating currents of choice and chance, while trying to figure out which direction we *want* to go."

"Maybe," I said, not buying Dave's watery metaphysics. This Laura was making him all touchy-feely and, I feared, a little soft in the head. "What's your point?"

"That Vance discovered he was going the wrong way," Dave said. "Tried to change course, but he hit some rapids, got sucked under and drowned."

"No," I countered. "He tried to drive while drowning in booze."

"That's just the way it happened," Dave insisted. "Not the *why*."

"Suppose you're right," I said, resisting the urge to tell Dave he was full of it. Didn't want to pick a fight with one of the only people on the planet who gives a rat's hind end about me. "Even if Vance quit stripping too late, so what? What are *you* gonna do?"

"Quit now."

"Quit dancing?"

"Yeah, but I'll give Derk time to find a replacement."

"Wow." I laughed and pointed at Dave accusingly, like a teacher fingering a cheater in class. "A couple weeks ago you swore you weren't gonna shake up your life because of Laura."

Dave grinned. "That was a couple weeks ago."

"Whatever, bro." I got up and padded out to the kitchen. "Want a beer?"

"I'm good."

I grabbed a brew and slammed the fridge. I didn't care if Dave quit stripping or not, but knowing he was doing it for *luv* made me want to upchuck. Back on the sofa, I grilled him like a crusading district attorney. "Aren't you worried quitting might piss off your roomie?"

Dave shrugged. "Derk won't care, as long as I pay my rent."

"Speaking of rent, what kind of job are you gonna get after two years of *dancing*?"

"Construction maybe. Tending bar. I'm not sweating it."

"Congrats." I lifted my beer in mock-salute. "That's quite a plan."

"I'll be fine, Adam," Dave said. "And believe me, this isn't just about Laura. I'm tired of playing fantasy stud. Tired of chicks who'll screw me, but wouldn't *dream* of getting serious, or even introducing me to their friends. Sure, it was fun being the Rock 'n' Roll Kid. *Lots* of fucking fun actually." Dave laughed and lit a Marlboro. "But the show's almost over."

"Just as well," I muttered. "Derk's gonna be out of business anyway."

"What?"

"Nothing." I considered telling Dave everything but sucked some suds and the impulse passed. "Just babbling."

"I have to make a grocery run. Wanna come?"

Dave leaves me alone for days then wants me to push a grocery cart? "No."

"Been keeping yourself entertained?"

"Oh, yeah, nothing but fun, fun," I said, glancing at the muted movie on the jumbo screen. A laughing frat boy was running down the beach holding a bikini top above his head, pursued by the girl he'd snatched it from. "'Til daddy slams the T-bird into a light pole."

"Sorry I haven't been around more," Dave said, ignoring the Vance reference. "Life's been unexpectedly nuts lately."

"Ain't *that* the truth?"

"How about going up to Boulder with me soon?" Dave asked, putting the bong away and digging out his keys. "I want you to meet Laura."

"When?"

"We'll figure something out," Dave said.

"Sure." I nodded. "Have your people call my people."

"Need anything at the store?"

"Nope."

I waved him out the door then the smile slide off my face. Let Dave enjoy his big romance, while it lasted. There are icebergs out there in the dark, big brother, and a collision is inevitable.

If I didn't get to be happy, why the hell should he?

59

I rattled the ice in my drink as *Blowjob Bimbos'* end credits scrolled by. An hour ago, I'd hoovered fat lines with Derk and his squeeze for the night, a blonde Valkyrie named Shannon. They soon retreated to his room and were probably now performing medieval sex rites.

I stared blankly at the screen, thoughts blowing through my head like tumble weeds. The twenty minutes or so of the video I watched hadn't done much for me, but I still craved blood flow to my groin to let me know I was alive. Something nasty for the zom-clone-drone.

I got the porn book and Rush from my backpack and hunkered down in the bathroom, where I could hear Derk and Shannon bumping around through the wall. I'd read *Cheerleader's Rape Night* cover to cover three days ago and now peeled off my t-shirt and sat on the john to scan for selected passages.

Cliff Notes: our heroine Jill is not only gorgeous, but a virginal honor student and church choir soloist, practiced at fending off the amorous advances of her football star boyfriend. This the reader learns in the first couple pages as Jill walks down a dark street toward her destiny.

Two brawny, muscle-bound brothers named Frank and Gordon Speck stopped to offer Jill a ride in their rusty old pick-up. She wisely declined, but the brothers weren't taking no for an answer.

"Yes, Derk," Shannon moaned through the wall. "Oh, yes."

Frank jumped from the cab and tackled the sexy cheerleader, scattering schoolbooks and scuffing her knees on the asphalt. The dazed Jill was hoisted into the bed of the pick-up and quickly blindfolded and gagged. As the truck roared away, she couldn't believe this was happening, yet despite her terror and confusion, something *stirred in the sweet unexplored cave of her cherry cunt.*

The prose was spare, seasoned only with the seven words you can't say on network TV. Jill fought valiantly for her honor through thirteen pages before Frank finally "bled her" in an abandoned gas station on the outskirts of town. Jill continued struggling, but in vain as the brothers took her every which way but loose. Against her will, the "leggy, tasty-titted pom-pom queen" started getting turned on as the Speck boys punched her secret buttons.

Frank and Gordon weren't just hung like the Mule Man, they got hard again "mere minutes after cumming like a fire hose" as they put Jill through her paces. She proved a quick study. After her first involuntary and unexpected orgasm, Jill belonged to the bros, was eager to be taken to their ramshackle farm outside of town and presented as a gift to their father, a fat old coot with a fourteen-inch cock.

When the Speck boys dropped Jill off back at the high school a hundred and eighteen pulpy porn pages later, she thanked them for "revealing my true sluttish self. For making me realize I'm a pig for cock, any cock. And I love it!"

Garbage, right? Implausible plot, piled atop moral degradation.

I strained to remember ever hearing of a rape victim who loved it. Nope. "Garbage," I whispered, dropping the book on the cool tile floor.

"Yeah, baby, I'm your rider!" Derk cried. Shannon neighed like a horse. "I'm the Lone fucking Ranger!"

Yet suppose a rape *could* happen like in the novel. No one would ever hear about it, because a happy cock convert like Jill wouldn't think of going to the cops, unless it was to get some big blue dick.

So riff on this, the little voice sighed, displeased. *You know you want to.*

Suppose that, just like with doctors and plumbers, there are bumbling rapists but also topflight pros like the Speck boys, wise in the ways of the Machine. Jill had felt dirty and degraded at first, but the brothers kept working to unleash the ravenous sexual animal within, the filthy 'ho in her soul.

But that would never happen in real life, right?

Shutting my eyes, I visualized the stunning brunette I saw at the pool yesterday, firm and fine in a bright orange bikini. She lived at Windhollow, maybe only a few doors away, and I imagined myself as a beast on the prowl, creeping up to her window. . .

138

"Who's my cowgirl! Woo woo!" Derk on sound effects. Panting and high-pitched little squeals from Shannon.

Petey came to attention as I imagined ripping off that orange bikini top, right at poolside. Dropping trou, I picked up the book and flipped to the page where Frank speared Jill for the first time. Did a big blast of Rush up both nostrils because the only rule is write your own. The words seem to pulse on the page. . .

With a victorious grunt, Frank grabbed Jill's taut and tender ass and lifted her off the rough wooden floor while savagely thrusting his hips forward. The throbbing head of his huge cock pierced the thin, fleshy veil of Jill's virgin cunt, tearing it bloodily asunder. "Yeah!" Frank roared with glee as he filled the gorgeous cheerleader with his twelve-inch torpedo. Jill shrieked with both pain and passion.

"Oh, Derk!"

Another Rush whiff and I almost left my body while erupting like Vesuvius as I gave it to Jill *and* orange bikini girl.

Take that, you God damned horny sluts!

My whole body shuddered, felt electrified by 10,000 volts. I geysered again, spewing cum and creation like the universe big bang being born!

Then scant seconds later: *Zap.*

The power goes dead all at once. The surge of transcendental ecstasy ends as abruptly as quarters running out in the arcade. I cursed and tossed the book toward the door. Completing the program left me feeling empty, icky, wondering how the hell I managed to become this big a screw-up. I was a nice kid once, right? Loved my mom, got good grades, thanked sweet Jesus every night at bedtime...

Over to the sink, I confronted my pale and pasty reflection in the mirror. I must have lost ten pounds since hitting Denver, and my ribs protruded like a stray dog's. My eyes were bloodshot slits and a big pimple sprouted from the four days' stubble on my chin.

Lovely.

I scrubbed my hands and face, desperate to feel clean while telling myself that porn was just fantasy. Freaky fun and games that hurt no one. Yeah, it was creepy, discovering some inner sicko I never knew existed, but I felt too wiped out to brood much about it.

Instead, I trudged upstairs to Dave's room, crawled into bed and pulled the sheet up to my chin. Soon starting to drift off, I heard Mom whispering, "Now I lay me down to sleep. . ."

I grunted and pulled the sheet up over my head, refusing to pray along with a runaway ghost.

60

At the liquor store I grab a quart of Coors and line up at the register behind a big Indian, who's paying for a bottle of Thunderbird with pocket change.

"Hey, Adam! How's your brother?"

I turn to see Vance, holding a quart of tequila in each hand. He's smiling broadly, no easy feat, considering that he's obviously dead. Flaps of torn flesh dangle from his face and windshield fragments glitter in the ragged wounds. One eye socket is an empty cave, the cheekbone below it a splintered mess after a high-speed impact with the steering wheel.

"Oh, Dave's fine," I say casually. "You?"

"I'm a corpse," Vance answers merrily, hoisting the tequila bottles. "But I still get thirsty."

"Sure."

The Big Chief leaves with his fire water. I flash my fake ID, pay for the beer then turn and ask Vance, "This *is* a dream, right?'

"Yeah, but dreams often come true," he tells me. "So do nightmares. Man, I'm thirsty." Vance cracks open a quart and chugs tequila, which dribbles out of a big hole gashed in his neck.

"You should really have that sewn up," I suggest.

Vance nods. "Good idea."

"Stay high, dead guy." Out in the parking lot, I make quick work of the beer then jog across Colfax to Kitty's. The front counter is now manned by an actual gorilla. The beast makes my change with a grunt, then leaps atop the counter and waves its long red penis.

"Thanks, Cheetah," I say, pointing to his King Kong dong. "And you pass the audition." Scooping up my quarters, I beeline for the arcade. Passing the live fantasy booths, I notice the phone babes have gone hi-tech. Heads and tits now jut directly from the back wall, while bellybutton phone cords lead to receivers cradled in open mouths. Quarters are to be deposited directly into coin slot cunts, accessible via a cut-out in the Plexiglas.

But I don't feel like talking, even to another zombie machine. Instead, I tromp to the last booth at the end of the hall and bolt the door behind me.

We're safe now, the little voice says. *We're home.*

"Yep."

The TV glows to life without being fed a quarter. Reaching for my jeans, I see they've vanished and that Petey is now *enormous,* putting even the Mule Man to shame. Cool dream! I sit down, grasp the monster between my legs with both hands and focus on the action.

A woman's hand reaches up from beneath a bank teller's cage and slowly unzips a man's fly as he counts out bills, "Twenty, forty, sixty. . ."

The camera swings around to reveal the woman, on her knees on a dirty tile floor, wearing only an apron that reads THE COOK WORKS FOR COCK. Mom strokes Fred Glaston's engorged member in time to his counting.

Click!

Wendy and her Cape Cod pal are fucking onstage at the Big House, while Tommy Weathers stands off to one side, jackin' it.

Click!

A camera slowly pans along the weathered tin roof of a barn, zooms in through a knothole, down at the hayloft below. Two sweaty, stripped-to-the-waist teenagers lounge on a thick bed of hay, sucking a bottle of gin and thumbing through skin mags.

Click, click, click!

I mash the channel button repeatedly, but it no longer works. The volume cranks all the way up as one boy suddenly launches himself atop the other.

"Kenny! What the fuck?"

"Exactly."

"Quit joking around!"

"No joke." Kenny laughs maniacally. "I'm gonna bone you up the ass!"

Tight close-ups of their faces, one pained and panicky, the other twisted with crazed, animal lust. Kenny's big hands fumble for the snap of my jeans.

I jump up and yank on the booth door, but it won't budge. Pain needles through my right shoulder, matching the on-screen action of Kenny twisting my arm behind my back. Dropping back on the padded bench, I look down, see that the monster between my legs has vanished.

I'm as dickless as a rag doll.

On-screen, Kenny slams my head against the floor of the loft, knees me in the right kidney then starts working my jeans down, inch by struggling inch. I thrash futilely beneath him, pinned like a bug to a board.

I hear Kenny unzip. He slaps his stiff pecker against my butt. Takes his hand off my shoulder to part my ass cheeks. There's an extreme close-up of the sudden penetration. Both on-screen Adam and I howl as a fireplace poker is rammed up my clenched rectum.

"Feels fine," Kenny groans, rocking into me. I bite my bottom lip, swallowing a scream. Soon he takes his knee out of my back, grabs me by the waist and tries to haul me up onto my knees. As he scoots me back, I spread my legs wider, manage to plant both feet firmly on the weathered planks. Every muscle in my body coils. My clenched teeth grind sparks.

The camera tracks overhead in slow mo as I stop trying to scrabble away from Kenny. Instead I lurch *backwards* with terrorized strength, driving him out of me with a final, ripping pain.

141

Arms flailing, he staggers back to the edge of the hayloft, seems to hover in mid-air for a moment, then tumbles down to the stalls below. The horses whinny in panic. Crawling to the edge of the loft, I look down to see a hoof catch Kenny squarely in the right temple.

Down the ladder and out of the barn, I glance toward the farmhouse, toward a phone and an ambulance. Then I turn the other way and break into a run. And keep running. I watch myself grow ever smaller on the porn booth screen, until I finally disappear over a hazy green hilltop.

The screen goes blank.

I slump against the booth wall, wrung out and trembling, but relieved that it's finally over. That I'll be waking up soon. But the booth door still won't open and after a moment the screen glows to life again. There's a barn in the distance, coming closer now as the titles roll for *Hayloft Homo Rape*.

I scream.

61

My legs were finally loosening up as I jogged by Windhollow's front gate for the sixth time. Despite weeks of heavy-duty partying, running remained a matter of motivation and getting warmed up. After that I could still go all day. Twelve times around the complex, twenty, thirty, but the laps brought no relief to my troubled mind, as if the psychic escape hatch running provided had been slammed shut.

On that hot August afternoon four years ago, I fled the hayloft in pain and shame and just kept going. I ran the two miles back to town, bypassed it on the interstate loop and headed down the dirt road beyond the dump. Garrison disappeared behind me. Scalding pain burned in my chest like battery acid but I didn't stop, spurred on by the sense that *something* up ahead could make things right, but to reach it I had to keep running, never look back, just keep going, because my salvation was out there, somewhere. It had to be.

I'd been running ever since and sometimes when I went through the wall and into the blank, there'd be a tantalizing glimpse of my deliverance, even if it remained always over the next hill.

So just keep going.

The sun was setting when I finished my last, no-longer-counted lap around Windhollow and collapsed in a sweaty heap on the grass beside the fountain, just inside the front gate. The concrete cupid looked down at me with an amused expression, as if he'd known all along what I had just realized. I could never run far enough to escape from Kenny. There was no salvation awaiting me over some distant horizon, no safe haven to run to.

And now I had more things to run *from*.

Wendy was gone.

How and why weren't important, just the bitter truth that the only girl I'd ever loved had dumped me like week-old junk food in the back of the fridge. I'd always love Wen, but part of me hated her now, too, not so much for giving me the boot as for claiming she'd never *really* loved me at all.

The Great Summer Road Trip had become a massive meltdown. On the bus west, I'd fantasized about all the fun Dave and I would have: hiking in the Rockies, hitting the town at night, just hanging out and becoming closer than ever, now that we were both adults. I'd conned myself into believing Dave would magically become the brother I'd always wanted but that he'd never actually been, except in my thirsty imagination.

And then there was this *other* thing. . . the newly revealed cirrhosis in my soul. I'd always loved books, journeyed between covers for fun and adventure, sure, but also for knowledge and insight into all the unvarnished truths most adults never speak aloud.

Most importantly, books had nurtured the hope that I could break out of my small-town cage, escape into a life only imagined in vague outline. Books kindled my hope that it wasn't just a matter of time until I was claimed by zombiedom. That one day I might even become the sort of man worthy of being written *about*.

Words had been my truest friends, yet I never imagined they could be arranged in perverse patterns like *Cheerleader's Rape Night* or suspected that pattern would appeal to me. That cruddy little book touched unknown anger and urges, proclaimed twisted lies that ached like some awful but undeniable truth.

So forget God damned Kenny Karanski. How was I supposed to escape from myself?

I got up and did jumping jacks by the fountain, glad for the example of Derk as a deterrent. He might be cruel and cunning, a ruthless hunter, but he was still going down. I'd already seen the cops at his door.

It was weird, but just then the thought of being clapped into a cell didn't frighten me. In prison the program was all laid out - eat, sleep, shit, everything scheduled down to the minute. Maybe prison is the ultimate zom factory, with the inmates being both the ends and means of production.

I trudged to the condo and showered, flashing back to the second time Wendy and I made love. Her old man had gone out of town overnight, so we had time to explore and experiment. It was amazing. Afterward, we took a long shower, camped out in the stall until the hot water ran out. I remembered her girlish squeal when the water went cold, bumps of gooseflesh rising on her thighs, the rhythm of her pounding heart next to mine as she held me close after we jumped out of the shower.

My Wen. . .

I started to cry and didn't fight it, glad that I had something left to mourn.

Drying off a few minutes later, I thought, okay, so I'm going through a bit of a rough patch right now. Yet once I get a grip, get back on an even keel, everything will be okay. My feelings for Wendy were curdling, so I had to figure out how to let them go before they turned completely rancid.

And having discovered something ugly inside myself, I had to purge it, too. If garbage attracts you, design a disposal.

I wasn't Derk and never would be.

The roomies were out, so I did a small bump from Derk's shelf, grabbed a Pepsi from the fridge then clicked on the news for a dose of non-me reality. Ronnie had said something dumb. There'd been another terror bombing in Paris and then a bulletin. . .

"Denver Police have arrested Scott Schulman, charging the twenty-nine-year-old contractor with four counts of rape in a series of attacks on metro area teens, with other charges expected. . ."

I stared slack-jawed at a handcuffed suspect being rudely bundled into a cop car on the big screen. He was tall and well-built, had long black hair.

Scott Schulman?

My first thought was that the stupid cops busted the wrong guy. Then it hit me: *I* was the stupid one. I'd built a sandcastle case against Derk and swallowed it whole, maybe as a subconscious defense against my own warped urges.

Good thing I didn't tattle to the cops, I thought, barking out a hoarse laugh. So much for the career in law enforcement, Inspector Clouseau.

I was out of smokes and decided to hoof it to 7-Eleven. Halfway there, I saw Derk buzz by in his red Corvette. Maybe he *was* an okay guy, just like Dave said. Sure, Derk could be an arrogant prick, but the world's full of them and with my own inner perv to worry about, I was in no position to judge anybody.

When I got back to Windhollow forty minutes later, a cop car was exiting the complex. I half-expected to see Derk in the back seat, but no. Scott Schulman was the Shopping Mall Rapist, which raised the question of why that cop was at the condo the other day. Hawking tickets to the policeman's ball, or did he just have an itchy nose? Screw it. The only thing playing detective had revealed was how deluded I'd become.

I strolled into 22-G, swung the door shut behind me.

"That you, Adam?" Derk called from the kitchen.

"Yeah."

"Get your butt out here!"

His voice was like a lash. I cringed, wondering if he'd discovered I'd been pinching magic powder. If so, I'd just have to fess up and offer to pay for it. Squaring my shoulders, I pasted a grin on my face and marched to the kitchen.

144

"What's up?"

Derk turned from the sink, smirked, then sucker-punched me hard, right in the gut. I gasped, couldn't breathe as the floor flew up to meet me. My head bounced off the linoleum. I gulped for air and rolled over on my back.

Derk straddled me, a steel-tipped boot digging into my left armpit. "You little shit," he hissed, raising the boot above my chest menacingly. He held it there a moment, then stepped over me and stalked off to the bar.

Still gasping, I managed to crane myself up off the floor and follow. Time to take my medicine. "W-What'd I do to deserve that?"

"Don't fucking play Mr. Innocent," Derk said, downing a shot of whiskey.

I retreated to the sofa, eyeing him warily.

"Getting into a fender-bender is one thing, Adam, but a god damned hit and run? What are you, a total fucking moron?"

"*Hit and run?*" I repeated incredulously.

"At the 7-Eleven."

Oh. This was about the Charger. I'd spaced out telling Derk the fender got dinged at the Big House. "I'm sorry," I said contritely. "I was a little buzzed that night and this guy started screaming at me. Guess I just panicked, but that's not a god damned hit and run."

"It *is* leaving the scene of an accident," Derk said, capping the whiskey. "Which is pretty damn close, legally, so guess what?" He came over and stood directly in front of me, muscles taut, his lips a hard line. "I just had to pay a cop five hundred bucks to make this go away, or I'd be on my way to jail right now."

"Derk, I..."

Couldn't think of anything to say. My encounter with Goatee and his Jag seemed like ancient history. Who knew he'd not only manage to scribble down the plate number but would actually call the police? That was hardly a winning defense, I knew, so time to cop a plea.

"God, I'm sorry," I said, hoping I looked half as miserable as I felt. "I really fucked up."

"No shit, Einstein." Derk scowled, slowly cracking his knuckles. "And helping yourself to my coke, is that just another fuck up?"

"Ahh..."

"You're a liar and a thief, Adam, and both *really* bug me."

"Listen. . ." I forced myself to meet his iron gaze. "I... I'll pay you for the coke. It was only a line or two, a couple times when I was drunk." Even while confessing, I was fudging the truth. Zombies gotta zom. "It's not an excuse, but I've been losing my mind since Wendy dumped me. Fucking up royally, but it never occurred to me that *you* might get in trouble over the Charger. That's the truth."

Those blue eyes bored into me. Derk said nothing.

"I deeply regret abusing your hospitality." My voice dropped to a whisper. "It was a major jerk move, but that's not who I am, not really." This wasn't an act. I was sick of myself and ashamed.

Derk continued staring at me until I finally looked down at the floor. "Just be glad you're Dave's brother," he said, finally walking away.

"And I'll pay for the coke," I offered again.

"I don't want your god damned money." Back at the bar, Derk racked the bottle of whiskey. "What I *do* want is you out of my house tomorrow morning, comprende?"

I nodded.

"Say you understand."

"I understand."

Having meted out my sentence, Derk stalked off to his room without another word, a slammed door punctuating his sentiments.

So this is it, I thought, rubbing my stomach. Out I go.

Maybe I was just over Denver, but I accepted my eviction calmly. It was a just and relatively light sentence. Sinking onto the sofa, I lit a cig and realized that if Dave was staying up in Boulder again tonight, I might not get to see him again before I split. But I was okay with that, too.

Hell, I'd come a thousand miles to visit and Dave had mostly just passed through the condo since shortly after I hit town. How long would it be, I wondered, before he even realized I was gone?

Grabbing my backpack, I finally counted my bankroll: two hundred and thirty-nine dollars. That plus whatever was in my pockets was all the money I had in the world. I considered finding a fleabag motel, but there was nothing for me here now. Time to hop a bus to Garrison.

Yes, the little voice agreed solemnly. *Back across the border.*

I'd sleep for a week when I got home, sober up and then go get a job, maybe even out at the damned tire plant, if Wendy didn't badmouth me to her old man. The plant paid the best money in town, and when you've got cash then girls, cars, and all other goodies follow, right?

All the real world gives a flip about is what's in your wallet.

Hell, if I wasn't now on his permanent shit list, I might take up Derk's offer to teach me to strip. Hit the gym and learn the old bump and grind, 'cause who better to replace the soon-to-be-retired Rock 'n' Roll Kid than his baby brother?

Another promising career nipped in the bud.

All I was worth to anyone was two hundred and thirty-nine bucks. That's what things had come down to for our hero, who'd been *this* close to winning fair Wendy forever by bringing SMR to justice.

What a joke.

I got the phone book and called the bus station. The next Greyhound home left at two twenty-five tomorrow afternoon. Eastward, ho.

146

With my immediate future mapped out, I stretched out on the sofa. Shut my eyes and decided that, seen from a distance, my Mile High miseries *were* pretty funny. Worthy of a sick-o sitcom.

"Hey!" Derk barked. "No time for daydreaming, kid."

"What?" I blinked up at him, looming over the back of the sofa. "You said you wanted me out in the morning, right?"

"If you have nothing better to do than zone out, maybe you should just hit the road now."

"Sure." I got up and dug into my backpack for the jumbo baggie that held my toiletries, relieved that this whole messed up misadventure was coming to an end.

"I guess you're really pissed at me, huh?" I asked Derk, who just glowered. The manhunt now seemed so absurd that I had to share it with someone, even, maybe *especially*, its intended target. "But pissed or not, I'll bet I can make you laugh."

Derk's expression charged from near-homicidal to bewildered. Score one for the kid. "What the hell are you babbling about?"

I got up and brushed past him, headed for the bathroom. "Is it a bet?"

"Why not?" Trailing me down the hall, Derk leaned against the door jamb, crossing his arms across his chest. "So make me laugh, comedian."

Loading toothbrush, razor, and deodorant into the baggie, I said nonchalantly, "I almost narked you off to the cops."

In the mirror, I could see Derk's mouth drop open slightly. For once he was at a loss for words.

"Yeah," I continued in a jocular tone, "I got the screwy idea *you* might be the Shopping Mall Rapist. Don't know if you heard, but the cops busted the real guy this morning. Scott Schulman." I smiled and slapped the countertop. Rim shot. "Pretty hysterical, huh?"

Derk didn't look amused. "What gave you that odd idea?"

"Nothing," I answered, cramming the rest of my stuff into the baggie. "Just an overactive imagination."

"What exactly what did you imagine?"

"Obvious shit," I said, unafraid of the ridiculous truth. "You have a black van, so does Schulman. He has long black hair, you've got a black wig. It was just mind games, mental masturbation while I was fuckin' high, that's all." I turned, ready to leave, but Derk still filled the doorway. My well-punched stomach sank to the floor.

We stood frozen in place for a forever moment before he finally stepped back so I could pass. I hurried down the hall to finish packing. Time to beat feet out of 22-G.

"You win the bet, Adam." Derk followed me to the living room. "That actually *is* pretty funny."

"Yeah." I forced myself to chuckle. "But what an idiot, right, to dream up such a wacky idea?"

147

"Dream up any other wacky evidence?"

Derk wasn't SMR, so why not tell all on my way out the door? "I glanced at your Bad Boys notebook. Thought maybe you did strip-a-grams in the same neighborhoods on the same nights those girls were attacked."

Now Derk *did* laugh. "That's a fucking stretch."

"It is," I agreed, zipping up the backpack. "But you can sell yourself anything when you're wasted."

"True," Derk said. "But even if I *had* been in the same part of the town, so what? So were thousands of other people."

"Exactly. Something obvious overlooked by the delusional detective." I grabbed the pack by the frame and made for the door, then decided to jerk Derk's chain one last time. I stopped, turned around and smirked. "But delusions don't explain everything."

"What's *everything*?" Derk's blue eyes X-raying me from across the room.

"The night we went to the Big House and you got a call to work that party? I got bored and started poking around in the van. Found handcuffs and some tiny panties."

He shrugged. "The cuffs go with my cop costume."

"I figured."

"As for the panties..." Derk laughed again, but his expression suggested he found this as funny as the plague. "They're an erotic souvenir, evidence only of my *Penthouse Letters*-worthy sex life. And that you *do* have one hell of an imagination."

"Yep." I nodded. "I'm gonna cruise. Always leave 'em laughing, right?"

"That's quite the giggle, Adam," Derk agreed, waving me toward the bar. "Pour yourself a stiff one for the road, because after *that* story I can't hold a grudge. And while you're getting a drink. . ." He started toward his bedroom. "There's something I want to show you before you motor."

"Sure." I'd enjoy a *very* generous pour for my final round of free booze. "Oh, do you have Laura's phone number?" I called, eyeing the bottles. "I need to get in touch with Dave."

"Yeah!" Derk yelled back. "I'll jot it down for you."

"Cool."

I poured myself half a tumbler of 101 proof Wild Turkey and took a sip. This was going to be my last drink for a while, because boozing wouldn't help ward off all the traps awaiting me back in Zomsville. I downed the rest of the shot and shuddered. Glanced into the mirror behind the bar and saw Derk returning from his room. Holding a gun in his right hand.

I whirled around to stare at the revolver, now pointed directly at my chest.

"Grab your stuff," Derk said softly. "We're going for a ride."

62

The three of us walked out of the condo in silence – me, Derk, and the pistol in the pocket of his Bad Boys windbreaker. I considered making a break for it, figuring Derk was just trying to scare me, extract some payback for my fender-scraping, coke-stealing sins. He certainly wasn't going to shoot me right there in the parking lot. Hell, the gun probably wasn't even loaded and I could have gotten away.

But I didn't try it.

"Get in," Derk ordered, opening the driver's door of the van.

I hoisted my pack into the back, climbed over the console and dropped into the passenger seat. "So," I said as Derk got in and shut the door, "are you gonna tell me what the hell's going on?"

He opened the console and fished out a pair of handcuffs. I didn't appreciate the irony. "Give me your arm."

"Now wait a sec, Derk," I said, holding my hands up in an *I surrender* gesture. "I know I've been a real ass and understand you wanting to teach me a lesson." My voice remained calm, and it wasn't an act. Having recently discovered a sick fuck hiding in my own head, Derk's tough guy posturing seemed like high school theatrics, right down to the prop pistol.

"And I *know* you could kick my butt six ways to Sunday," I continued, "and I probably deserve it. I dinged the Charger, took some coke, so just punch me a couple more times and I'll be out of your hair forever."

Derk looked at me calmly, zero emotion on that movie Nazi mug. "Hold up your arm."

"Just tell me how to say uncle, okay? I'll say it. . ."

He pulled out the .38 with an exaggerated sigh. "Your arm, Adam."

"Okay," I said, realizing Derk was determined to play this little game out. He cuffed my left wrist, attached its mate to a strut under the seat, then went back to the mini-fridge and returned with a sixer of Coors cans. Cracking two beers, he handed me one and casually dropped the rest on the floor by my feet.

I took a healthy pull off the beer, not concerned right then with my alcohol intake. Derk started the van and we were off. "Where we goin'?" I asked as we exited Windhollow. "Or do we have to play twenty questions?"

"I just need to tie up some loose ends." Derk gnawed on one of his little cigars as we reached Colorado and turned left. "But don't sweat things," he said softly. "It won't hurt."

"What won't hurt?"

"Drink up."

Good advice. I slurped more beer then asked again, "What is it that won't hurt?"

Derk just frowned as we headed south, away from downtown.

"What?" I demanded, my voice spiking up an octave. If Derk meant to scare me, he was giving a very low-key performance. *That* kinda scared me because he knew how to put on a show, so if it wasn't that. . .

"You can't mean getting shot." I tried to laugh but managed only a strangling sound. I slugged down more brew. "It can't be that," I insisted. "Because I bet it would hurt a lot."

Derk glanced at me with a forlorn grin. "That deductive mind is what got you in trouble in the first place."

"You can't be serious." I was still half-convinced he wasn't, because it didn't make any sense. "Shooting me over some lines and a scratched fender would be insane."

"Yes, it would," Derk agreed, sipping his beer. "But this isn't about that."

"Then what?"

We stopped at a red light and he trained those baby blues on me. "You really don't get it, do you?"

"No." Glancing at the car beside us, I tried beaming a telepathic S.O.S. to the driver, but I failed the Kreskin test. The light changed and the car sped away. "What's there to get?"

"You were right, Adam." Derk's smile was all teeth now, like a hungry shark. "A gold star for the junior G-man."

I shook my head, feeling dumber by the minute. The last of my cool evaporated as it hit me that whatever his game, Derk might really be playing for keeps. "Right about *what?*"

"Me," Derk said as we turned onto I-25 and headed west, toward the mountains. "You were right about me."

"You mean. . ." I bit off the words, suddenly not wanting to know. Instead I fumbled out a smoke with my right hand. Derk offered me a light then sparked his cigar. I took a deep drag, exhaled and finished my thought. "Are you saying the cops busted the wrong guy for the rapes?"

"Oh, no," Derk said with a wink. "Denver's finest got their man."

"Then I still don't get it," I said, suddenly wondering if there was anything *to* get. What if Derk wasn't playing minds games, but had completely lost his instead? That was terrifying, because a Norman Bates nutter *could* murder me to avenge car fender and cocaine. "You've lost me."

"My plan exactly." Derk seemed to swell up in his seat, like he was gonna bust soon if he didn't spill his secret.

"What plan?"

"Crime without punishment," he said grandly, obviously enjoying my befuddlement. "Rape without risk."

"What, are you partners with Schulman?"

"No." Derk's voice dropped to a conspiratorial whisper. "I'm *him.*"

150

I downed more beer and stared out the windshield. Smoked in silence until the light finally when on. "Holy shit! You were doing copycats."

"Give the lad a cigar!" Derk exclaimed, waving his stogie under my nose. I flinched away, only to be jerked back by the handcuff's metal bite.

"I've raped a couple three chicks before," he continued, changing lanes to blow past a VW bus full of young stoners and old dogs. "The first time, around your age, I nailed this blonde at a kegger up in Deer Creek Canyon. It was impulsive and sloppy, plus the bitch gave me crabs." Derk scowled at the itchy memory.

"Bummer."

"But that's the great thing about sex crime. . ."

"Crabs?" I asked, an auto-pilot smart-ass comeback.

"No," Derk said, ignoring my wisecrack. "What's great is that even a teenager or a moron can get away with it, nine times out of ten."

"Yeah?" I polished off the beer and grabbed another off the floor. Pressed the can between my knees and opened it one-handed.

"Then you're no longer young, dumb, and full of cum," Derk went on, "and ninety percent odds aren't good enough for someone who values their freedom as much as I do. But what if you could improve those odds?"

Derk looked at me expectantly, like this was some sort of test. I figured acing the final was my best hope to still be breathing come morning. "So you whittled away at that ten percent," I guessed, pointing to the police scanner under the dash. "Listened in on the cops, stealing their plays."

"A scanner is useful, sure, but that's not the secret weapon," Derk said, puffing his cigar. "I hang out in cop bars a couple times a month, have for years. And like in any bar, if you're buying, you're making friends."

"Covert action," I whispered.

"Whenever T.J.'s wants a bodyguard for a girl working a potentially sketchy party, I hook them up with off-duty cops who don't mind naked girls and booger sugar." Derk tapped his nose. "In their eyes, a free buzz from a friend who gets you work is hardly a crime."

"I wouldn't think so."

"Our boys in blue *love* telling war stories after a few rails," Derk said. "Sharing offbeat details about crimes, or inside dope on cases big enough to make the news."

"So you've been working the refs for years," I said, impressed by such long-range planning. Derk made SMR seem like an amateur.

We continued west, the Rockies growing ever larger in the moon light.

151

"The few details reported last year about the Mall Crawler - that's what the cops called Schulman before the press renamed him - were enough to tweak my interest," Derk explained. "He was about my size, twenty something, long black hair, black van. Intrigued, I upped the partying with my cop pals and learned the Crawler's m.o., one detail at a time. Like he approached his targets on foot and carried a map, pretending to be a lost out-of-towner. The chicks he snatched were the ones who stopped to help him. He lured them to his van on various pretexts, like *wanna see my puppy*?"

"Pretty slick."

"I calculated that once I knew enough to copy the Crawler's playbook, those ninety percent odds would improve enough to make me damn near bulletproof."

"Brilliant," I told him, meaning it. "But what I don't understand... I mean, you were already getting tons of pussy, right?"

He glared at me like I'd insulted his mother. "Metric tons. So what?"

"So why do it at all, whatever the odds?"

"Because of the challenge," he said simply. "And because I can."

"I - I get that," I muttered, scared that maybe I did.

"But this is about much more than tearing off a random piece of ass, Adam. It's about *power*, the primordial imposition of one's will. It's about man in the raw, accepting and embracing his animal nature."

"Yeah?"

"Power is the only thing in this world that's real. All the hearts and flowers crap about *love*..." Derk spat the word contemptuously, like he'd bitten into a rotten peanut. "...are fairy tales spun by horny poets, hustling to get laid. It doesn't matter which pussy you're pounding, what matters is the power to take it, *fuck* it, when and how you want. Live as you will shall be all of the law. Everything else is tinsel."

I stared at him, appalled but fascinated. "But I believe in love," I whispered.

"Like with Wendy?" Derk snickered. "How's that working out?"

I bit my bottom lip and said nothing.

"Love's a handy fiction," he said, putting his cigar in the ashtray. "A magic word aging businessmen chant while mounting fat wives and fantasizing about nubile daughters."

"What about them?" I asked. "The daughters, the rapees?"

"It doesn't have to be rape, but the principle remains the same," said Derk. "Uptight, patriarchal society tries to keep young chicks clueless about their sexual nature. It's a control mechanism. That's one of the only things I don't like about Reagan, the anti-sex propaganda, draping curtains over nude statues, while the fake preachers supporting him hype the phony value of an intact hymen." He flashed the shark smile. "But one hard cock can cut through a whole lot of bullshit."

Derk was growing excited as he spoke, a revival tent pervert, wound-up by his own sermon. "Pussy's just another way of keeping score, kid. Sometimes sweet, whispered words uncross a girl's legs..." He hammered a fist on the dash. "And sometimes a man just *takes*!"

"That's intense."

"As life is meant to be," he declared. "Lived on the edge, sometimes with your ass hanging out over it. All men know this, deep in their gut. Most are too timid to honestly admit that, let alone act on it, and that's all to the good." Derk laughed and nudged my shoulder. "It leaves the spoils to the brave and the bold."

I shut my eyes, his words ringing in my ears. Here was theory, but what of the practice? I had to know. "The mall rapes," I ventured, "how many were yours?"

"Just three and a half," Derk said, sounding almost apologetic.

"A *half?*"

"One chick managed to break free before I got her aboard," Derk said, tone of voice like a fisherman, resigned that a big one had gotten away. "But I already had my hand down her pants." He shrugged. "Maybe that only counts as a quarter."

"So three and a half," I said, honoring his original score. "Out of how many attacks?"

"Ask Scott Schulman," Derk said with a snicker. "The cops will announce a number at some point. Maybe unsolved cases they want cleaned up will be added to the total. Fine by me. The bigger monster they make Schulman, the more invisible I become. Any minor inconstancies in the evidence will be papered over as the cops trumpet their big win. And with the dreaded SMR behind bars, there'll be no more attacks."

"You'll stop, just like that?"

"Of course." He tossed his empty beer can out the window and asked for another. I handed him one. "This was conceived as a precision campaign, not a banzai charge. Aping Schulman eliminated virtually all risk, except extreme bad luck. Now that he's stopped, so will I."

"And skate away scott free," I said, hearing what sounded like admiration in my voice. "What a perfect plan."

"Almost perfect," Derk amended. "I didn't game plan for having a snoop under my roof. *You* are the extreme bad luck in this scenario, Adam."

"*Me?*" I asked indignantly. "Hell, Derk, I'd never say anything."

He rolled his eyes. "You said you almost called the cops on me."

"*Almost*," I stressed, waving my free hand like a magician, desperate to make my own words disappear. "And that's ancient history, before Wendy's letter and... a lot of stuff. Trust me, Mr. X, your secret's safe with me."

"Maybe so," Derk said softly. "But my freedom being contingent on your silence is not an acceptable risk. Sorry."

"So what then?" I croaked, my throat suddenly sandpaper dry. I quaffed more beer. "You're just gonna take me out and shoot me?"

Derk stared out the windshield.

"But you can't do that," I said, trying to channel F. Lee Bailey. "Legally, murder is much more serious than rape. . ."

"Let me explain the math," Derk said. "The equation is now one plus one. "One crime, one mouth, comprende?"

His total was "three and a half" crimes, but I wasn't about to quibble over the math. "Okay."

He aimed his index finger at me. "But *bang*. We get a final score of two crimes and no mouth. And zero is my lucky number."

I had no comeback for that. We drove on in silence, ever west.

"Listen, it's not like I *want* to do this," Derk finally said. His voice was quiet, almost sympathetic. "If you can come up with another solution to our problem, I'm all ears."

"Good," I said, nodding eagerly, but all that occurred to me was the horrible idea of having Derk cut out my tongue. But then he'd have to hack off my hands, too, so I couldn't write. Not a mutilation road I wanted to go down.

Then find a better route! the little voice yelled.

"No duh," I whispered, dropping my head into my right hand. Shutting my eyes, I tried to glimpse any path leading away from my upcoming murder.

"This sucks for both of us," said Derk.

"Sure." It was my turn to smirk. "Maybe a bit more for me."

"Touché," Derk said. "But it's like I mentioned before, all medical evidence suggests a shot to the head is instant and painless."

"Well, *that* makes me feel better!" I cackled like a lunatic, thrashing wildly in my seat, yanking against the handcuff chain with all my might. Metal dug deep into my skin, ground against bone, the pain underlining the horrible truth that this was no game. Derk was taking me up into the mountains to kill me.

I cursed softly and slumped back against the seat.

"Here." Derk dipped into the console and produced a half-pint of whiskey. "Drink up."

I grabbed the bottle and did a blast. We were climbing into the foothills now, the night air growing cooler as the Denver lights faded behind us.

154

"Honestly, Derk, I'd never say anything." I gave the Boy Scout salute and summoned every lesson learned in debate class. "Think about it, will ya? If I was *ever* serious about calling the cops, I would never have mentioned it to you, right? The whole thing was a big joke, like I said at the condo. Doesn't that make sense?"

"Except now you know that I *wasn't* joking, and that changes the equation."

"I'll never say a word," I repeated, realizing my defense was going nowhere. "*Never*. I just want to go home. Hell, drive me to the bus station and watch me leave. I'll be five hundred miles away by this time tomorrow, lips forever sealed. And you'll have no worries."

He chewed his cigar, pondering, but then ruled against me. "You can pick up a phone from anywhere. No, distance doesn't solve this."

Point to Derk.

I glanced out the passenger window, now seeing every gully and stand of trees off the interstate as a possible execution site. Traffic was light. Derk could take any exit and five minutes later we'd be far from any witnesses. But we kept going, so I kept thinking, spinning out worthless ideas like pinwheels until I had a eureka flash.

"Derk, what if I convince you. . ." I began, bouncing on the seat like an excited ten-year-old catching his first glimpse of Disneyland after three days in the backseat with an annoying little sister. "*Really* convince you I'd never say shit, then you wouldn't have to shoot me, right?"

"In theory, sure," he agreed. "But I don't see how. . ."

"Just listen!" I yelped. "I'll never nark you out because I know you're right. Right about love being bullshit, about power being the one true thing, right about *everything*. And you don't just talk, Derk, you *live* your truth. You're strong enough to just grab some little bitch and screw her silly, but you're also smart enough to do it as the Invisible Man. That's fucking *brilliant*, man." I took a deep breath. "And maybe the coolest god damn thing I've ever heard."

"Think so?" he said, looking pleased by my testimonial.

"Absolutely," I said, hope rising that I might actually have a chance. "You're like a dark prophet, stripping away all the bullshit fairy tales, whittling things down to core reality. God, to be like you would be great. . . Strong enough to write my own rules."

I did another blast of whiskey, then delivered the punch line.

"Strong enough to rape any chick I want." I winced a little inside, just saying that, but there was no condemning clap of thunder, nothing but the van's wheels humming along the highway.

Derk blew a smoke ring and grinned, not one of his smartass smirks, but with genuine amusement. "A for effort, kid."

"Y-You don't believe me?"

"Believe what? Your chick back in Hooterville dumps you, so you're gonna go all Night Stalker?"

"I never said that!" I protested, taking my turn to punch the dash. "And maybe it's not so sudden. Maybe you helped reveal things inside of me that have been there all along."

"Huh." A noncommittal grunt.

More whiskey and I shook my head because all this was just too weird. Until an hour ago, I'd been desperate to kill off my dirty dreams, but now my survival might hinge on convincing Derk I dreamed them at all.

"You need to see something, Derk. Pull over." I knew this was a big risk, because once we were stopped. . .

He shook his head. "I am not going to fall for any tricks from the late, late show."

"No tricks," I pledged. "You said you'd welcome another way out of this, right? If that's true, then goddamn it, let me show you something."

"All right." Rather than continuing to the next exit, Derk moved into the right lane, hit the blinker as we slowed down then eased the van off onto the wide shoulder. He shifted into park and left the motor running, "Make your pitch, Adam. I'm all ears."

I asked him to grab my backpack and tried to slow my racing heart. I knew this was it, that if I couldn't sell him *now* this might be very close to the place where I would die. Unzipping the pack, I pawed through my stuff one-handed, digging down to the bottom.

"Here," I said, brandishing the book like an unholy relic.

Derk puffed on his cigar, then grinned as he reached for *Cheerleader's Rape Night.*

63

We were parked along a lonely dirt road, a mile or so off the interstate, sucking on beers and sipping whiskey after having hoovered several jumbo lines of coke. The .38 rested on the dashboard in front of Derk and my fate had come down to this: of what significance was a porno paperback?

"Rape fantasies are very common," Derk said, flipping through the book distractedly. "I don't see how this changes anything."

"Look closer then, because it changed *me*. Hell, I never even saw a skin flick before I got to Denver, so reading this. . ." I pointed at the novel. "And hearing you spell things out, it was like a burning bush moment, comprende?"

Derk rubbed his nose. "Maybe so."

"I've taken shit all my life," I told him, voice rising with anger. "Been laughed at and putdown by dumb jocks and bubbled-headed chicks." I slapped my knee. "Well, the joke's over and I'm not gonna take it anymore!"

Derk closed the book, tossed it in back and looked at me with curiosity. "What do you want to do instead?"

"Get a little payback." I looked deeply into his eyes, saw myself reflected there. "And get some power of my own."

"Always a worthy goal," Derk agreed.

"You've shown me it's possible to not just write your own rules, but actually live them out. That's all I've ever wanted, Derk, to discover how to do that."

He picked up the gun, opened the chamber and spun it. It made a soft clicking sound, like a roulette wheel. "You talk a good game, Adam," he said, "but it's still only words." Derk flicked his wrist, snapping the chamber shut. "And *other* words of yours could still land me in the penitentiary."

"Damn it," I said, knowing I was losing the debate. "How can I make you understand?"

"But I *do* understand." he said sympathetically. "You have potential. Hell, I recognized it when we first met. You have this vibe, an angry spark. Oh, it's tamped down, suppressed for sure, but still there. Still ready to be ignited."

"A spark, exactly!" Here, here: I gaveled the dash in agreement. "I've always tried to control it, since it usually got me in trouble when I didn't. But I never wanted to stamp it out, 'cause that seemed like it would be killing an important part of myself."

Derk nodded as he studied my face.

"But *you* don't just keep the spark alive, you make it blaze, use it to light your own outlaw path, define your own truth." I finished my beer and tossed the can out the window. "It may sound dumb, but I've been trying to figure out what's true my whole life. That's always seemed to me the most important thing there is. You've shown me some truth, understand, so there's *no* way that I'd ever betray that. Or you."

Derk stabbed a fresh cigar between his sensual lips. "I believe you."

I sagged back against the seat with relief. "Great."

"I believe you wouldn't drop a dime on me in *today*, tomorrow, next week." Derk's expression grew as hard as stone. "But neither of us can be sure about what you might decide to say next month, can we?"

"I. . ." couldn't deny the obvious. Instead, I despaired over the paradox of pleading for my life *and* claiming to embrace Derk's cold-blooded credo, since my possible murder would be the ultimate expression of his philosophy.

Some catch, that Catch .38.

"This genuinely sucks," Derk said quietly, then finished off the whiskey and flipped the bottle into the back of the van. "Had things gone differently, we might have become good friends." With that *what if* declaration, he offered me his hand.

Weird, right?

And I shook it, because just then Derk didn't seem like a monster, but rather someone who was vividly human, with nothing of the zombie about him. He said he didn't want to shoot me, and I believed him. The lines and drinks he kept offering were a stall, delaying the final act that he didn't want to perform.

I shut my eyes and weird animated images unspooled in my head. "Funny," I whispered, "I just had a vision of a sick Saturday morning cartoon."

"Yeah?" Derk pocketed the pistol and went back to the mini fridge for more suds. "Do tell."

"It starred us as superheroes. You were Molester Man and I was your sidekick, Jack-Off."

"That's one sick sense of humor." We both chuckled as he sat back down and handed me another beer. "I'll be doing society a favor, saving it from that twisted mind."

He was the only one who chuckled at *that*.

We drank. Derk lit the cigar, puffed on it contemplatively for a minute or two, then took the keys from the ignition and uncuffed me. "Let's go take a walk. Bring your beer."

"But cartoons have happy endings," I protested.

"The show's been cancelled," Derk whispered. "I dig your taste in literature, but fantasy is just not enough." He opened his door and got out, motioning for me to follow. "Let's go."

I sat there. Slurped beer and started to tremble.

"Take a minute to get your head together," Derk said, glancing away. "But no longer than that."

I started to say something but only managed a grunt.

Be as brave as you can, the little voice urged. *And it probably won't hurt.*

Chugging down half the beer, I considered making Derk drag me out of the van. But that might well turn into begging and bawling, and I resolved not to do either. After slowly climbing over the console and hopping out of the van, I leaned over and stretched, loosening up for one last sprint. What odds, I wondered, would Coach Hansen give me on outrunning a bullet?

Derk started around the front of the van, motioning for me to follow, but then he stopped abruptly, face lighting up like he'd just spied a long-lost friend.

"What?" I asked, hungry for any shred of hope. "Did you think of something?"

"Yeah," Derk said with a smile. "And you, Adam, just got a reprieve."

"What?" I was desperate to believe him but feared some final *fuck you* joke before he shot me right between the eyes. "How?"

"Your cartoon," Derk said, eyes shining in the moonlight. "Molester Man and Jack-Off are about to step off the screen and into real life."

64

As we sped back toward Denver – with me now handcuff free – Derk explained his idea. The only way to guarantee my silence, he reasoned, was for us to commit a crime together. So we were off to kidnap and rape a girl, comprende?

"You may have gotten worked up over a porn novel, but you won't *really* understand until you get a taste of the real thing," Derk predicted, puffing thunderheads from his cigar. "Then you'll crave seconds."

"I'm hungry *now*." We rounded a wide downhill curve and Denver again appeared below us, ablaze with 100,000 lights, stretching away to the horizon. I was feeding Derk's ego, sure, but slipped into the role so easily, like a comfy old t-shirt, that I wondered if maybe *this* was what I'd been running toward, not just the last four years but maybe my entire life.

"Some chicks just lay there like a dish rag and let you do your thing," Derk said, old pro perv lecturing the eager apprentice. "But squirmers are the best, thrashing around under you like a fish on the line. God, it's an epic rush."

"Do they get into it after a while?" I asked, thinking of cheerleader Jill's cock-loving transformation.

"Sometimes, if you do them up right," Derk said. "It's akin to breaking a horse. Ride 'em long and hard, and they know who's boss."

I nodded, wondering if Kenny would have "broken" me in. Don't think so, because men and women have a natural tab A into slot B biological connection, it's hardwired, so "riding them right" might break down all inhibitions and taboos, triggering pure carnal desire. Resistance is useless.

Pound, pound, pound.

A state trooper suddenly blew past us, siren off but lights whirling. I jerked back in my seat, startled by the unwelcome reminder that this wasn't some skin flick fantasy. Derk and I were gearing up to commit a *real* crime, and real policemen would try to lock us up for it. I sipped my Coors and said, "What if we get caught?"

"We won't, unless you fuck up." Derk hiked a thumb over his shoulder. "Hey, we can always turn around if you want…"

"I won't fuck up," I swore.

"Then we won't get caught."

"No, we won't." I knew only a small percentage of rapists were ever arrested, let alone convicted. Plus, if we somehow *did* get busted, I'd just tell the truth: that I was participating under threat to my life. As terrifying as the whole idea was, it suddenly struck me as liberating as well. It was hunt with Derk or eat a bullet, right? Since I didn't have any choice, why flinch away from life in the raw?

Experience it instead. Remembering Gina Kelly ditching me at the dance, I muttered, "Too bad that bitch is a thousand miles away."

"Don't sweat it," Derk said. "The world's ripe with snatch."

"Yeah," I agreed, feeling almost giddy. Faces flashed through my mind, all the girls who'd ignored me, snubbed my fumbling advances, made me feel two inches tall. Once in eleventh grade, I found the nerve after history class to ask the well-endowed and popular Jenny Dobler (who I allowed to cheat off my tests) why girls didn't like me very much.

"Oh, Adam," she chirped, a hint of compassion in her doe-like brown eyes, "If you haven't figured that out by now, you probably never will."

We'll see about that, bitch.

I stared down at the city, crazy quilt of electric jewels. All that power, I thought, fuel for little Adam's spotlight as he avenges old slights, fresh heartbreak. Doesn't every religion demand a sacrifice to appease the gods? Maybe the offering to come would silence the demons that had been howling after me since I scrambled down the ladder from the hayloft.

Hard times demand hard truths. Kenny had been my friend, so what good was friendship? Wendy had been my lover, so what good was love? Cracking my knuckles, I recited a Next lyric, stripped of the singer's condemnatory tone.

"Track the free ones down, check the malls, the school playground."

"That's the spirit!" Derk enthused. "Which is why I'm going to let you select our target."

"Well, hell," I said, blindsided like a lazy student unprepared for a pop quiz. I looked down at my feet. "I don't know any girls here."

"Not an issue," Derk said. "You *never* want to target someone you know anyway, because the risk factor skyrockets."

"Makes sense." I nodded. "It's just that…" My voice trailed off. I had no idea where that thought was going. We were close enough to civilization again to hit our first red light. As we slowed to a stop, Derk eyed me skeptically, like a hanging judge.

"You're not going all squishy on me, are you, Adam?"

"No." I shook my head for emphasis, then finished my beer and flung the can out the window. "It's just… you're the expert. You know what to look for, how to do the mall crawl."

"Forget malls." The light changed and we sped off. "That was Schulman's hunting ground, so the last thing we want is the cops scratching their pointy heads over a similarly themed assault, right after they bagged SMR."

"Make sense," I repeated, again impressed by Derk's cold-blooded strategy of piggybacking on someone else's crimes. Maybe he *was* an evil mastermind. And maybe he was right in insisting that only power can raise you from the zombie ranks. Brute take-it-if-you-dare aggression, red in tooth and claw.

"No malls," I echoed, steeling myself for whatever lay ahead. "What's the alternative? We just cruise around until I spot a likely..." I swallowed the word *victim*.

"Something like that," Derk said. "Opportunities always present themselves, to those with open eyes. Maybe we'll check out the Big House and Herman's, do Colfax."

Mention of Colfax reminded me of bubbled-headed Tish and her demand that I pay for the privilege of her sparkling conversation. I smiled like a landlord about to foreclose on a widow with six kids.

"What?" Derk arched an eyebrow. "You get an idea?"

"Maybe."

If Jack-Off had to go into action with Molester Man to save his skin, so be it. With that as a given, the *last* thing I wanted was to spend a couple hours cruising, searching for some random, vulnerable girl, an innocent type, eager to help a lost schlub clutching a map. . .

We might not have to do that, not when I knew someone far more deserving of our attention. It made perfect sense.

"Yeah," I said, amending my *maybe* as I gave Derk a punch in the shoulder. "I think I've got our chick."

65

Derk laughed at the punchline of my porn store pick-up: Tish offering a discount rate to listen to my sad sack woes. He was up for her as the object of our exercise, *if* the logistics worked out.

"First, we hit Kitty's to see if your girl is working tonight," Derk said, glancing at his watch. "It's nine-thirty now. If she *is* working, let's hope it's not until they close at two."

"Yeah," I agreed. "Even downtown is pretty dead by then."

"Except for the police."

"Right."

"Hey, don't sweat it, Adam. It's a good idea, but if your greedy little tartlet isn't available, we have plenty of time to find another contestant."

"Suppose she does get off early," I wondered as we headed north toward downtown on Santa Fe Drive. "What's the plan?"

"I don't have one yet," Derk admitted, puffing on his cigar. "But things fall into place, one way or another. Hunting requires patience. You watch and wait, and when the moment's right, you strike!"

"Kinda like a race," I suggested. "You try to stay close to the leaders, then kick near the finish line."

"No, this isn't like *anything* else," Derk said, shaking his head. "It's life lived at full throttle. And it makes a Big Statement, thumbing your nose at the lies of little men."

"How's so?" I asked, hanging on every word.

"Most people need lies, pious pabulum and Madison Avenue myths to keep the world's terrors at bay," Derk proclaimed, voice like a rising wind. "Lies to keep their eyes averted from the fact that life itself is a lie, just a temporary illusion. Only the strong of heart can admit that humanity simply doesn't matter. We're dust specks, unloved and ignored by a vast and uncaring universe."

"If that's true, then what's the point of anything?"

"The point," Derk explained, "is that there is *no* point. No gods, no rules, so *my* will be done!" He shook a defiant fist out the window. "My will, until someone or something bigger comes along to squash me, which is inevitable. And I'm okay with that because until that moment arrives, I'm the rarest motherfucking thing in this world."

"Which is what?" I asked.

Derk beamed. "A truly free man."

"Yeah." At that moment, it all made perfect sense to me. "Free."

"Know what I appreciate about you?" Derk slowed down, changing lanes to follow a station wagon full of high school girls, either scouting prospects or just for the fun of it. "You don't seem scared of things that would send your brother screaming for the hills."

"I used to be scared of lots of things," I admitted, watching the teen queens turn into a Burger King parking lot. They were laughing, no doubt at guys like me. "But not anymore. It's time for somebody else to be scared."

"That's the spirit," Derk said, raising his beer. We clinked cans.

At the next stop light, we pulled up beside a copper-colored Trans Am. There was a gorgeous blonde behind the wheel. I stared at her and when she caught my gaze, I pulled a crazy smile and kept staring. The light changed. She mashed the gas and roared off.

I laughed, having just discovered that where fear is concerned, it was better to give than receive.

By the time we parked on a side street close to Kitty's fifteen minutes later, Derk had brainstormed a strategy. Step one was recon. I'd enter the store first, with him soon to follow. He didn't mention that we'd remain in close enough proximity that if I tried to bolt, he could easily run me down or gun me down. He didn't have to.

162

And it occurred to me that I could try something nutty, like vaulting over the front counter while screaming at the Gorilla to call the cops. As we exited the van and strolled toward Colfax, I realized Derk had bought into my conversion enough to be confident that I'd try no such stunt. And he was right. Jack-Off wasn't going to bolt.

He was reporting for duty.

66

Per instructions, I remained in the front section of Kitty's, skimming a Ray Bradbury interview in *Playboy,* until Derk strolled in about five minutes later. That was a longer time lag than expected and I wondered if it was some sort of test, or an expression of trust.

It didn't matter. Amped out of my gourd on coke, booze and Derk's twistoid gospel, I was all in.

With a nod in his direction, I re-racked the *Playboy* and proceeded through the black curtains in the southeast corner of the store, was halfway down the long hall before remembering this side was all videos, no phone bims.

I stopped dead, my gaze tracking up to the EXIT sign above the rear door, just twenty feet away. Then I lit a smoke and headed back up front. Crossing the dingy industrial green carpeting to the other arcade, I glanced at Derk eyeballing bondage gear before ducking through the curtains.

There were three live girl booths on each side of the hall. No sign of Tish, but she could be entertaining behind any of four
currently closed doors. Not wanting to hang out in the hall – cruising turf for pervs like Shirttail and Tommy Weathers – I returned to the front of the store.

I shrugged at Derk to signal I didn't know yet if Tish was on-duty. Had I shaken my head *no* and started for the door, we would have been off in search of Miss Plan B.

It was a hot summer night, with no air conditioning in Kitty's. I was sweating through my black Kinks t-shirt but still played things *cool,* smoking a cig as I strolled slowly past the rows of hard-core mags, eyeballing the cover photos like a dutiful shopper. After snubbing out my butt in a corner ashtray, I paused to knead my eyes.

Some of the cover girls I'd just ogled – two big-Afroed black girls, a buxom blonde with pig tails and giant lollipop, and a trio of punk rock vamp/tramps – sashayed by inside my eyelids, eager to audition in the back of Derk's van. Unconsciously conjuring up mental porn was apparently Jack Off's superpower, and it struck me again how crazy this whole thing was, a coked-fueled meat-beatin' fantasy. . .

Derk coughed, reminding me that his .38 was as real as ass cancer.

———

Back to check the phone booths again. All the doors but one were now open, and there on a ratty mattress sat Tish, middle booth on the left. She was fussing with her make-up and didn't glance up as I walked by but. . .

A problem occurred to me that hadn't before, given my general elation over not being shot dead in the mountains. Tish had no reason to remember most customers who passed through her booth, but she'd spent time with me away from Kitty's. I'd also told her my name repeatedly, kicked her out of a car *and* been cursed for it, so I was hardly just another anonymous dick-fiddler.

Emerging back through the curtains, I shot Derk a thumbs-up and headed for the exit, anxious to let Molester Man handle the problem of my not-so-secret identity.

***

Derk listened as we slowly ambled around the block beneath ancient shade trees, the bustle and noise of Colfax seemingly far away. Then he dismissed my worries. "Even if she recognizes you, Adam, your girl can't actually identify you in any meaningful way."

"But Tish knows my name," I repeated for the third time.

"*If* she remembers it."

"The way she screamed it after *fuck you,* I'm pretty sure she'll remember."

"So what if she does? It's only a first name and not an exotic one." Derk shrugged. "And a jerk booth skank is not going to go to the cops anyway or get much sympathy if she did."

"She knows I'm from out of town, too," I said, more concerned with my personal exposure than Derk's opinion on the compassion of policemen.

"Which narrows down where you're from to the rest of the fucking world," Derk said with a smile. "Hardly a hot lead."

I scowled, fretting that he was either going to just blow this off, or suggest we head back to the hills for a three way with his pistol.

"Still, I understand your concern," Derk decided, stroking his chin. "Your girl getting a good look at you would not be optimum."

"No shit. Better safe than sitting in a cell."

"Jesus, you're a drama queen."

"Just trying to cover all the angles," I said. "Like you did, with all your homework on Mall Crawler Schulman."

Derk nodded like he appreciated my response. We walked on in silence. I didn't want to interrupt what I figured was more strategizing.

"We've got two things to accomplish before fretting over your girl's power of recall," he said, pausing to bend down and smell a flower garden bordering the sidewalk. "First, I'll find out when she gets off work. If it's early enough, part two is convincing her to go out with me afterwards. If my charm fails…" He gave me a wink. "…an unlikely proposition, but it *could* happen, then waving a fifty in her face should do it."

"I'm sure it will."

We turned right at the corner of 16th and Clarkson, heading back towards Colfax. An old black guy in a Broncos t-shirt was hobbling toward us on the uneven flagstone walk, leaning on a cane. Derk give him a long sideways glance as we passed, and I braced for a snide comment or worse, but my movie Nazi broke character.

"That must really suck," Derk muttered.

"What, having to use a cane?"

"No, being black in this redneck country," Derk said. "I wouldn't last a fucking day."

"Oh, *that*," I said, disoriented by this flash of empathy. Then I remembered our mission and got the conversation back on track. "If Tish gets off early, *of course* she'll go out with you."

"Perhaps."

"Come on. You're *Derk*, dude," I said, prompting an *ah-shucks* grin from him. I shook out a cig and sparked it.

"You really should quit," Derk said, making a smell-the-fart face. "Those things will kill you."

I swallowed a crack about his .38 being none too healthy either and instead said, "Assuming your charm works it magic, when you get Tish to the van, we're back to my ID problem."

"It's solved," he said breezily. "There's a Lone Ranger mask in the bar you can wear. And it will be dark." He laughed and feigned a punch at my shoulder. "Just don't ask her rates for talk time and we'll be good."

"Yeah, okay," I agreed, scared to fully acknowledge what "good" would mean now that the sex crime commutation of my death sentence seemed more and more like something that might really happen.

At the corner of Clarkson and Colfax, we stopped by unspoken agreement to listen to a band tear through the last couple guitar-army minutes of "Freebird" through the open door of Pete's Cactus Lounge. As the final chords faded away, we turned the corner and moseyed back down to the candy store.

67

Forty-five minutes later we were sitting in the van, waiting for Tish's shift to end. Derk laid out two small lines on a cassette case. "A taste of crystal for an extra boost," he said, snorted his and handed me a rolled-up ten. "We want to be plenty energetic for your girl, right?"

I nodded and did the speed. It burned, but the line was small enough that my nostril didn't feel totally napalmed. I rubbed my nose and glanced at my watch. Tish would be off work in fifteen minutes, with Derk there to meet her.

"She's up for a party," he'd reported after spending maybe ten minutes in her booth. "It didn't take much of a sales pitch, but I gave her a nice rock to maintain the enthusiasm."

"She'll be raring to go," I predicted. But what about me?

When Derk leaves to meet Tish, the little voice advised, *you can still play hero by summoning the cavalry.*

Fuck heroes, I thought darkly, washing down the nasty Drano drip with a gulp of Coors. They're all fakes, from Jesus and JFK right on down to absent brothers and faggy guitar players. I ain't summoning shit.

Then run away, the little voice said. *We know you're good at that.*

Nope. Jack-Off doesn't leave Molester Man in a lurch.

I was high as a kite, sure, but that had little to do with me staying put. It was more like, sometimes we're gripped by forces we barely understand, except to acknowledge powers at work far beyond our own. The only thing I knew just then was that the story had to be played out to the end.

Besides, right or wrong doesn't exist for zoms. And I *wanted* to rape the hell out of Tish, live out the dirty book creed Derk so enthusiastically championed. I needed to feel something besides Wendy's dagger in my heart, melt it away with a white phosphorus eruption, hot enough to cook off eighteen years of failure and frustration, maybe even my alien sense of otherness. The feeling that either I'm a fake human or everybody else is.

So strike a match.

I glanced at the Lone Ranger's mask in my lap and flashed on the ultimate porno: Derk and the Speck boys tossing Wendy into the back of a pick-up. I shuddered and sucked down more brew.

"Are you scared, Adam?" Derk asked.

"No."

"Bullshit."

"Maybe a little," I admitted.

"Good," he said with a smile. "Lying is a useful tool but try to never lie to yourself, particularly about being afraid. It's a natural defense mechanism, so embrace it, let it flow through you. Become a conduit for fear, not its final destination."

"Yeah, that makes sense." As a speed rush raced down my spine, I resolved to let my fears run through me like a river, bound for distant seas. Fear for my immortal soul, which I don't even believe in. Fear for our guest-starring booth girl, even if Tish was a dumb little bitch. Hell, even fear for ringmaster Derk, who's glad to see ya *and* has a pistol in his pocket.

"Don't you think, Adam?"

"Huh?" Shaking off the mental chatter, I saw Derk was digging through the console bin.

"I asked if you thought some mood lighting was in order."

"Sure."

Producing a small screwdriver, he quickly removed the dome light's cover, swapped out bulbs and screwed the cover back into place. "And now. . ." Derk paused as he reached for the keys dangling in the ignition. "Romance!"

The van's interior was bathed in dim red light.

"Welcome to the netherworld," I whispered.

"Crouch down at the end of the bar when you hear us approaching," Derk instructed, pulling the rearview mirror toward him. "Between the low light and the Ranger mask, your secret identity is safe, Jack-O."

I had to grin at the comic book lingo. "Sounds good."

Derk made a kissy face in the mirror and pushed it back into place. "And you've got the tape and rope ready?"

He'd watched me prep them, but I just said, "Roger." The *rope* was actually several lengths of nylon cord, each about four feet long and now positioned right behind my seat, along with duct tape, the edge folded back on itself, so there'd be no fumbling to find the end of the roll. "Ready to rock."

"And so I am," Derk said, popping his door.

"Hey." I hadn't planned to say anything, but the word had just emerged from my mouth.

Derk stopped halfway out of the van, dropped back into his seat and looked at me expectantly. "Yes?"

I considered just wishing him luck, but there was something I had to know. "You won't be back for maybe twenty minutes, assuming she's on time. . ."

"So?"

"How…" I grabbed the refilled half-pint of whiskey off the floor and took a swig. Wiped my mouth with the back of my hand, which tasted sour and metallic. "How do you know I'll still be here when you get back?"

"I don't," Derk admitted. "But I got faith in you, Adam." He winked and stepped out into the street. "You get a certain look in your eyes."

68

Derk might believe I wouldn't run off, but that didn't mean he trusted me with the keys. After he left to rendezvous with Tish, I sat there in the dark, trying to ignore my jumbled thoughts and think of nothing instead.

"Just experience," I mumbled like a mantra.

The little voice, his advice ignored and no doubt horrified at events now unfolding, remained silent.

I pulled on the Lone Ranger mask. Checked the rearview and saw in the dim street light filtering through the trees that I was only recognizable as an anonymous creep in a cheap Halloween getup.

I sat and smoked. Realized when reaching for another one that I'd lost track of time and had better get into position. Climbing over the console, I shoved my backpack further behind the bar then sat down on the thick shag carpet, trying to *just experience.*

No good. I couldn't ignore the fact that this moment – *right now* – was my last chance to boogie, to change the story, to *not* do this. I stood up...

But only snatched a bottle of Bacardi from the mahogany rack behind the bar and took a swig. I re-racked the bottle and sparked a cig. Peeked out the tinted back windows and absently fondled Petey through my jeans. Nothing going on down there yet.

I sat back down. The cigarette made me hack, so I snubbed it out and sucked my bottom lip instead. I'd like to claim some big epiphany, that I found a thread running through my chaotic existence, from fucked-up family and Kenny's *Hayloft High Jinks* to breaching the Zomtown border and escaping out into the world, only to be knifed by Wendy and somehow get sucked into a sick puppy porn novel. . .

But there's no thread to discover when everything unravels, just random data, chance encounters and robotic repetition. Memories of my life paraded by like an out-of-step marching band.

I saw myself shivering in the November wind outside our garage, hoping that if the old man was going to try to asphyxiate himself in the Riviera, he'd *get on with it* so I could rush in and save him, then get out of the god damn cold and call the rubber wagon.

I flashed on the Saturday morning in July, between first and second grade, when Mom took me to the Garrison Library to get my own card, key to the kingdom! She turned me loose amid the stacks for a glorious half-hour, free to hunt up any three books I wanted. And every Saturday until I was old enough to go alone, Mom took me back for more books. I'll always love her for that.

And I wondered if I should jizz on Tish's face or tits, no doubt exploding like a fire hose behind my black rebel mask. . .

A troubling thought struck me. Derk had spent ten minutes in Tish's booth, up close and personal. He wasn't disguised, then or now. Why would a master schemer who buddied-up to cops to help him plot his crimes suddenly be so unconcerned about being recognized?

Maybe because Derk had a .38 caliber method of shutting Tish up...

"Baby, if you want steak, we'll get streak!" Derk proclaimed loudly, alerting me that he and Tish were approaching the van. "Three inches thick!"

"Yummy," Tish said.

"Just experience," I whispered like a prayer.

69

Hearing the rattle of Derk's keys, I hunkered down at the end of the bar, any sense of erotic anticipation overcome by my newly hatched fear that he might have terminal plans for our co-star. Possible new math: three minus one equals two.

"Wow!" gushed Tish, poking her head inside the van for a pre-boarding peek. She seemed to be staring right at me and I half-hoped she'd scream and haul ass, but all she said was, "Nice ride, Bobby."

Bobby must be a fake name Derk had given her. Some master of disguise.

Tish climbed up into the swivel chair, no doubt with Derk's helping hand on her ass. In her reflection on the windshield, I saw Tish was wearing a Twisted Sister t-shirt and faded, knees-out jeans. The passenger door *chunked* shut and Derk strolled slowly around the front of the van, grinning like a car salesman who's just taken your keys.

He got in, turned over the ignition without starting the engine. The red light came on, so dim it didn't illuminate the darkness so much as give it a bloody tint. Barely audible on the radio, Robert Plant moaned about getting his lemon squeezed until the juice runs down his leg.

Still crouched by the bar, I bounced on my toes and remembered the cords and tape on the floor behind the passenger seat. I had to fully commit to our plan, not despite my Tish-gets-murdered fears, but because of them. Trying to abort the kidnapping would almost certainly result in Derk pointing his gun at someone *now*, no matter what he had planned for later.

"You know what sounds even better than steak?" Tish asked as I began inching up behind her.

Derk cut his eyes toward me then smiled impishly at Tish. "What, honey?"

She leaned across the console and put a hand on his thigh. "Another line, Bobby-Boo. Can we?"

"Sure, sweet thing," Derk said, glancing back to make sure I was in position. "But first. . ." His unseen left hand pushed a button. The passenger door locked with a *thunk*!

The next few seconds seemed to unfold in slow motion.

Tish's head swiveled toward the door, no doubt to confirm what she thought she'd heard. Her body listed slightly in that direction.

Derk's right hand shot up in a blur, cupped the back of Tish's head and slammed her face against the window.

"Ranger!" he barked, jerking Tish upright by her hair. "Tape her mouth."

I sprang up like a jack-in-the-box. Almost dropped the tape, but managed to unspool six inches or so that I tore free with my teeth. Glancing left, I saw Derk's right hand on Tish's shoulder, the left clamped over her mouth. Holding the strip of tape with both hands, I leaned over the right side of the seat.

"Ready?" he asked.

"Y-Yeah."

Derk jerked his hand away. I slapped the tape across Tish's mouth, then ran my hand over it to secure the seal. Her quivering lips beneath my fingers felt like they were trying to scream.

"Move back," Derk ordered, reaching over with his left hand to crank up the tunes. Not enough to attract attention, but loud enough that anyone strolling by on the sidewalk would hear Zeppelin instead of the Diabolical Duo.

I stepped back and sideways, pasting myself against the carpeted side of the van. Gripping the squirming girl under her armpits, Derk rose in a half-crouch and lifted Tish off the seat. Her legs kicked out wildly, left foot hitting the rearview so hard that it broke off the windshield, bounced once on the dash, and spun away toward the floor.

I watched bug-eyed as Derk slapped her, then tried to hoist Tish into the back while simultaneously stepping over the console. He couldn't quite manage it, lost his balance and let go of Tish to keep from falling. She tumbled to the floor, then scuttled on hands and knees toward the rear doors.

"Ranger!"

His shout jolted me like a cattle prod. I seemed to fall forward, landing on the back of Tish's legs and stopping her cold. Glancing up, I saw her grasping hands were maybe three inches from the door latch.

"I got her!" Derk called, now clutching Tish's ankles. I rolled off her, panting and sweating as adrenaline surged through me. As Derk dragged her back from the doors, Tish yanked the tape off her mouth and let loose a feral scream.

Derk smothered most of it by releasing one ankle and using the free hand to smash her face into the floor with a lot more force than when he banged her off the window. Deep carpet or no, that had to *hurt*. Tish groaned and her legs stopped kicking.

"Re-tape her mouth," Derk ordered, "then help me hogtie this little piggy."

Moving on what felt like autopilot, I teeth-ripped more tape, stuck it in place when Derk flipped Tish onto her back.

"Tie her wrists," he said.

"Wrists," I echoed, fumbling for a length of cord. The sooner Tish was tied-up, I realized, the safer she'd be. I set to work, but she began thrashing around, recovering from her *wham-bam* close-up with the floor. I managed to loop the cord around one wrist, but Tish wasn't having it. Her other hand flew up wildly and caught me square in the throat. With a strangled cry, I stumbled back, gasping in panic before realizing I could still breathe.

"I-I'm okay," I croaked, neck hurting like hell.

"Fuck this," Derk decided, grabbing Tish's left arm and wrenching it behind her back. He fumbled behind his seat with his other hand and came up holding the revolver. I expected him to go full gangster and press the barrel against her head, but instead Derk pulled Tish into a sitting position and held the .38 a couple inches from her face, barrel pointing up at the van's roof.

"Be still or be dead," he said softly, voice all velvet menace. "Understand?"

Tish nodded and stopped moving. Blood oozed from her right nostril, a red trail running sideways along her top lip.

"Good girl." Derk slid open the bar's middle drawer and pulled out another set of handcuffs, making me wince with familiarity. "Now lay down and put your arms behind your back." Tish compiled and was duly cuffed. "That's just until we get where we're going, honey," he said, patting her ass and then rolling Tish onto her back. "Same for the tape on that sweet little mouth."

"Sweet," I heard myself parrot. But as I stared down at the bloody-nosed, handcuffed girl, she didn't look much like a slutty cheerleader, about to take a magical journey to Cockland.

"Ranger," Derk said, patting my shoulder as he moved toward the driver's seat. "Tie your girl's ankles and then grab us a couple beers."

70

We turned into a warehouse complex off Santa Fe, a few miles south of downtown. Derk parked by the last prefab building in the last row of the complex. A sodium lamp thirty yards away cast everything in a sickly yellow glow.

"Let the games begin," Derk said as he killed the engine and turned on the red light. Flashing a wolfish grin, he climbed over the console, pistol in hand. "Right, Ranger?"

"Yep," I said, following him into the back.

Planting a foot on either side of Tish, Derk squatted down slightly, holding the gun so that the barrel jutted toward her at crotch-level. Then, maybe in some perverse show of professional courtesy, he began doing a slow bump and grind, top Bad Boy performing for a booth girl who diddled herself behind glass, at five bucks a throw.

"Get some whiskey ready," Derk told me, hips swiveling as he produced the handcuff key and held it out toward Tish like an ice cream cone to a kid on a hot summer day. "Want me to unlock you?"

Tish nodded vigorously. Derk told her to turn over, face down. When she did, he removed one cuff, but left the other attached to her right wrist, like a leash. He then untied the cord binding her ankles and flipped the girl onto her back.

Circling around them to the bar, I rubbed my throat and plucked the Wild Turkey from the bottle rack, but Derk was too busy with our co-star to have a drink.

"I'm only going to tell you this once, girl," he said, pulling Tish up into a sitting position. "When I untape your mouth, whiskey is going in. What *won't* come out are shouts, screams or other lamentations, understand?"

Tish's head bobbed affirmatively.

"And I'm going to put this away," Derk said, waving the pistol in her face. "Don't make me have to get it out again."

She grunted agreement and continued to nod.

After stashing the .38 under the bar, Derk leaned over and ran a finger down Tish's right cheek. "Whiskey, Ranger," he said, slowly peeling the tape off her mouth. I uncapped the bottle and gave it to him. Derk lifted her chin. "Bottoms up."

"Sure," Tish mewed, then opened her mouth and leaned back slightly. Derk poured the booze directly down her throat. She gulped along as best she could, but after three big swallows started to choke.

Derk stopped serving and handed the bottle back to me. After giving Tish a chance to catch her breath, he told her to lose the t-shirt. When she did, Derk wadded it up and used it to gently dab booze and blood off her face. This small, unexpected tenderness made me flash on something I'd read in a World War II book, about a guard at Auschwitz who gave children a sweet while they waited in line outside the gas chamber.

I took a big slug of whiskey and watched, spellbound.

"Now close your eyes and open your mouth," Derk said, tossing her shirt aside. Tish probably expected the same thing I did, but instead of reaching for his fly, Derk pulled a tiny black box from his jeans, extracted something from it and popped it in her mouth.

"Swallow," he said, enforcing this instruction by clamping a hand over her face. Tish struggled briefly then thought better of it and gulped loudly several times until he was satisfied and released her.

"W-What was that?" Tish whispered, and I idly tried to remember if they'd ever caught the Tylenol killer.

"Just a little acid, honey."

"H-How much?" asked Tish.

"One hit of blotter, but it was cut up," Derk said, "for those times when I only want a little bit of heaven."

"Oh," Tish said.

Behind his back, Derk flashed four fingers, I assume to signal me how much LSD he'd *really* given her. Never had a chance to try the stuff and after hearing a couple of Dave's tripping stories, not sure I'd want to. I already know how fucking ludicrous reality is.

"Ranger." Derk snapped his fingers. "Another drink."

"Roger."

Derk tapped the neck of bottle against Tish's cheek. "Open Sesame." She opened her mouth real wide, like at the dentist. In went more 101 proof Wild Turkey. Gobble, gobble, glug, glug.

After handing off the bottle again, Derk peeled off his own shirt. "Behold the prize," he said, flexing his pecs. I wasn't sure if he meant the helpless girl beneath him, or if he was talking to Tish and meant *himself.* She sure didn't look like she had won anything.

Ever the performer, Derk now struck a series of poses, even throwing a couple kung-fu punches, and then got down to business. He unsnapped Tish's jeans, briskly worked them down and pulled them over her ankles. She wasn't wearing panties. Spreading her wide like a human wishbone, Derk buried his face between her legs.

My heart was thumping like mad, yet there was zero cock-twitch excitement in *my* jeans as I watched the dirty dream unfolding before me. Had I believed in a wish-granting god, I might have prayed for a big boner and Tish's transformation into a cock-pig, 'cause wasn't that the only happy ending to a fuck fairy tale?

Doing her best to go with the flow and get through this, Tish moaned loudly as Derk ate her out, her "Oh, yeahs!" right out of bad porn acting 101. "Feels *good!"*

"Quiet," Derk commanded. Reaching toward the bar, he slid open a drawer and pulled out the billy club that went with his cop costume.

"B-Bobby," Tish panted, likely ignoring his *hush* directions in the hope that slutting things up would help. "Eat my pussy. Eat me!"

"I said. . ." Derk whacked the club across her stomach. "Shut up!"

"Oww!" Tish yelped, fake pleasure replaced with real pain.

"Silence, cunt!" Another belly whack, then he ran the tip of the club slowly between her breasts, traced a large S across Tish's stomach and continued on down to her heart-shaped bush. Then, grinning in the bloody red light, Derk suddenly rammed the billy club up inside her.

Tish cried out. Derk slapped her, laughed and worked the club faster, each brutal thrust making it clear he had absolutely zero interest in her pleasure.

Pound, pound, pound.

Her mouth was clamped shut, but Tish couldn't completely contain her whimpers. I shut my eyes and smelled molding hay, horse shit, Kenny's Beefeaters breath. . .

Blinking all that away, I re-focused on Derk, who now stood up and shed jeans and jockeys. Maybe this is the moment to get in the game, I realized, time to show Wendy and all the rest, to get some power and payback. . .

My left hand dropped to my crotch and squeezed. Nothing down there but numb.

"Ranger!" Derk called. "Whip out your gun and get busy, son."

"Yeah," I said, thinking that Tish, little caterpillar cunt, must have more cock to free the butterfly whore from her cocoon.

Derk was in her mouth now. I unsnapped my jeans, knelt down between Tish's legs and moved the abandoned billy club out of the way. Ran my left hand slowly along her inner thigh while stuffing the right into my underwear, but still nada down there. Petey was so shrunken, he'd almost retracted up into my pelvis. What was wrong with me? Shouldn't I be sporting a diamond-cutter hard-on?

"Take me deeper, slut," Derk grunted, holding the back of Tish's head as his hips bucked. "I'm on a submarine mission for you, babe. Dive, dive!"

Snuggled inside a booth at Kitty's, I probably would have cranked the volume on a scene like this, but now the sound of Tish gagging made me want to hurl. I shut my eyes again.

Look at it! the little voice commanded. *This is the truth, not your stupid jerk book. So look!*

"The truth. . ." I mumbled as I stood up, almost tripping over Tish's left leg as I lurched past her on my way to the passenger's seat. I wanted to flee, but just dropped onto the seat and cranked down the window, gulping fresh air that didn't smell like sweat and sex and fear.

"You squirt that quick?" Derk asked.

I thought about lying but didn't. "No," I croaked, pulling the Ranger mask down off my sweaty face. It hung around my sore neck on its elastic cord. "I just need a couple minutes," I panted. "T-The speed and everything has me over-amped."

"No hurry, Ranger," Derk said, as casually as if we were sitting in a booth at the G&M Cafe. "We'll be here awhile."

"Great," I whispered.

What's wrong? the little voice sneered. *"Your girl" not transforming into a world-humping nympho?*

No.

I realized that after this Tish would be left – assuming she survived – more damaged and screwed-up than before, a precious part of herself having been snatched away. I figured others had gnawed on her soul, before she landed in a jerk booth at Kitty's.

Now Derk and I were taking a bite.

71

"Fuck, fuck, fuck," Derk moaned like a dark incantation, having been at Tish for what seemed like hours. I'd been back and forth to the passenger's seat several times and sat there now, staring out the window at a rat scurrying along the lip of a dumpster, three feet away. It paused to fix me with a black-eyed glare until I looked away.

How low can you go? Let's hope losing a rat stare-down is rock bottom.

My nosed burned, stomach churned, head throbbed with awful truth the little voice didn't have to announce. I was wrong, maybe always had been. Becoming a zombie isn't a small-town disease, or something you can shed with distance. In these twisted times of go-go greed and off the books wars, maybe everyone has to struggle to stay human, to not settle for a belly full of McBurgers and a quick cum squirt in a porn booth.

And Derk was wrong *squared*, despite his strange, toxic appeal. I still believe that life *does* have meaning. Maybe our job as humans is to define what it is at any given moment, however incompletely, to add a microscopic speck to the story of the Universe Understanding Itself. Not that we'll be rewarded with Big Answers in return, but so what? Maybe the search for meaning pays some dues on our incredible luck of existing at all, let alone being gifted with even a *glimpse* of a cosmos bristling with Big Questions.

And back down here among the grubby little anthill of humanity, I believe that despite our King Kong egos, blustering ignorance and open wounds, most people desperately want to fight off encroaching zombification, which isn't a matter of geography at all.

It's a choice, like waving a white flag.

I groaned over this terrible knowledge, wanted to vanish up my own ass, but Derk had other ideas.

"Ranger, I'm spent," he called from the back of the van. "It's your turn."

"L-Listen. . ." I stammered, swiveling the chair around so I could see him.

"*You* listen," Derk said sharply. "We have a deal, remember?"

"Yeah." I glanced down at Tish, sprawled on the carpet and muttering acid-fried gibberish. The van reeked of booze, sweat, cum, shit – like a Kitty's booth, plus cat box – and I desperately longed to be anywhere else in the world.

175

Derk was leaning against the bar, naked, holding the Wild Turkey. He lifted the bottle and smirked in the bloody red light. "You're up, slugger."

"I can't. . ."

"Bullshit," he hissed. "Get busy."

Instead of arguing, I climbed over the console, unzipped and yanked down my jeans. "I'm so fuckin' high," I whispered, pointing to shriveled worm Petey, "I can't even *feel* my dick."

Derk raised an eyebrow, but then just chuckled. "It doesn't matter if you fuck her or not. Legally, you're already guilty of kidnapping and attempted rape." He took a big drink of whiskey. "Comprende?"

"Absolutely," I said, pulling up my jeans. "I do."

"Too bad, kid," Derk said, sounding disappointed. "I've got her all wet and ready for you." He pulled Tish back up into a sitting position, lifted the bottle to her lips and poured.

I don't know whether it was the sudden movement or a fresh infusion of alcohol, but Tish snapped back to reality, with a vengeance. She spit the whiskey right in Derk's face and sprang to her feet.

"My eyes!" he bellowed.

"Out!" Tish screamed, bolting for the rear doors. "Gotta get out!"

"No!" I leapt at her, managed to grab Tish around the waist and pull her against me. "Don't run or he'll hurt you worse," I whispered in her ear, desperate to stop her before Derk's did.

Tish couldn't know I was trying to protect her. She twisted out of my grasp then wheeled around and tried to punch me, but the handcuff still attached to her right wrist went flying and made contact first, inflicting a gash above my left eye. I flailed at her, blood running down my face, but Tish kicked me in the stomach. The air *ooof*ed out of me and I reeled backwards, crashing into Derk.

"Fly away!" Tish cried, flinging the doors open. She jumped out of the van and took off running across the parking, stark naked. I saw this with blurred vision, my eye tearing up to wash out the blood.

Derk shoved me into the side of the van. "Fucking cunt," he growled, rubbing *his* eyes with one hand, while groping over the top of the bar with the other.

"Derk, no!" I yelped, pressing a finger against my wound. "Don't kill her."

"Not unless I have to." Sweeping the .38 over the bar, Derk scrambled into his jeans and took off after Tish.

She was yelling something unintelligible but there was no one around to hear, except us rapists. She was flying on acid and adrenaline, but small girl vs. Nordic Super Villain still wasn't much of a foot race.

Derk caught up with her maybe eighty yards from the van. True to his word, murder wasn't his mission. He *did* use the .38, bashing Tish in the back of the head with the pistol grip. She stumbled forward a couple more steps and then dropped like a sack of rocks.

Hopping down from the van, I glanced around nervously and gingerly took my finger off the cut above my eye. It had almost stopped bleeding. The late-night emptiness of the industrial park made us more vulnerable, or at least it felt like it. Then I realized Santa Fe was a half mile away, beyond two rows of buildings, another complex, and the Platte River. I couldn't even hear any traffic.

We might as well have been on the moon.

"Hey, Jack-O!" Derk called, but I no longer found my *nom de porn* amusing. "Are you going to help me with your girl, or do I have to drag her?"

"Coming!" I sprinted over to join him, looked down to confirm Tish was breathing, sighed with relief when I saw she was. "Uh, do you want me to grab her feet or. . ."

"You just keep an eye on her," Derk decided. "I'll get the wheels."

"Okay."

As he sprinted back to the van, I knelt down beside Tish and lightly touched her flushed, freckled cheek. She snuffled and jerked her head away. I took it as a good sign that she was reacting to stimuli, even while out cold. A drop of blood splashed on the asphalt, and I realized running across the parking lot had caused my wound to start bleeding again. I pressed my index finger against the gash for a few seconds then wiped the blood on my jeans.

Tish's naked body was drenched in sweat, and I wished I had something to cover her. By the time I decided my t-shirt would be better than nothing, the van was pulling beside me and *my girl*.

Derk had used that term all night, a constant reminder, whether he intended it to or not, that *I* had put Tish into the back of the van. Some guys are such genius jerks, they can yank your chain on instinct alone.

After we loaded the unconscious Tish back into the van, Derk dusted his hands then glanced toward the warehouse and pointed. "Look at that shit on the dumpster."

Spicks n niggers sux! read the spray-painted graffiti.

"Assholes," I muttered.

"Yeah," Derk agreed, "but it gives me an idea." He slammed the van doors and slapped me companionably on the back. "Don't sweat the equipment failure, Adam. I know you'll get it right next time."

72

Derk is wrong.

As I examine the scab over my eye in the dingy bus station mirror, maybe the only thing in the world I'm certain of right now is that there will *never* be a next time. One Molester Man mind-meld is enough. Too much. Yet fool that I am, I hope to claw my way back to being human after mainlining pure zom juice, with whatever passes for my "soul" intact, if much the worse for wear.

Rewind and rot: before we left the warehouse complex, Derk handcuffed the unconscious Tish again and had me tie her ankles. Safety first! We soon hopped on I-70 and drove dead east for. . . forty-five minutes? Ninety? Time's fluid for a whacked-out rape-o.

Once we hit the interstate, Derk had me grab some paper towels and a bottle of water from behind the bar and wash the blood off my face. Tish finally came to well outside of the city but wasn't a problem. The pistol-whipping on top of the booze and drugs had taken the last of the fight out of her. Her occasional acid babble didn't bother us. Derk and I didn't talk much. Mostly listened to random tunes as he clicked among stations. Pink Floyd, Donna Summer, Vermin Squirm.

Eventually we got off the interstate by some tiny bugfuck town, maybe six blocks long. Drove through it and on down a dirt road that reminded me of home. Derk seemed to know where he was going but might have just been winging it. I didn't ask.

Oh, I forgot to mention Derk's idea back at the industrial park, prompted by the racist graffiti. After we first got back in the van, he grabbed a can of silver spray paint from under the bar and used Tish's back as ad space.

Dont sux off niggers bitch!!

I noticed he aped the bad spelling.

"Just a little misdirection," Derk said, admiring his handiwork. "On the off chance your girl winds up in a cop shop, they'll think any alleged assault was racially motivated."

"What if she doesn't date black guys?"

"Like the cops would believe that," he scoffed. "Or care if they did." Touching her back gingerly, Derk nodded with satisfaction. "Quick drying."

And we were on our way.

About ten minutes on the far side of Bugfuck, we pulled over at a wide spot along the washboard dirt road. Not a house or farm building in sight. As a final touch of mind-fuckery, we called each other a variety of names while getting the woozy Tish back into her jeans and t-shirt. *Raoul. Felix. Dino. John-Boy. Kenny* was one of my contributions.

Derk stuffed a twenty-dollar bill in the back pocket of her jeans. Then we topped Tish off with a final whiskey gargle, set her on unsteady feet in the middle of the road and drove away.

178

It was after two when we got back to Windhollow. After parking, we quickly searched the van by flashlight, finding Tish's keys and hand-tooled leather wallet. "Litt'l Angel" it read, above a crude rendering of a smiling girl with devil horns. Derk pocketed her belongings, and we headed in to 22-G. Dave of course was up in Boulder with what's-her-name.

Once inside, Derk went through the wallet, finding Tish's ID, wrinkled photos, phone numbers on scraps of paper and a hundred and thirty-four bucks. Derk gave me the money, pocketed the keys, then burned the rest of the stuff in the fireplace, using a couple patio newspapers as kindling.

We made drinks, did some lines, then Derk decided we should burn our clothes, too, fearing that lab tests – on the unlikely chance any were ever conducted – could turn up bodily fluids that had splashed around. It was only then I realized the Lone Ranger mask was still around my neck. I laughed. After all my worrying about Tish recognizing me, once I pulled the mask down in the front seat, I'd forgotten all about it.

"You owe me ten bucks for that," Derk said when I tossed the mask in the fireplace.

I paid him without comment. Having to burn my Kinks t-shirt sucked, but I couldn't argue with Derk's logic. Better safe than in a cell.

He sent me outside to see how much smoke we were producing on a hot summer night, but there was barely a puff, and nobody was around to see it. As the fire burned down, Derk went to his bedroom, returning with a fresh notebook and three pens. He started making a copy of the dance log, in three colors of ink.

"Different ink to make it look written at different times?" I asked.

Derk glanced up from his task and winked. "You're a natural, kid." He told me several strip-a-grams would be deleted from the new version of the log, while tonight's business would show him working a party in Castle Rock, twenty miles south of Denver, around the time Tish got off work at Kitty's.

It took Derk about a half-hour to write out this new edit of reality. Once finished, he burned the original log and made sure it and whatever was left of everything else was reduced to ash by adding some Bacardi 151 to the fire. Then he made us fresh drinks, whiskey sours.

We clinked glasses and Derk toasted "our eventful evening."

"And to still be breathing," I added, and we toasted to that.

Didn't crash until four, but Derk shook me awake at eight-thirty, handed me a steaming mug of coffee and said we had work to do. While I got caffeinated, he destroyed Tish's keys with bolt cutters. Then we drove to City Park – with me tossing bits of keys out the window along the way – where we scrubbed down the van's interior with Pine-Sol and Windexed every window, all to better inhabit our new alter-egos as Invisible Men.

Soon after we set to work, Derk said, "Now's your chance, Adam."

179

"For what?" I asked, sponging down the bar.

"A debriefing." He wiped down Tish's face-plant window, re-Windexed and wiped it again. "Ask for tips, unburden yourself, whatever you want to talk about."

"Ahh..." I considered this for a moment, but decided there was nothing more from Derk that I wanted to know. "I'm good."

"That's fine, but understand this..." He fixed me with his blue laser stare. "After we're done here, I never heard of your girl and was working in Castle Rock last night, from ten to midnight. Which can be verified, if need be."

"I don't doubt that." I grinned without intending to. "Molester Man is a fuckin' genius."

Derk beamed and tossed his cleaning rag at me. "I love that name!"

"Well," I said modestly, "some things write themselves."

"Still, when we're done..." He ran two fingers across his lips, zipping up. "I don't want to hear it again."

"Hear what?"

He smiled and I flipped the rag back to him. We worked in silence for maybe ten minutes then he again took my temperature. "So no questions about *anything*?"

"Why would I have questions about something that never happened?"

"Exactly."

From that moment on, we never mentioned Tish again. If she went to the cops, it hasn't hit the media. I've checked both *News* and *Post* closely the last three days and have watched tons of local news.

Mr. X/Molester Man/SMR II made good his escape, with Derk flying to San Diego yesterday afternoon for some "quality beach time." His parting words to me were, "Happy hunting, Adam, and keep it hard," which sounded like both a perv-o pep talk *and* a taunt about my "equipment failure."

Given Derk's *I me mine* creed, punk nihilism meets '80's boomtown greed, I doubt he can imagine how glad I am that I *didn't* fuck Tish, though I certainly raped her. Yet at least I live in a world where Basic Humanity matters a lot more than getting a nut. He'd no doubt call that philosophical blather, an excuse, a loser's limp-dicked lament.

Well, fuck him, because it doesn't matter anyway.

We're both guilty.

Dave is moving in with Laura, up in Boulder. I saw him yesterday afternoon for a couple hours, helped him load his Camaro with stuff. We grabbed burgers for lunch, made small talk, hugged before he took off. My bro didn't seem surprised that I was cutting my visit short, and he was done apologizing for being MIA for so much of it.

Funny how I can still get upset about that, when Dave's "sin" is so trivial, compared to my own.

I splurged and took a cab downtown this morning around ten, walked around awhile, and have been hanging around the bus station ever since, almost three hours. Chain smoking and reading random selections from my Thompson and Ellison paperbacks. Ate a lunch counter chill dog that tasted like it contained real dog.

The dispatcher finally calls my bus, says boarding will begin in five minutes. I squirm on the uncomfortable plastic chair, which reminds my sore ass of a too-small school desk.

We're ready for your report, Mr. Freeman. What did you learn on your summer vacation?

Moral collapse, Mr. Wilson. Evil of a bestial, brutal kind, served up with self-help slogans and a corporate raider's compassion. And I discovered a monster lurking inside the dumb-ass kid from Garrison, a heartless stumble bum in cum-crusted pants, even if I'm not a natural like Derk.

Sure, I unintentionally sniffed-up zombie Adam with cocaine and Rush, summoned him with buckets of booze and suck-fuck fairy tales, but he could never have shambled forth if an embryonic bad seed hadn't been gestating inside me all along.

Derk *controls* his dark impulses, hones them like a well-designed magic trick, to be trotted out only on special occasions. Hell, it's his personal liberation movement. He may be horribly wrong, a moral black hole, but Derk doesn't believe intangibles like *right* and *wrong* even exist, and what gods will tell him otherwise?

While he may be more "evil" than me, that's *not* what flashes in those electric blue eyes. I don't know what to call it, some combo of jungle law license, unchecked appetite and geometric cunning, all fueled by an absolute belief that it makes him the freest man on the planet.

And by his lights, the bastard may be right.

All *I* can do is work like hell to be less wrong.

Maybe some good will come from having embraced my inner jackal, in discovering how easy he is to awaken, snapping at the leash with fangs bared. Maybe *becoming* zombie Adam – in fact not just theory – was a necessary first step toward killing the son of a bitch for good.

We'll see.

Thinking of Wendy is still agony, but I think of her a little less, every day. That I was wrong about us is hardly a surprise, eh? What I thought we were, never was. Or if it was, I ruined it. Or she did. We did.

Puppy love gone sickly, needing to be put down.

But whatever she said in that letter, I know Wen *did* love me, before ultimately deciding I'm missing too many pieces, am *incomplete,* like one of her unfinished paintings. And of course she's right.

As for Tish. . .

I pray–yeah, even without a personal call center god–that she gets off the dark road we dumped her on. Isn't doomed to flee down it forever, like me from the hayloft.

But *sorry* ain't worth shit, I know. Derk may have threatened my life but in my black heart, I'll always know that I fingered Tish like an eager Judas. She did nothing to deserve it.

That what happened to her probably saved my life doesn't make it much better, because *none* of it would have happened if I hadn't been in training to become Derk's sidekick all along. But enough self-flagellation for now. . .

I've been running ten miles a day, with no drink or drugs since that night. Not that I'm gonna go straight full-time, but a clear head feels marginally better right now, and I'll take every bit of *better* I can get.

I also feel a little less like killing myself today, so that's good. Don't know if the off-myself impulse stems more from devolving into a drooling perv, or knowing nothing awaits me back in Garrison. Either way, I'll take *less* suicidal as another millimeter victory, even if the notion of suicide is probably more self-loathing wallow than serious death wish.

And hey, I'll have two days on the bus to work up a "reasons to live" list.

Maybe, the little voice suggests as I glance over at the pay phones beyond the lunch counter, *you can start right there.*

"Nah, I'm nowhere near strong enough for that," I mutter, thinking about the phone call I've fantasized about making the last three days.

"Operator, get me the Denver police. . ."

I grab my backpack and slowly inchworm across the lobby, trying to work up some nonexistent courage. It's one thing to confess between your own ears, something else entirely to go naked in front of clustered news cams, for Dad and Dave and everyone else to see. Hell, *me* knowing what a wretched piece of shit I am makes me want to run in front of a truck, so I'm going to shout that news to the whole fucking world?

I imagine a stern but pretty reporter on the courthouse steps.

". . . trial of dirtbag sex criminal Adam Freeman, who hopes ratting out his partner will spare him the guillotine."

What little resolve I have evaporates before I get halfway to the phones. I slouch back to the hard chairs like a loudly scolded little dog.

Deserve it, the little voice murmurs insistently as I sit back down.

I grunt and dig into a pocket, fishing out change as the dispatcher calls my bus again.

"...now boarding at bay five."

I only have fifteen cents. The phone takes twenty.

Sorry, Tish, but sometimes destiny decides. And it's left me a nickel short.

I head out the lobby doors to the loading bays, inhale the exhaust fumes of idling engines. I find my bus and line up behind the fifteen or so people with luggage to be loaded.

The line moves slowly. The long wait at the station has left me sluggish and dozy, but when my eyes flutter shut, I see Tish's stunned, blood-speckled face. Blinking her away, I shuffle forward with the line, feeling like a Nazi war criminal ready to board a tramp steamer for Argentina.

The driver stops loading luggage to speak with a passenger, then trots back into the station. I grab my pack and wander off to have a cig. Standing on the curb outside the lobby, I spark up with my last match, stroll over to a trash can and toss in the empty book. Take a deep drag and glance down.

There's a nickel on the sidewalk, an inch from my left foot.

I freeze, feel a cold stab of panic, but then it melts away as I embrace the whims of destiny. Bending down to pick up the coin, I think of my trips to the hospital to see Kenny over the last four years, remember how glorious the summer we met had been, before that afternoon in the hayloft.

But the hospital visits weren't about reliving good times. I went to make sure the horse kick hadn't worn off. It's very therapeutic, knowing the guilty have been punished. Yeah, it was horrible seeing Kenny with a dented head, reduced to little more than a drooling moron, but *satisfyingly* so.

The reason I'll never go back to the hospital is that during the last few visits I was starting to wonder if maybe he'd been punished enough. I don't want to start hoping Kenny gets a miracle. Maybe someday, but not yet.

Not today.

Tish, I'm quite certain, would love seeing me and Derk kicked where it counts. She deserves seeing us marched into court, sure, but I have to do this for *me*. Do it for a chance to–not make things right; I know *that's* impossible–maybe be worthy of anything good, ever again.

Clutching the nickel in my fist like a nugget of gold, I stride back inside the station, heading straight for the pay phones. I feel lighter with every step, almost giddy, as I realize there's now one other thing in the world that I know for sure.

It's time to stop running.

THE END

**ALSO BY
MARK BARSOTTI**

ROCK IS DEAD

THEY SAY...

Interviews & Opinion From Rock's Last Wave

VOL 1
2nd EDITION

MARK BARSOTTI

"I like (Barsotti's) writing a lot." – Charles M. Young

EXCERPTS FROM
ROCK IS DEAD THEY SAY. . .

"If rock's jackboot beat and howling guitars were the clanging, cacophonous soundtrack of the Late Industrial Age, then it's well past its sell-by date anyway. Ashes to ashes, rest in peace, Major Tom, amen. "

BILLY CORGAN: ". . . almost went out of his way to piss on punk in the early '90s, when the flannel-clad grungsters were bowing at its gob-stained altar. . . can still toss off top shelf alt-rock ear candy whenever the mood strikes him."

VAN HALEN: ". . . snobs like Bob Christgau often missed the obvious – in this case recognizing Van Halen as super nova saviors of pop savvy hard rock, led by a generational talent on guitar."

MEGADETH: "Dave Mustaine's Deep State boobery *is* cringe-worthy... but I can enjoy his hot rod guitar without endorsing his Z movie worldview."

JACK WHITE: "*Boarding House Reach* begrudgingly serves up a meaty three second riff here, a bleat of guitar noise there, but it's a near-starvation diet, when it comes to satisfying our minimum daily six string essentials."

THE CLASH: "I'd have killed for more, assuming in some alt-reality Strummer and Jones patched things up – risked the band becoming bloated superstars or a touring oldies act, just for another junkie-itch fix of the *good* stuff."

THE '90s: "One actually had to go out and hunt down rock movies in meatspace, like some Neanderthal with an overactive boogie gland."

ALICE IN CHAINS: "Killing bolt nihilism, corrosive, cauterizing. . . If *my* job was singing the Alice In Chains songbook every night. . . I might well kill myself, too, even without the heroin."

AVAILABLE ON AMAZON

AVAILABLE ON AMAZON

PRAISE FOR YAKETY YAK

"…captures all the raw, throbbing… electrifying power and vitality of an audiovisual medium and blasted it onto the printed page… you can dip in anywhere and not emerge until after many hours of fascinating revelations and amusements, edifications and bewilderments… Barsotti's book fully merits its place in the rock arena, like Lester Bangs "playing" his typewriter onstage with the J. Geils Band.
– Paul Di Filippo, author of RIBOFUNK, THE STEAMPUNK TRILOGY, etc.

About the Author

Originally from Colorado, Mark Barsotti was born in Denver and now lives in San Diego, California with his cats Ed and Harlan. His short fiction has appeared in *Ellery Queen's Mystery Magazine* and *Alien Skin.* He is the author of *Rock Is Dead They Say… Vol. 1, 2nd Edition* and *Yakety Yak Rock's Greatest Quotes Sex, Drugs & Everything Else.* His rock writing appeared in *Westword, Musician, Request, Livewire, D.J. Times, Syracuse New Times, Bad News,* and *New Times.* He's currently working on a semi-comic dystopian novel and *Volume II* of *Rock Is Dead They Say.* He can be reached on Facebook and Twitter @ marconi451.